KUMARI

GODDESS
OF SECRETS

For my daughter

Thanks to my agent, Peter Cox, and to everyone at Piccadilly Press, especially Brenda Gardner, Mary Byrne, Melissa Patey, Vivien Tesseras and my editor Anne Clark. I would particularly like to mention the excellent Jane Burnard, my copy editor, and wish her luck in her new career. A big thank you, as ever, to my family and friends for putting up with authorial angst. Most of all I would like to acknowledge all the brilliant booksellers, librarians and readers I have had the privilege to meet since Kumari – Goddess of Gotham *was published. Your feedback has been wonderful and it makes it all worthwhile.*

First published in Great Britain in 2008
by Piccadilly Press Ltd,
5 Castle Road, London NW1 8PR

Text copyright © Amanda Lees 2008

A catalogue record for this book is available from the British Library

ISBN-13: 978 1 85340 989 9

1 3 5 7 9 10 8 6 4 2

Printed and bound in Great Britain by Bookmarque Ltd.
Cover design by Anna Gould and Simon Davis

Set in Stempel Garamond and Trajan

KUMARI

GODDESS
OF SECRETS

AMANDA LEES

Piccadilly Press • London

THE STORY SO FAR

Kumari is a goddess-in-training who lives in a secret valley kingdom. She is destined to stay young for ever, unlike people in the World Beyond. But it's pretty lonely in the palace, where her only friend is a baby vulture, and there's nothing to think about, except the mystery of her Mamma's death.

It's hard to kill a goddess, but someone did, so Kumari tries to summon Mamma back from the dead and find out the truth. Things go badly wrong, and Kumari finds herself in New York, running for her life. She has only a year and a day to get back home – or die.

Taken in by Ma Hernandez, Kumari starts a new life in the World Beyond. She goes to school, makes her first real friends, and meets a boy called Chico. But her life is still in danger, and not only because of the march of time. Simon Razzle, a crazed cosmetic surgeon, plans to carve her up to find the secret of eternal youth. Yet he is not Kumari's deadliest enemy: the Ayah, her beloved nurse in the Hidden Kingdom, is revealed as a murderess eaten up by jealousy and hatred. Kumari faces death at her hands, until her Mamma comes to save her in the nick of time.

Kumari has only twenty-four hours until her year and a day runs out. She must say a sad farewell to the World Beyond and return to the Hidden Kingdom, where her destiny as a goddess awaits her.

Behind her, the friends she would never see again.
Ahead lay her home, Happiness and Papa.

Time to avenge Mamma.

CHAPTER 1

Kumari perched in the jacaranda tree, hardly daring to breathe. Directly beneath her stood a palace guard, calling out her name. Luckily for her, the branches were thick with purple flowers that screened her from the guardsman's view. There was no way she was coming down. She would spend the rest of her days up a tree.

All right, maybe that was a bit extreme. But she would at least stay here until nightfall. Although by then Papa might be getting worried. He was very anxious about her these days. Probably something to do with her having been kidnapped and whipped off to the World Beyond, although frankly, now she was back, she could see no reason to fuss any more. But in a funny way it was nice. Too often Papa had been so distracted by affairs of state that he had paid little attention to his only daughter. Granted, it could not be easy

1

being a king, but he was her Papa too – the only parent she had left. The thought made Kumari's eyes sting as tears rose, unbidden. She blinked them back fiercely.

'Aaark!'

Badmash's squawk nearly sent her spiralling off her branch.

'For goodness' sake, Badmash,' she croaked. 'You'll give us away.'

Badmash opened his beak and looked plaintively at Kumari. For a baby vulture he had one adult-sized appetite and a belly to match.

'OK, OK,' she muttered, as the guardsman's voice grew more distant. 'Have the last honey cake.'

Great. Stuck up a tree with no rations. Her own stomach let out a growl. How long had it been since lunchtime? Since the RHM, Papa's Right Hand Man, dropped his bombshell? Kumari had no idea, but the memory stiffened her resolve. Hungry or not, there was no way she was coming down. Not until they dropped their ridiculous idea, at any rate. Palace School, for heaven's sake!

Who had dreamed that one up? She could make a good guess. All she had asked for was to go to school with the other kids, like she had back in the Bronx. No special treatment, no girl-goddess stuff. Just an ordinary member of class. At first Papa had been horrified. No member of the royal family had ever gone to school before. A trainee goddess must be tutored at the palace, just as tradition dictated. But then the RHM had stepped in and the result was this compromise.

Bring school to the palace.

A genius idea.

Not.

For one thing, they would pick the nerdiest kids, those least likely to offend. She would be stuck in a classroom with a bunch of losers, pretending to ignore their stares. Not that she was judgemental, but, really, there were limits. And there was no way she was going to hang out with the goof buckets. She had said as much to Papa but he had stared at her as if she was speaking a foreign language which, in a way, she was.

That was the other thing. No one seemed to understand her any more. Like, *really* understand her. Must be the accent she had picked up in the World Beyond, not to mention the vocabulary. Kumari sighed. Of course she was happy to be home. And yet she missed her friends, she missed Ma. She missed Chico.

A ferocious rustling snapped her out of her reverie. The branches to her left were swaying and dipping. There was something clambering about in amongst the leaves. And it was heading straight for her. It could be a sharp-toothed monkey. Possibly even a leopard. Kumari steeled herself. Beside her, Badmash cringed. A head popped through the purple blossoms.

'Kumari.'

'Papa!'

Her Papa up a tree? *Unbelievable.* Papa was a king. Kings did not climb trees. Yet here he was, his head poking up between the branches.

'I thought I might find you up here.'

'You did?'

Bizarre.

Papa's face was pale, his breathing ragged. Fearing for his already frail health, Kumari scrambled down until she was crouching closer to him. Papa's feet were wedged in a low-lying branch, his fingers clinging, white, to the main trunk.

'Yes indeed. I'll let you into a little secret. I used to climb up here too, when I was a boy. A little higher than I can manage now, unfortunately.'

'You used to climb trees?'

'Hard to imagine, I know.'

Papa's face broke into a rare smile. It made his face seem all the more wan.

'When I was your age I was always hiding away from my tutors. These trees offered the best view. You can see right down into the town.'

'And all the way beyond,' said Kumari.

'And all the way beyond,' echoed Papa. 'Were you looking for something in particular?'

'Um, no. Not really.'

'Just . . . looking?'

'Yeah, kind of . . .'

She could not meet Papa's gaze. She knew that he knew that she had been looking out to the western frontier. He did the same himself, every evening. She could see him silhouetted against his window, staring out into the night. There were rumours of an invasion by the warlords who terrorised the lands beyond the border to the west; whispers of rebellious citizens gathering within the kingdom, ready and willing to aid the warlords' passage. It was unheard of, unthinkable. An uprising against the king! Against her Papa, for goodness' sake. No wonder he looked worried.

'It's amazing what you can see when you look properly,' said Papa. There was a definite teasing note to his words now.

Kumari pondered this a moment.

'You used your Powers to find me, didn't you?'

Papa looked her straight in the eye. 'No, Kumari, I did not.'

'Why not? I would have done. I mean, Power No 2 is perfect. The Power of Extraordinary Sight means you don't have to waste time on ordinary *looking*.'

'Looking for you would not be a waste of time. You forget I spent a year and a day doing precisely that.'

Papa spoke quietly, but the pain blared, still raw, from somewhere behind his eyes. Instantly, Kumari felt terrible. She laid a tentative hand over Papa's.

'I'm sorry,' she murmured. 'About everything. Truly.'

'Don't be. I'm glad you're safe. That is all that matters to me.'

The smile was back, this time soft with understanding. This was a side of her Papa Kumari had never seen before. Another symptom of change. So much had altered in her absence and yet her homeland looked the same. The valley still unfolded, lush, between the soaring, snow-capped peaks. Life continued at the same rhythmic pace. The gods reigned on the Holy Mountain. Maximum National Happiness remained the ultimate goal. Beneath the surface, however, there was this bubbling, the ripples of discontent. In the skies, Kumari could see scarcely a puff of smoke from the holy fires. The haze of Happiness was far too thin.

5

An icy hand clutched at her heart. The haze of Happiness was their lifeblood, as essential to them as oxygen. It concealed them from the World Beyond like an overarching canopy, shielding the valley Kingdom and its borderlands beneath its camouflaging cloak. While it allowed light to permeate, it hid the Kingdom from spying eyes. The haze of Happiness held Time at bay, protecting the people from its ravages. The thinner it got, the closer the World Beyond drew. Lose it and they would be defenceless. The microcosm that was the Hidden Kingdom would no longer exist. Kumari had seen for herself what Time could do, had witnessed its cruelty. She could not bear to see her Kingdom surrender to its relentless march, to have to watch all she loved perish.

Her Papa seemed to have sunk even deeper into the depression to which he had succumbed after Mamma's death. It was as if their year apart had wounded him still further, sapping him of what little divine power he had left. He should be tending the fires of Happiness. Perhaps then all thoughts of rebellion would be quelled. Instead, he was here – gaunt, a grey cast to his skin, the violet circles ever more evident under his bloodshot eyes. He had not slept properly since the day Mamma died, but now it seemed something more than that was troubling him. For a split second, she wondered if her Papa was seriously ill. No, god-kings did not get sick.

Except that was not entirely true. Mamma, after all, had perished, thanks to some mysterious malaise. What if Papa had somehow caught it too? But that was impossible. Mamma had been murdered. Kumari even knew the culprit and was poised to take her final revenge. The Ayah was dead, for heaven's sake. There was no way she could hurt Papa now. Even so, the fear refused to leave, lurking stubbornly in her gullet. If Papa died she would be alone. *Papa was not going to die.*

'Kumari, you're hurting me.'

'Am I? I'm so sorry.'

As she removed her hand she could see the livid marks on Papa's wrist where she had squeezed too tight.

'Not to worry, my child. It's been a difficult time, hasn't it? Now, I think you should climb down before they send out a second search party.'

'I can't,' said Kumari.

'Why? Because that would be giving in?'

Kumari squirmed. Sometimes it seemed Papa knew her far too well.

'I'm not going to Palace School,' she muttered.

'Why not? Do you think you're too good for it?'

'No! It's just . . .'

'You want to be like the other children. You want to go to school in town like everyone else.'

For a heartbeat Kumari wondered if he could read her mind, so piercing was Papa's gaze. None of the Eight Great Powers covered thought-reading.

'Um . . . yes,' she gulped.

'Trust me, my child, it is not possible at this time. Now, will you do it for me? Will you at least try Palace School?'

Kumari looked at her Papa, really looked, and saw again the translucence of his skin. It was as if the blood had all but drained away, leaving a paper-thin carapace. Her fingers fluttered forward, seeking reassurance. She had to touch this mask that was once her Papa's face, make sure it was still flesh. And then Papa's mouth twitched. The life flooded back into his features. It was her imagination after all. It was probably all in her head.

The Kingdom was fine. The people were happy. The rumours of rebellion were just rumours. Papa was simply a little tired, that was all. Everything was going to be all right. She would ignore the heaviness in her heart, the fluttering in her stomach.

Everything was going to be all right.

So why did it feel like a lie?

KUMARI'S JOURNAL
(TOP SECRET. FOR MY EYES ONLY.
EVERYONE ELSE KEEP OUT!)
THIS MEANS YOU!

My bedroom

Two days until the First Dark Moon of the Year

It's so quiet in the palace I can hear my heart beating. At least, I think it's my heart beating. Could be some kind of weird drumming I suppose. Ever since I got back, strange things have been happening. I walk along and I'm sure I hear someone behind me, but when I turn around there's no one there. And there are all kinds of shadows that never used to be here, like those shadows under Papa's eyes. He insists he is fine, but he is so obviously not.

Like today, when we got down from the tree, I could see that his legs were shaking under his robes. For a moment there I thought Papa might pass out, but then the RHM appeared. Papa kind of pulled himself taller and pretended nothing was wrong, but I could see by the RHM's face that he was not fooled at all. He gave Papa his arm and helped him inside without saying a word. I suppose I should be grateful – the RHM was too distracted to tell me off. I would rather Papa was well, though. I'd go through ten tellings-off for that.

I'm so frightened it's something serious. I could not bear to lose Papa too. I can't let myself think like that. Papa's going to be all right. Is he though? Really? Nothing feels certain any more. I mean, even the Kingdom feels different, like someone threw a grey blanket over it. I know Happiness is nowhere near Maximum. Papa knows it too. Every day he tries to tend the holy fires but they're getting lower and lower. It's like he doesn't have the strength to keep them going. That's why I'm so afraid.

If Papa doesn't have the strength to keep the fires going then things are really bad. Cook told me of another rumour today, something about the warlords already being here. The RHM says it's just talk, that these rumours mean nothing. Why won't he even discuss it with me? It's like he still thinks I'm a stupid kid. After what happened in the World Beyond I thought he saw me differently. He even told me he was proud of me, for heaven's sake! Said I would one day make a *worthy queen. But all that's forgotten now we're back home. It's business as usual. Palace School is all his fault and now I've promised Papa I will go.*

Oh my god – what is that weird snorty noise? It sounds like a demon pig or something. Get a grip, Kumari. There's no such thing as demon pigs. Actually, there might be, or so the Ancient Abbot says. We were just studying demons today during my Entities lesson. I asked him if the Ayah counted as one. He said she probably did. Well, there are only two more days to go and then I can perform the Banishment Rite. Two days until the Dark Moon. I wonder if the rite works on demons.

There'll be no Entities class with the other kids. They don't get to study goddess stuff. In a way, I wish they would. It might liven them up. I just know they're going to pick the most boring saps they can find. There'll be no one like Charley or Hannah. No one like Chico either. But then there is no one like Chico. When it gets really bad, I take his necklace out and hug it to my heart.

There it is again – snuffle, snuffle, snort, snort. I must just check it out . . .

It's OK – it's only Badmash. I've never heard him make that noise before! I think he must have a cold. Poor thing's been kind of depressed ever since we got back. He's missing his doughnuts and all the attention he used to get from my friends. Not that I don't give him attention – I'm constantly telling him he's the greatest baby vulture that ever lived. It's important to work on his self-esteem. I mean, I am kind of his surrogate parent. Anyway, he's not the only one that's depressed. It's less of a fun palace here than ever.

CHAPTER 2

As soon as Kumari opened her eyes, she remembered. This was the first day of Palace School. Even less reason to get up. She turned over with a sigh.

'Skraark!'

'Oops! Sorry, Badmash.'

How was she to know he'd be lying with his beak practically up her armpit? Ordinarily, Badmash kept to his side of the bed. He must have had a bad dream. A memory pricked at her sleep-fugged brain. It was not Badmash who had had a dream. She could recall the snorting of a thousand demon pigs, fangs bared as they chased her. Badmash must have cuddled close as he often did when she cried out in the night. In the early days after Mamma's death she often woke to find his head resting on her heart, one wing stretched out across her chest.

'Oh, Badmash,' cooed Kumari. 'You were only trying to comfort me.'

Badmash flopped on his back and opened one eye. His stomach let out an ominous growl.

As if on cue, the door opened.

'Good morning! Breakfast is ready,' beamed Cook, her rounded cheeks flushed with the warmth of the kitchen. Cook was unceasingly good-natured, even when Kumari tried to steal a freshly-baked treat or two.

She set the tray down beside the bed.

'Extra rations to see you through school.'

Kumari peered at the tray. On it, Cook had set a bowl of yak yoghurt, thick honey drizzled across in the shape of a smiling face, a strawberry set to form the nose. Alongside, a plate piled high with pancakes, each one dusted with cinnamon. Next to that was a dish for Badmash, overflowing with sticky pastries. It was not the dead mouse the Ayah used to bring him, but Badmash did not seem too bothered.

'Thank you, Cook,' said Kumari. 'How is my Papa this morning?'

'His holy majesty is well,' said Cook.

At least that was something.

Kumari tucked into the pancake, then waited until Cook had left before she passed the plate to Badmash. She would hate to hurt Cook's feelings but a stack that size was way too much for her. While Badmash gratefully tucked in, Kumari looked about for something to wear. Anything would do. It was not like there would be any competition on the fashion front. Here in the Kingdom all the kids wore a tunic top and trousers. It was a world away from New York.

Kumari smothered another sigh as she pulled on some crumpled robes. Charley and Hannah would laugh out loud if they could see her now. Robes were not what you would call cool. They hung to her ankles, swishing out around her sandalled feet. To match her mood, she'd chosen a particularly drab set – colours muted, fit saggy. Who cared what she looked like anyway? Certainly not a bunch of losers.

'Come on, Badmash. Time for school.'

Badmash kept his beak buried in the pancakes.

'Badmash! School. Now. Or no honey cakes.'

It was a threat that never failed.

She marched down the corridors, jaw set, Badmash clinging to her shoulder. Somewhere down in the town, the other kids would be going to school. The normal kids. The fun kids. Kids like Tenzin, for instance. OK, so she hadn't seen him since she got back. Tenzin was still bound to be the coolest kid around, not to mention the cheekiest. She would never forget the bold look he had once slid her in the throne room when all other eyes were respectfully cast down. Tenzin made her laugh. Once upon a time he had made her tingle. But that was before she met Chico. Now she knew how tingling really felt.

Her hand was on the door latch. *OK, brace yourself, Kumari. This is no longer your personal classroom. You now officially share it with a pack of losers.* One, two, three, push. The door swung open. The hum of chatter within subsided. *Fantastic. Great start.* The silence resounding in her ears, Kumari picked her way to her desk, now simply one of many. She could not look left or right. Instead, she kept her eyes fixed to the floor.

A few more steps and she was there. She could make out blobs all around. Human-shaped blobs. Blobs that sat, gawping. Carefully, she slid behind her desk. Why couldn't someone say something? Anything, just to fill the yawning void. To stop them all staring. It was even worse than she had anticipated. Day One and she was a freak. The Great Goddess Show had arrived. Maybe they'd get bored in a minute. And then she noticed a scrap of paper on her desk. Was this someone's idea of a joke? Warily, she turned it over.

'Look behind you,' it read.

This definitely had to be a joke. Double great. A set-up. Well, there was no way she was falling for it. They could find another goddess to be a laughing stock.

'Kumari.'

Just ignore them.

'Kumari, turn round. It's me.'

Me? Me who?

Kumari inched her head to the left, bracing herself for whatever was coming next. OK, she'd play their game. Reluctantly, she lifted her eyes. Looking straight into hers was another pair – almond-shaped, copper-coloured. Glinting in them, a hint of amusement that was echoed by the curl of an upper lip. Only one person in the Kingdom looked at her like that.

'Tenzin!' she gasped.

KUMARI'S JOURNAL
(TOP SECRET. FOR MY EYES ONLY.
EVERYONE ELSE KEEP OUT!)
THIS MEANS YOU!

My bedroom
Eve of the Dark Moon

How embarrassing was that? I mean, there's me in my worst possible robes. I didn't even brush my hair, for heaven's sake. And there he is. Tenzin. I thought I'd got over that tingling thing. I thought Chico had out-tingled him. But, well, Chico's out there, in the World Beyond, and I'm here. And so is Tenzin.

Is that so very disloyal? It's not like I can help tingling. And Chico still makes me tingle in my head. But I can't live in my head for ever. The RHM would say that's all I do, but what would he know about tingling? I can't imagine him feeling anything when he looks at someone, except maybe how to improve them. Anyway, now what am I supposed to do? It's like I have to change my whole strategy. The other kids aren't losers at all. Well, maybe one or two, but whatever.

In any case, I never had a strategy, so there's nothing to change except my outfit. Aaaaargh – I can't believe I did that. That robe makes me look like a walking carpet. Maybe Tenzin likes walking carpets. He did seem pretty pleased to see me. Anyway, I don't care what Tenzin likes or doesn't like. I am my own girl-goddess. And I have far more important things to think about, like the Banishment Rite, for instance. Tomorrow it will be the Dark Moon at last. The perfect time to finish things off.

The Ancient Abbot says you have to make sure a spirit is sent to outer darkness otherwise the person it belonged to still lives on. Only when nothing remains of the Ayah will Mamma be free to ascend the Holy Mountain. I can't bear to think of Mamma in limbo any longer. I have to get this ritual right. Straight after school tomorrow I'll head down to the lake. I must just read through my ritual book one more time.

CHAPTER 3

The book lay open at the appropriate page, marked by a lacy feather. It was the tail feather of a lyrebird and Badmash viewed it with disgust. The thing was long, curly, magnificent, in contrast to his own baby vulture fluff. Kumari was, however, far too busy trying to get her Banishment ritual right to notice Badmash sulking. She was putting the final touches to the Ayah's death mask, ready to consign it to the deep.

The construction of the death mask, read the instructions, *is the first stage of the Banishment Rite. It represents the soul to be banished. Care must be taken to include some relic of the person now deceased. If performed correctly, the effects of this ceremony are irreversible.*

Kumari glanced out over the lake. In it, she could still see the reflection of the Holy Mountain. The moment the sun slipped behind its peak, she could begin the second part of the Banishment Rite. In the meantime, she would settle down under the dragon tree and take the time to have a Think. Thinking was a skill she had acquired in her time in the World Beyond. It seemed to work equally well in the Hidden Kingdom. And there was plenty to Think about here. Her new classmates, for instance.

She stared back at the palace, its seven pagodas just visible beyond the frangipani fields. The lake lay at the feet of the mountains, some way from those gilded spires. Her ritual could not be completed until sundown. She would be returning home in the dark. There would not even be a moon to light her way. The Banishment Rite could only be performed when the moon was entirely absent.

Somewhere beneath the pagodas was the courtyard outside her classroom. She had passed through it on her way here, deliberately strolling so as not to attract attention. Except, of course, it had not worked. She had heard Tenzin calling her as she reached the far corner, had forced herself not to turn, knowing if she did she risked everything. Eyes constantly watched, most of them on Papa's orders. The girl-goddess must not go anywhere alone. Luckily for Kumari, she had her methods.

The palace was peppered with doors and windows, far too many to watch over. Time it right and the guards were easy to avoid. Tenzin was a different matter. She could still hear him calling as she slipped through an archway on the far side of the courtyard and began weaving through the warren of passageways that would take her to an unbarred window through which she planned to escape. Each time she stole away from the palace she varied her route, conscious of the dangers. So far it had worked. An hour's hard marching later, she had made it unscathed to the lake.

It was the perfect place to perform her ritual, to release her Mamma from the limbo to which she had been consigned. Sever the last threads of the Ayah's influence, and Mamma could at last ascend the Holy Mountain. The two of them had spent so many happy afternoons here picnicking under this very dragon tree. Mamma had loved splashing in the lake, swimming beside Kumari, guiding her flailing arms, soothing away her fears. Mamma had been afraid of nothing, not even the legendary creature that lurked beneath the waters. It was said that the creature thrived on evil, that it would swallow the souls of the wicked. Feed it the Ayah's spirit and Mamma would be free at last.

As they both stared at those waters now, Badmash let out a delighted squawk. He had spotted a tasty morsel. Plunging into the shallows, he emerged with it dangling from his beak. So enthusiastic was his attack on the thing, Kumari took a closer look. As soon as she realised what it was, she let out a gasp. To Badmash's dismay, she snatched it away and held it up. There was absolutely no doubt. This was a doughnut. But how on earth had it got here? There were no doughnuts in her homeland.

In fact, they were the single thing Badmash missed most about the World Beyond. And yet here was one in the lake. The doughnut was already half chewed, which meant another creature had got to it first, possibly even *the* creature.

It was soggy from the water, but not so soggy it had been in there too long. Something or someone had recently brought this doughnut into the Kingdom.

Kumari's puzzlings were interrupted by a flash of light from the water. The sun was bowing out to the moon. The day was all but over. As the orange blaze began to dim to burnished gold, Kumari hurriedly gathered her things together. Placing the sacrificial dish in the correct spot, she pulled a small bundle from her robes. Wrapped within it, a strand of the Ayah's hair she had found in the woman's old room.

Picking the strand up between thumb and finger, Kumari tied it firmly to the death mask, fighting back a surge of disgust. The woman had tried to kill her and now she was handling her hair! The mask was made of papier-mâché. Ordinarily, a death mask would be made of wax. In the absence of the Ayah's body, however, Kumari had had to improvise. She thought she had done rather well. The mask bore a distinct resemblance. Same broad cheeks and lumpy nose. She had even added an evil twist to the mouth.

Laying the mask upon the sacrificial dish, Kumari scattered Banishment Powder all over it. She had borrowed some from the Ancient Abbot's stock. It looked exactly like charcoal dust. Taking up the lyrebird's feather, Kumari wafted it over the dish counter-clockwise, stirring round and round for seven complete revolutions. Then, carefully, she applied the firestick. Once, twice, three times she tried. The wretched thing refused to catch. Oh great, it must be damp. Now what could she do?

She peered at her book. The light was diminishing. She

could still make out the words: *Destroy the death mask*, it said. Well there was more than one way to do that. If it had been made of wax, she would have melted it. In this case, she could rip it up. Without another thought, she began to tear, destroying what had taken hours to make. Working at it, teeth clenched, hearing the satisfying sigh of paper giving way, all the while thinking of Mamma, of the Ayah, of revenge. At last it was done. She could make the tiny scraps no smaller. They lay in her open palm like dirty snowflakes, sullied with flecks of grey.

Kumari glanced at the sky. The sun had slipped behind the Holy Mountain. Unusually, she could see the proud outline of the summit, tinged by fire, the last rays setting it ablaze. For once the clouds that generally obscured it had parted, exposing the home of the gods to view. This had to be a sign. Kumari rushed to the lake's edge. Casting the tiny scraps upon the water, she chanted with all her might, visualising her last sight of the Ayah, clamped between the jaws of a flying lion.

'OM GARE TARE SARWA
SHATDRUM BIGANEN MARA SEHNA . . .'

She could see Mamma on the lion's back, could hear the crowd screaming. Kumari squeezed her eyes tighter shut. She was doing this for Mamma. Get the Banishment ritual right and she would have avenged her properly, casting the Ayah's spirit into oblivion, ensuring she could never return. It was a drastic action, not to be undertaken lightly. And Kumari was the only one who could do it, who could perform this last duty for her Mamma. Not even Papa shared Mamma's blood. That was Kumari's privilege alone.

21

'HUNG BINDA BINDA PEH . . .'

Yelling at the top of her lungs, calling forth the creature. She dared not look but still she willed it to come. If she looked it might not work. Did this creature even exist? It might be nothing more than a myth. All of a sudden, she felt something hit her cheek, a stinging slap and then another. Kumari opened her eyes. The sodden scraps of paper were being flung in her face. The waters heaved, swollen by a presence, then were sucked down as if by a drain. They rose once more in a whirlpool, spiralling round and round.

A strange, flat light licked at gathering clouds in the sky. There must be a storm approaching. Just her luck on the night of the darkest moon. A spot of rain glanced off her face. Another followed and then another, mingling with the tears of frustration that began to fall. It was the storm that had stirred the water. This creature was never going to appear. She threw back her head and howled. Tropical in intensity, the rain pounded louder, reverberating off the lake. It was like that night on top of the Empire State Building, the time she had tried to renounce her goddess status. The same feeling that something was amiss. That this just might not have worked.

'How could you!' screamed Kumari, shaking her fist at the Holy Mountain. 'This is some kind of joke, right? Well, it's not funny! It's not fair!'

Of course, no answer came. She was hardly the gods' favourite. So far precisely one of her big attempts had worked and even that was with her mother's help. If Mamma had not appeared on her lion at Madison Square Garden, then the Ayah would probably have struck Kumari down.

OK, so she was not the greatest trainee goddess around, but it was time they cut her a break.

Soaked to the skin, Kumari squinted up at the summit. Raindrops clung to her lashes, making it hard to see. *Give me a sign*, she begged in her head. *Something, anything, to keep me going.* It was hard enough carrying out this vengeance thing, even harder to feel so alone. The rain was easing off, its power dissipating. If that was a sign, she needed something more. Something really startling.

From the rocks and crags the birds began to circle, the last hunting pass before night. Two particularly large ones drifted across the sky, getting closer and closer. Curiously, these birds did not move like the rest. For one thing, they appeared to be waving. Then Kumari realised these were not birds at all. These were two colourful canopies.

Beneath them, two tiny specks dangled. As they drew closer, the specks took shape, forming human figures. Or at least, they appeared human, bundled up as they were in silver outfits, their faces covered in balaclavas and goggles, snowshoes strapped to their feet. The figures had obviously spotted her and were steering in her direction. Mesmerised, mouth open in shock, Kumari gaped as they picked up speed. All of a sudden, the air currents caught them, sending them spiralling into freefall. Borne on those same air currents, a sound like a scream.

Closer and closer they came, in a last rush towards the ground. At last, with a bump, they landed in a heap. For a moment, no one moved and then the heap started to groan. First one staggered up then the other, hauled by its companion's gloved hand. As they stood, Kumari could see one was tall, the other shorter and rather squarer. This second figure kept up a litany of moaning and muttering that sounded strangely familiar. As both tore off their goggles and bala-clavas, Kumari's jaw dropped another fifteen centimetres. Rooted to the spot, she let out a strangled squeak.

Poking out from under the puffy outfit, a purple scarf scat-tered with glitter. Silver nails raked at flattened hair, its wild strands tipped with neon pink. The other figure was less exotic, but no less recognisable. As both faces broke into big smiles, Kumari blinked hard. It couldn't be. But it was. Oh my god, here, in her Kingdom. Impossible. But true.

'Ma, Theo!' she gasped.

CHAPTER 4

The acres of Ma's bosom felt more pillowy than ever which was probably something to do with the puffy snowsuit in which she was encased.

'Help me off with this darn thing,' commanded Ma once she had smothered Kumari in kisses. Hopping around on one leg, she tugged at various toggles, ripping and unzipping and achieving very little, trying to kick off her stubby snowshoes, which appeared to be stuck fast.

'Allow me,' said Theo, gallantly stepping forward and concertinaing his lanky frame.

Too late. With a screech of annoyance, Ma tumbled into the grass.

Smothering a giggle, Kumari helped Theo haul her back to

her feet. Patiently, Theo undid the straps on Ma's snowshoes and helped her wriggle out of her snowsuit. Finally divested of her down chrysalis, Ma emerged like a demented butter-fly, colours not so much clashing as annihilating one anoth-er. A candy pink sweater topped off a pair of puce leopard leggings, emblazoned across the sweater: *Bronx Babe*. On Ma's feet, fluffy boots that, for all the world, resembled two electrified cats. On her hands, a shrunken pair of orange gloves that spelled out *HOODOOHAIR* across the fingers.

'Lola knitted them for me,' said Ma, catching Kumari's glance. 'She's looking after the salon. Said these would remind me it's in safe hands. Darn things don't even fit right.'

Placing her gloved hands on Kumari's shoulders, Ma stud-ied her long and hard. 'What they been feeding you, child?' she said softly. 'You look like you're starving.'

'Yeah, well, things have not been too good around here lately.'

Around her waist, Ma wore a gold pouch which exactly matched the glittering extensions corkscrewing wildly from her hair. Delving into it, Ma pulled out a squashed doughnut.

'Emergency supplies,' she declared. 'Cinnamon apple. Your favourite.'

Before Kumari could take it, Badmash let out a desperate whimper. His belly growled, his wings flapped and the doughnut was snatched from Ma's hand.

'Let him,' said Kumari. 'He loves them so much.'

At least that explained the doughnut in the lake. It must have come from Ma's stock.

What it did not explain was what on earth Ma and Theo were doing here.

'It was all Theo's idea,' said Ma.

Theo's dark eyes twinkled. 'I had a little help with the details. Once Ma came and told us what was going on, we had to think pretty fast.'

'We? We who?' Kumari was none the wiser.

'Helen . . . Ms Martin and I. She so wanted to come see you, but she has her teaching commitments and no one else was free. Your friend Chico, he was desperate to come too, but there was no way they would let him out of school. It turned out we were the best choice. OK, the only choice.'

Chico? Chico had tried to come and see her? Disappointment stabbed at Kumari's guts. But wait, at least Ma and Theo were here, although they still had not told her precisely why. Kind, clever Theo, flakes of snow dusting his mop of raven curls. Had they climbed all the way up to the borderlands? It was an arduous trek. Kumari was surprised Ma had made it. Those extensions must weigh a ton.

'We flew up to the plateau,' said Theo, helpfully filling in the gaps. 'Crazy pilot said he could land us there. Then a Sherpa took us as far as he could through the snows. I remembered the rest of the route. I knew we couldn't get in through that petrified waterfall, but I thought we might be able to get over it if we judged it right and jumped off the rocks above. It took some persuading, but Ma here finally agreed.'

Ma shot him a look. 'Didn't get much choice, did I? Unless you call pushing me "persuading". Anyways, we're here now and not a moment too soon.'

'What do you mean?' said Kumari, still coming to terms with a vision of Ma parascending.

'That Simon Razzle, he's sent someone to snatch you back, child.'

'Simon Razzle? But that's ridiculous. I mean, how do you know this?'

Oh my god, so this was why they had come. The deranged cosmetic surgeon was making one more try to carve her up? Kumari shuddered at the memory. She could still see the stark white walls of Simon's surgery, in which he had held her captive, helpless, drugged and bound, ready to be dissected and sold off like prime cuts of meat.

'It was Sonny, he told me. After I twisted his arm.'

From the glint in Ma's eye, Kumari could tell she was speaking literally.

Still, none of this made sense. Razzle's heavies couldn't get to her here in her homeland.

'But no one can get into the Kingdom. It's impossible,' said Kumari.

'We just did,' said Theo.

Kumari gaped at him. She couldn't argue with that. She glanced at the sky. Somehow Ma and Theo had got through the protective canopy. The haze of Happiness must now be so thin it could be physically penetrated from beyond. From the World Beyond in fact, which meant they were all in danger. Kumari, Papa, their people. The very Kingdom itself. Maybe not immediately. It was hardly likely anyone else would come parascending by. Sooner or later, however, someone would figure it out. Once the haze disappeared altogether, the hidden Kingdom would become visible. No longer shielded, but exposed to the prying eyes of spy satellites, to the gaze of the World Beyond. Open to all who sought to enter, including the warlords waiting on the western frontier.

Kumari let out a shudder. Things were worse than she had thought. And now something else to contend with, the threat of a Razzle henchman appearing.

'But how does Razzle even know where the Kingdom is?' she demanded, looking first at Ma then Theo.

'He stole my notes and my drawings,' said Theo. 'Had Sonny break into my apartment.'

Kumari gaped at him, horrified. This was getting worse by the minute.

'And Sonny told you this?' she stammered.

'Once I sat on him,' said Ma.

Kumari winced at the vision. Ma was an awesome presence in more ways than one. Served the scrawny rat right, though. It was hard to believe he was Ma's offspring. Thanks to Sonny, Simon Razzle now knew where to find her. The very thought made her skin crawl. She had thought she was at least safe from him in the Kingdom, and it turned out she was anything but.

'Sonny got scared,' continued Ma. 'Soon as he realised Razzle was out to silence him. Couldn't leave any loose ends untied, the stakes being that high. Tried to hide out in my apartment, telling me he missed his ol' Ma. Then these heavy dudes came knocking and I realised what was what.'

Kumari could hear the pain in Ma's voice. A part of her would never stop hoping Sonny would go straight. It was about as likely as Ma taking up tiddlywinks, but no one had the heart to tell her that.

'But even if Razzle's men got into the Kingdom, they'd be

spotted,' said Kumari. 'It's a small place, you know. Strangers are forbidden here. They'd stand out at once. I mean, there are not exactly many other foreigners walking around. At least not apart from you two. And you've only just arrived. If they were here, I'd have heard about it.'

'Sonny said there's someone on the inside,' said Ma. 'Which could mean they're in hiding.'

Kumari gaped at her. Someone on the inside? In the Kingdom? No way! Then again, the Ayah had been on the inside, and look what she had achieved. Murdered Mamma, kidnapped Kumari, leaving a lasting legacy of suffering.

'Oh great,' muttered Kumari. 'Just what we need. Another traitor.'

'Now don't you go worrying,' said Ma. 'It's going to be OK.'

'Of course it is,' echoed Theo. Neither seemed convinced.

Kumari looked from one to the other. It was so great to see them. But however welcome, their presence brought its own problems. Like what to do with them, for instance. The minute the palace guards saw them, they would be deported. The only thing to do was somehow smuggle them into the palace and throw herself on the mercy of Papa. It was a long shot, but, to be frank, it was the only one they had got.

First things first. They had to hide the snowsuits. No point in trying to sneak into the palace sporting acres of silver nylon. And Kumari knew the perfect place: the bowels of the dragon tree. Bundling the snowsuits up with the canopies, they shoved them as far as they could up the hollow trunk.

'Hey, wait a minute,' said Ma, retrieving a cylindrical metal object. 'That's my Yankees travel mug. Where I go, it goes. Keeps my coffee steamin' hot.'

With the mug carefully stowed in Theo's backpack, they set off. Luckily, very few people ever came that way. Still, it was going to be quite a task getting Ma safely across the meadows and through the frangipani orchards. Kumari could only hope that anyone who happened to be watching would assume she was some kind of giant moth in full flight.

Sending Badmash ahead to scout a safe path, Kumari led the way. Quietly, Theo brought up the rear, shouldering both bags. Dusk was giving way to night and the air was alive with insects – dragonflies skimming out over the water, cicadas tuning up for their evening song. Now and then Theo would murmur in appreciation as he spotted a particularly interesting specimen, but otherwise they walked in silence, Kumari's ears ever alert. Which was why when Ma let out a shriek it proved particularly startling, propelling Kumari into the air in shock before she whirled round to see what was happening.

'There's a . . . *thing*. With horns. Over there, between those trees.'

Kumari peered through the frangipani branches. A shaggy face peered back.

'It's only a yak!' she hissed.

'A *what*?' Ma hissed back.

'A yak. Bit like a cow but hairier. It won't hurt you. It's too stupid.'

Well, that was the theory, at any rate.

She glanced at Theo, who was shaking with silent laughter.

'Come on,' said Kumari. 'We have to keep moving. Anyone spots us out here and you guys are toast.'

Sobering, Ma and Theo once more fell in behind Kumari. They wound their way along the edge of the wildflower meadows, white poppies dancing eerily in the twilight. As they came within sight of the palace, Kumari decided upon a detour, taking a wide loop through the forest that encroached upon the eastern fringes of the royal lawns, threading their way through teak and sal trees. Now and then Ma would stifle another squeak as the branches caught at her precious hairdo.

As they descended towards the palace walls, Kumari's heart kept up a steady thump. At the edge of the forest they watched and waited before at last breaking cover. There was no one around. No one, that is, apart from the herd of yaks, happily chomping. They would have to pass between them to reach the eastern door.

'Don't panic and don't run,' Kumari whispered. 'They won't hurt you so long as you don't disturb them.'

'B-but those horns . . .' Ma's voice quavered.

'Harmless,' Kumari lied, gripping Ma's elbow and steering her firmly through the herd.

They were halfway to the door when Badmash let out a warning squawk. Instantly, Kumari froze, straining her ears. Nothing. False alarm. She took another few steps. And then she heard it, the crack of branches breaking. Something or someone was in the forest, coming after them. It could be just another yak. Somehow she did not think so.

'Run!' she hissed.

'I thought you said not to run,' muttered Ma.

'Never mind what I said,' hissed Kumari. All this hissing was making her throat sore.

'There's someone coming,' murmured Theo. 'Come on, let's do it.'

And with that, they took to their heels, racing for the eastern door.

Their pounding feet acted like a starting pistol on the yak herd, sending them charging in circles. Round and round they raced, one or two scattering off at a tangent. From somewhere in the mêlée Kumari heard a shout. Their pursuer had collided with a yak. Then another shout from further behind. There was more than one of them. *Great.*

She could see the door and the latch now, within metres. Kumari lunged, grasping for it. The door swung open just as Ma let out another shriek.

'Let go of me! How dare you!'

A thud and then all three of them were falling through the door, Kumari slamming it after them. As she slid the bolt in place, someone rattled the lock. Picking herself up from the marble floor, Ma whooped in triumph.

'I got the sucker,' she declared. 'One punch and the guy was down.'

The door rattled again.

'They're not giving up,' said Theo.

And then, echoing towards them along the corridor that led to the eastern door, the sound of yet more footsteps. They were trapped inside the vaulted entrance hall, unable to go forward or back.

Oh double, double great. It had to be a detachment of palace guards. Get caught by them and the game was up.

'Follow me,' whispered Kumari. 'Quick, both of you. Up here.'

By the time the patrol appeared, they were well and truly hidden, teetering among the carved rafters that soared into the vaulted roof of the entrance chamber, Ma's foot wedged in a wooden demon's mouth. It had taken every ounce of Theo's strength to shove Ma up there. Grimly, he clung on to a creaking dragon. They watched as the guards halted by the eastern door, inspecting it with suspicion.

The rattling from the outside had stopped. Their pursuers must have given up. Her legs wrapped around a lacquered snake, Kumari's mind worked overtime. No one had known she was going to the lake. She had not even told the Ancient Abbot. Which meant that someone had followed her. She could only hope they had not seen too much. It was a feeling she had got used to since her return home, the sense that she was being watched. But by whom, she was not yet sure. Could it be Razzle's men were already here?

Unable to find anything wrong, the guards eventually shrugged and moved on. Kumari gave it a good five minutes more before finally sliding down from her perch. Landing beside her none too daintily, Ma let out a deep sigh.

'Lord, child, is it always like this round here?'

'It is now,' said Kumari.

'So who were those guys who chased us?' demanded Theo.

'That I have to find out.'

And find out she would, one way or another. But for now she had a bigger problem on her hands, two problems in fact. Her friends had barely arrived in the hidden Kingdom and it looked like someone had already blown their cover.

CHAPTER 5

A lamp burned by Papa's bed, illuminating the pilasters that rose from each corner. Etched into the ornate headboard, faces of the gods watched over Papa as he slept. At the foot of the bed was another lamp, set in a shallow copper dish. Apart from the magnificent bed, the room was simply furnished. Papa preferred it that way.

Softly, Kumari tiptoed to his side. He was breathing deeply and evenly. Even in sleep, he looked regal, his nose patrician, his mouth firm. Above his eyes, his brows arched, one slightly higher than the other. It lent his face an interesting quirk, softening his stern expression. Except Kumari knew Papa was not really stern. More preoccupied. She watched his once broad chest rise up and down. At least he was no longer gasping for air.

Sometimes, when he was tired, he did that. It seemed that whatever was ailing him did its worst at night. For once, though, Papa was resting peacefully. So peacefully, in fact, that Kumari could hardly bring herself to wake him. But wake him she must. This was important.

'Papa,' she whispered, gently stroking the hair from his forehead.

'Papa,' she said again. They did not have much time. Any minute now the night patrol would pass once more. If they even suspected the king had been disturbed they would be upon them in an instant.

'Kumari?' Papa was smiling at her, sleep-befuddled. Then his eyes opened wider. 'Kumari, is something wrong? What are you doing here my child?'

'Everything's fine, Papa. In fact, something wonderful has happened. My friends are here, Papa, from the World Beyond. The ones who helped save my life.'

Kumari held her breath. A look of consternation crossed Papa's face.

'Your friends here? I don't understand.'

'They've come to see me, Papa.'

All at once the king was sitting bolt upright, his face thunderous. This was not going to plan. Desperately, Kumari seized his hand.

'Papa, this is Ma and Theo. They've come to warn me, to help me. That man, Simon Razzle, has sent his men to snatch me back. The cosmetic surgeon who wanted to cut me up and find the secret of eternal youth. Anyway, he plans to try to take me away again to the World Beyond and if he does that you know I'll die. I mean, I've already had my year and a day out there. Ma and Theo know it too, which is why they've risked everything to come and tell me.'

The king's expression, although still severe, had softened a fraction. His gaze shifted to Ma and Theo, hovering uncertainly by the door.

'Come closer,' the king ordered. 'Come here where I can see you.'

Ma plonked herself on the end of the king's bed.

'I am *so* pleased to meet you,' she said. 'Kumari, she talked about her Papa all the time. It's an honour to be here, your excellency. Heck, I mean your holiness. Your majesty. Whatever. Say, can I just call you Pops? That would be a whole lot easier.'

Papa's face took on an interesting hue, somewhere between pink and purple. His lips worked, but no words emerged. Finally, he spat a couple out.

'*Pops?* And you are . . .?'

'Ma Hernandez. Well, actually, it's Salome, but everyone calls me Ma on account of my hoodoo.'

'Ma. I see. And you?'

'Theo Kreouzis at your service.'

At your service? Had everyone gone mad? You'd think they'd never come across a god-king before.

'It was Ma's apartment I stayed at in New York,' said Kumari. 'And Theo's the scientist who helped me find my way back here.'

'Scientist? I don't approve of science, but I'm very grateful for what you did for my daughter.'

37

Papa's face had now cleared, but he had yet to smile. *Oh please*, begged Kumari silently, *please let them just stay tonight. Don't give them over to the guards. These are my friends, Papa.*

'Well, thank you for coming,' said the king. 'But I'm afraid you must leave now. It's good of you to travel all this way to warn us, but, really, there is no chance of anyone penetrating our Kingdom.'

'If you'll excuse me, sir,' said Theo. 'There is every chance someone might get in. After all, Ma and I managed it. What's to stop Razzle's men?'

That crease was back between Papa's brows. 'And how exactly did you get in?'

'They, uh, flew,' said Kumari. It was better to leave out the exact details. Suddenly, Papa looked very tired. 'I . . . I need to speak with my advisors.'

He leaned over and tugged at two cords by his bed, one for the RHM and one for the Ancient Abbot. Fab flippin' not so 'tastic. Now they had three people to convince. It was a toss-up as to which one would object the most. Within moments they were there, hurrying to the king's side – the Ancient Abbot with his long locks all askew, the RHM pristine in night robes.

The Ancient Abbot was still fumbling for words when the RHM spoke loud and clear.

'What on earth are these people doing here? Get them out of the king's chamber at once!'

He stared at Ma in particular, a glimmer of recognition dawning.

'You remember Ma,' said Kumari.

'Indeed I do.'

'And Theo here, he flew with us back from the World Beyond.'

'Ah yes. The scientist. It is good to see you again, sir. I am afraid, however, that your presence has come as a shock. If you'll excuse me, I must speak with the king.'

With that, they were dismissed, banished to the dressing room where Papa's robes were kept. The RHM's demeanour had not boded well. Nervously, Kumari chewed her lip. Even with an ear pressed to the door, she could not hear what was going on.

'They don't seem too happy to see us,' whispered Theo.

'No, no, it's just . . . protocol,' said Kumari.

What felt like a whole moon cycle passed and still they were waiting. Badmash had fallen asleep in one of the king's bejewelled headdresses when finally the door swung open. There stood the RHM, beckoning them back to the king's bedside.

'His holy majesty has made a decision,' announced the RHM.

Papa waved a feeble hand.

'Your friends may stay,' said the king and Kumari let out a whoop of joy. 'The RHM tells me the threat from this Razzle person is all too real and it seems we must ask for your help.'

The king looked at Ma and Theo. Was that a plea Kumari could see in Papa's eyes? Surely not. The king would never beg. Then again, these were dire times.

'I apologise for your lack of welcome but your entry was most unorthodox.'

'Hey, no problem,' said Ma. 'It's not everyone drops in by parachute.'

Too late, Kumari's kick landed on Ma's ankle. Mercifully, the king let that one pass. His strength was fading fast.

'Permit me to continue,' he said. 'You will be allowed to stay for a maximum of one moon.'

'One moon? How long is that? I only bought a one-week ticket.'

The RHM's cool gaze flicked to Ma. 'One moon is the equivalent of one of your months in the World Beyond.'

'A month! I have two daughters. A business to run. A non-refundable air ticket. Y'know I'd love to stay, Kumari, but it's impossible, honey.'

'We would be very grateful,' said the RHM, 'if you would consider altering your plans. I can arrange for messages to be sent to your daughters and your, ah, colleagues, if that would help. And we would, of course, reimburse any additional expenses. We feel that Kumari's safety depends on your presence here. We are, madam, sir, asking for your help.'

'Surely you can protect Kumari?' said Theo.

'Only from threats we understand. In this Kingdom, we are not used to crime. Kumari's kidnapping was shocking to us. You know the ways of the World Beyond. You will be able to give us insights into this Simon Razzle. As you are a scientist, you will also be able to help us with our work. We are attempting to classify our entire ecosystem. I have persuaded his majesty this is necessary.'

At this, the king sighed and shut his eyes, his face as white as his pillow. Papa did so hate to break with tradition. Kumari could see the pain on his face.

'As part of this study,' said the RHM, 'we will examine how our plants, animals and minerals interact. We plan to identify the factors that make our Kingdom such a special place, that keep us all so youthful.'

Kumari saw the gleam in Theo's eye. A new scientific challenge! One that was absolutely unique. He was already champing at the bit.

'You will be accommodated in the monastery,' the RHM went on. 'There you may blend in with the monks, and the Abbot can look after you. We already have a laboratory within the building which is dedicated to the study of the medicinal and magical properties of native plants and minerals. We would be honoured if you would bring your expertise to our studies and give us a new perspective.'

Theo inclined his head. *A done deal*, thought Kumari. *Clever old RHM. He knew exactly what to say.*

'And madam,' the RHM had turned to Ma once more. 'I have a special request for you. Kumari has been without an Ayah since the . . . unfortunate incident with her previous one. We would consider it a great service if you would take the post of her guardian temporarily. That way, you could keep a close eye on Kumari at all times. As you can see, the child needs someone to care for her now that her Mamma has departed us.'

Bingo! The RHM had hit the right button again. Ma's eyes misted over.

'I sure can,' she said, crushing Kumari to her chest. *Letting me breathe would be a good start*, thought Kumari. Still, it did feel good to get another of those huge hugs. Cuddles had been thin on the ground lately.

'We'll stay,' declared Ma. 'Won't we, Theo?'

Theo nodded enthusiastically, his scientist's mind already seeing possibilities.

'In that case,' said the RHM, 'I shall make immediate arrangements.'

'The girls will be OK,' said Ma. 'CeeCee and LeeLee, they're nearly eighteen and my neighbour is looking in on them. In fact, they probably won't even notice I'm not there. All they do is study at the moment. As for Sonny, well, he's gone. Took off the minute I let go of him. Maybe you could just get a message to the girls, tell them not to worry. And another one to Lola at Hoodoo Hair. That's my beauty salon.'

'I remember,' said the RHM. *But how?* thought Kumari. She couldn't recall the RHM visiting Hoodoo Hair.

'I am on sabbatical,' said Theo. 'But perhaps you could inform my family. And my, ah, girlfriend, Helen Martin. You may recall her.'

'Indeed I do,' said the RHM.

Girlfriend? So now they were official. Kumari slid a sideways glance at Theo. Ms Martin, her old teacher. Miss Dangly Earrings and A-line skirts. She and geeky Theo made a good couple. But how was the RHM going to let everyone know? It was not like there was an international postal service in the Kingdom. In fact, all contact with the World Beyond was forbidden. Perhaps the RHM was just saying that to make them stay, in which case he was doing wrong. Should she say something now? And risk Ma and Theo leaving?

All of a sudden, a choking sound bubbled up from Papa's throat. The Ancient Abbot let out a gasp. He grasped the king's wrist, feeling for a pulse. Kumari's hand flew to her mouth. Papa's head had slumped to one side. His face had taken on the sheen of marble, more statue than living being. His body spasmed into rigidity, his eyelids clamped tight shut.

'Your holy majesty,' cried the Abbot. He turned to the others. 'He's not moving. He's not breathing.'

'His lips – look at the colour. And this paralysis. He's been poisoned,' said Theo. 'Shouldn't we call a doctor?'

'I am the palace physician,' said the Abbot.

'Then what should we do?'

'Whatever we can to save him.'

Without waiting for further instructions, Theo bent over Papa and placed his hands flat on the centre of his chest. Ignoring an outcry from the RHM, he began rhythmically to pump. What felt like for ever passed until, all of a sudden, Papa's chest rose and fell of its own accord. Within a few more minutes he was breathing unaided, although the rest of his body still lay unmoving.

'We need to keep a close watch on him,' said Theo. 'Although I think he's out of danger for now.'

'But how could this have happened?' said the Abbot. 'Everything his holy majesty eats is tasted first.'

'Who makes his food?' asked Theo.

'A woman I would trust with my life: Cook.'

'You sure about that?' said Theo.

'Entirely sure,' said the Abbot. 'Cook has been here almost as long as I. She loves the royal family as her own.'

'We need to step up security measures at once. Double taste anything and everything.' The RHM's mouth was a grim line. 'We cannot allow someone the chance to slip him another dose.'

Her Papa poisoned? It was too much to take. Kumari's sobs began to fill the room.

'Hush now, Kumari. He's going to be all right. Ain't that so, Theo?'

Ma rocked her to and fro, holding her tight. Theo looked at the Ancient Abbot and almost imperceptibly shook his head.

Kumari flung herself across her Papa's chest and let out a wail. But, as she slowly raised her head, gazing in disbelief at his beloved face, she thought she saw his lips move. Bending her ear very close, she just about heard him murmur.

'You must fetch the Secrets of the Kingdom. Only way to save us all. Your Mamma, she guards eight. Tell no one, my darling.'

The Secrets of the Kingdom? Eight? Papa must be delirious.

And then he was silent, his lips moving no more.

'Papa . . .?' she croaked. 'Please, Papa, don't leave me.'

'It's all right, Kumari,' said Ma. 'Look, honey, he's sleeping.'

Through streaming eyes, Kumari stared at her Papa, at last seeing the breath flutter in his chest. So slight it was like the stirring of a moth's wing, but a breath nonetheless. She took his limp hand in hers.

'Come on, Papa,' she murmured. 'I'm strong enough for both of us.'

But despite her brave words, abject terror clamped her tight in its grasp. She could not, would not lose her Papa. She would hold on, help him cling to life, give him all the love she could muster.

'Oh Mamma, help me,' she prayed.

What was it Papa had said? Something about Mamma

44

guarding secrets. But the Secrets of the Kingdom were kept in the temple vault. It did not make sense. Just at that moment there came a loud hammering on the door. Before them stood a monk, terror choking the words as he tried to get them out.

'It's the fires, sir, the fires!'

'And what about them?' snapped the RHM.

The monk trembled as he stared at the floor.

'The holy fires have gone out.'

CHAPTER 6

'You must not speak of this to anyone.'
The RHM's eyes bore into the monk's.

'Yes sir. I mean, no sir.'

The monk was practically gibbering.

At least Papa appeared to be breathing freely once more. Kumari dared not drag her gaze from him. It felt that, if she did, she might break the fragile thread with which he clung on to life.

'Kumari.'

The RHM was addressing her. And still she ignored him, staring at her Papa, willing him to keep breathing.

'Kumari,' repeated the RHM.

It was no good. She was not listening.

'My child,' said the Ancient Abbot.

Even his words fell on deaf ears.

Go away, thought Kumari. *Just go away, all of you. Come on, Papa, that's it. One breath in, one breath out.*

'Kumari.'

It was the RHM again, one hand on her shoulder this time. Impatiently, she shook it off, but still he kept talking. 'Kumari, I know you don't want to hear this but we need to take immediate action. If the fires have gone out then it is not only your Papa who is in mortal danger, but the Kingdom as well.'

'But it's my Papa who's lying here,' sobbed Kumari.

'I know, child, but duty calls. Your Papa would not want you to desert your people in their hour of need. Besides, this is for his holy majesty as well. Believe me, Kumari, this is life or death. We must restart the fires or the haze of Happiness will soon disappear. What residual Happiness there is can only last one more moon at most. It was already thin before this happened. If it disappears then all is lost. The World Beyond will begin to encroach, polluting this special place. The Kingdom will be lost for ever. All of us here will succumb to Time. For a living god like your Papa this means that divinity will be extinguished for ever more. The haze of Happiness acts as divine oxygen.'

A tiny bell rang in the recesses of Kumari's mind, its knell resounding. The RHM was right. Duty called. She was, above all, the girl-goddess. Which meant she, as well as Papa, faced certain extinction if the fires remained unlit. Being one per cent mortal, she might last a little while. But in his weakened state, Papa would succumb immediately.

It's not fair! she wanted to yell. *Why me? I'm all on my own right now. Mamma's in limbo. Papa's unconscious. I'm the only one left.*

'It's OK, honey, we're here for you,' said Ma, ever intuitive. Kumari could feel the loving warmth that seeped from her, soothing her soul. She could do this herself for Papa, for her people.

'So how do we restart the fires?' muttered Kumari, still keeping one eye on Papa. His lips twitched slightly. Surely that was a good sign.

'We must retrieve the Secrets of the Kingdom from the temple,' said the RHM. Kumari's spine stiffened. Papa's words resounded in her head. She must tell no one what he had said. 'Or rather, you must, Kumari. Only those of holy blood are permitted to enter the innermost sanctum. We should leave at once.'

Kumari bent forward and gently placed her cheek on Papa's chest. She could hear his heart beating, oh so slowly. Was it stronger, though? Just maybe. Her own felt like it might tear in two. Shakily, she forced herself to her feet.

'Come on, then. Let's go.'

'I'll stay with your Papa,' said Theo.

Kumari smiled at him in gratitude. Papa would be safe with Theo.

'I'm coming with you,' said Ma, in a tone that brooked no argument.

Seizing the moment, the RHM bundled them out of the room. The monk was stationed outside the door, with strict orders to send for them if necessary. 'If necessary' did not sound good, but she had to do this, for Papa and the Kingdom.

The RHM was practically running, Kumari keeping pace alongside him. Ma fell back with the Ancient Abbot, some distance behind. They raced through the courtyards and corridors that linked the royal quarters with the temple. What was normally a short walk suddenly felt like an endless trek. But here they were at last, at the temple doors, guarded by bejewelled lions. Between the lions stood two monks, each bearing a ceremonial sword.

'At ease,' commanded the RHM. 'Bow down for the girl-goddess.'

At the sight of her, their heads dropped, practically sweeping the floor in obeisance.

Oh, for heaven's sake, thought Kumari. *Just get the doors open.*

And then they were swinging wide, admitting them to the outer chamber of the temple. A thousand flames flickered from every wall, amplified by the bronze bowls in which they floated, illuminating the gods painted twenty metres high, scenes of the heavens soaring into the gilded ceiling. Their eyes seemed to follow Kumari as she darted after the RHM. From behind she could hear panting. It sounded as if the hounds of hell were on their tail.

She turned and saw Ma and the Ancient Abbot, puffing and wheezing as they put on a spurt. Reunited, the little party gathered at the door to the inner temple. The RHM rapped the lion-shaped knocker once, twice. They could hear a latch rattling. From within, a voice called out: 'Who's there?'

'The girl-goddess. Open up.'

The sound of a key rasping in the lock and then another figure bent low.

'Your holy highness,' murmured a muffled voice, the hammered bronze door half open.

'Yes, yes,' said the RHM, trying to push the door wider.

'Wait!' cried out the temple attendant. His knees shook but he stood firm. 'None may enter the innermost sanctum save those of holy blood.'

'The girl-goddess will go alone,' said the RHM.

The man was only doing his duty. Even so, Kumari wished he would hurry up. Every second was another spent away from her Papa. The attendant led them through an antechamber to another, heavily-bolted door and produced a huge bunch of keys. He fiddled with the first lock, finally getting it to turn. Four locks later and Kumari was suppressing a scream. The attendant must not pick up on their urgency. Walls had ears within the hidden Kingdom and most especially within the palace. Should anyone even guess the holy fires had gone out, everything would be lost. Rumblings of anarchy had already stirred the people up. Such a catastrophe might prove the last straw. The ensuing panic would lead to chaos. *Keep calm*, Kumari thought. And then, *I wonder if Papa's OK?*

At last the final bolt gave way and they were faced with yet one more door, this time of plain, uncarved wood. It did not appear to have a lock at all. How on earth were they supposed to get through? Correction, how was *she* supposed to get through? The RHM was already pushing her forward.

'But . . . ' Kumari began.

And then the door simply opened.

Just like that, at her approach, as if it had been waiting for her footstep. It reminded Kumari of the automatic doors she had so loved in New York. But in the Kingdom? Surely not. Nervously, she hesitated on the threshold, glancing back at Ma and the Ancient Abbot. Ma's teeth bared in an encouraging smile. The Abbot merely nodded.

'You'll find the scrolls within the dragon's mouth,' said the RHM. 'It is written so within the Temple Lore. Hurry now, Kumari. There is no time to waste.'

Gingerly, Kumari put one foot over the threshold. It was awfully dark in there. Darker still when the door closed with a sigh behind her. A solitary lamp illuminated a steep flight of stone steps that led down into nothingness. Oh great. Now all she had to do was break her neck. Keeping one hand on the wall, Kumari made it to the bottom. With her eyes growing accustomed to the gloom, she peered about, searching.

No dragon's mouth here. In fact, no animals of any description. All she could see was a bare stone plinth, just visible in the dim light. The chamber was only about the size of Papa's dressing room. She might as well go back, tell them all it was a waste of time. This was obviously the wrong innermost sanctum after all. Besides, it was pretty creepy. Was that a cobweb brushing against her face? Or something worse . . .

She swatted the cobweb aside. Strange. That was one thick cobweb. Groping about, she grasped hold of it again. This was no cobweb. It was a cord. Experimentally, Kumari tugged. It was as if a veil had been swept aside. Curtains above the plinth parted to reveal an enamelled imperial dragon, its back arched, cat-like. Poking from the dragon's mouth, a long, red tongue, curling upwards as if to cradle

51

something. Only there was nothing there, no ancient scrolls, no Secrets. Maybe they had fallen out of the dragon's mouth. Desperately, Kumari scrabbled around.

But there was nothing else on the stone plinth nor on the smooth floor that surrounded it. Perhaps her first thought had been right. This *was* the wrong innermost sanctum. Unlikely, though. After all, how many could there be? As for innermost sanctums with imperial dragons, the probability of there being another was rather low. About nil, in fact.

Stomach plummeting, Kumari stumbled back up the steps and out through the door.

'They've gone!' she cried to the waiting party.

'Gone? What do you mean?' The RHM looked alarmed.

'Gone, as in gone. Disappeared. They're not there, in the dragon's mouth. I mean, they're not anywhere. Someone must have taken them.'

'Impossible,' said the temple guardian.

'Impossible,' echoed the Ancient Abbot.

'I am telling you,' said Kumari. 'Why don't you go see for yourselves?'

At this, the temple guardian looked profoundly shocked.

'That would be sacrilege,' he stuttered. 'Only those of holy blood may enter. But no other such person has been here, I swear. Her holy highness must be mistaken.'

'Are you absolutely sure they're not there?' said the RHM.

'Of course I'm sure. I looked everywhere. I mean, it's not exactly a huge place.'

The RHM looked at the Ancient Abbot.

'In the circumstances, is there any way we can breach the sanctuary and see with our own eyes?'

The Ancient Abbot placed a hand on Kumari's shoulder. 'I see no need. If Kumari says the Secrets have disappeared then I take her word for it. We must organise a search party without delay.'

For once, the RHM appeared at a loss. Kumari met his eyes and saw something that instantly squeezed the breath out of her throat.

The Secrets of the Kingdom had disappeared and the RHM was afraid.

If the RHM was afraid, then things were very bad indeed.

CHAPTER 7

'So what exactly are these Secrets?' asked Theo. They were huddled in the corridor outside Papa's bedroom. Inside, he lay sleeping peacefully, as he had done all the while they were at the temple. Except that this seemed more than just a deep sleep. Another reason to worry.

Papa was a god-king, after all. Gods were supposed to be invincible. A tiny one per cent of him remained mortal until the day he ascended the Holy Mountain. And something was slowly killing that one per cent. Now the haze of Happiness was thinning, the immortal part of Papa was also under threat. If the fires of Happiness remained unlit he would not be strong enough to survive. Her Papa would be snuffed out like a light.

'The Secrets of the Kingdom,' said Kumari, 'are kind of

like the blueprint for how this place works. Within them are supposed to be the recipes for Happiness and longevity and all the other things that make the Kingdom so special. There is also perhaps the greatest Secret of them all, the Secret of the holy fires that feed everything.'

'Recipes?' said Theo. 'You mean there are specific formulae for these things?'

'So they say,' said Kumari. 'Of course, I have never actually seen the Secrets. Until now, there was no need. They are kept locked in the temple until a time of crisis.'

'Well, you sure got one of those,' said Ma, letting out a long, low whistle.

'Shhhh,' said Kumari. 'Someone might hear.'

She loved Ma to bits, but she could be awfully loud. Still, they had to stick around here. They were officially guarding Papa while the Ancient Abbot and the RHM questioned all the monks in the temple. Kumari could not imagine anyone trying to defy the RHM in his present mood. He was truly terrifying. His eyes had gone all steely, like they were sharp enough to stab you. She had never seen him quite this angry, even when he showed up to rescue her in New York.

'OK,' said Theo. 'What's in these recipes?'

'That, no one knows except the gods. At least, not until the Secrets are read.'

'Are you telling me no one has read these Secrets before?'

'No one has needed to. There has never been a situation like this. Normally everything in the Kingdom is hunky dory. Well, it was until recently.'

Theo looked at Kumari, but his mind was elsewhere. She could see it ticking like a clock. Thank god she had left *those* behind in the World Beyond. Kumari hated clocks. They scared her, the way they counted off the days. Here, they lived by the rhythms of the moon. Eternal. Tidal.

'So,' said Theo slowly. 'There is a chance the Secrets might be total nonsense.'

'Absolutely not!' said Kumari.

'Hey, don't look at me like that. I'm only approaching this as a scientist. And, as a scientist, I have some serious questions.'

'Ask away,' came a quiet voice from behind them.

Kumari whirled round. There stood the Ancient Abbot. Unfortunately for Theo, he was one of the few people in the Kingdom who spoke English.

'Hey, Abbot,' said Ma.

The Ancient Abbot inclined his head. Kumari noticed the smile he bestowed upon her. Seemed like the Abbot was a fan. And look, Ma was smiling back.

'How you getting on with those monks?' said Ma.

'No progress as yet. The RHM is still questioning them. I thought I would check on the king.'

'He's still sleeping,' mumbled Kumari miserably.

'Yes, child, I know. That's why we must find the Secrets.'

The Ancient Abbot looked at Theo. There was a glint in his eye Kumari had never seen before.

'The Secrets of the Kingdom, sir, are sacred to us. They needed to be set down for situations such as these. The gods are prudent, you see. They foresaw there might one day come a disaster of these proportions.'

'Shame they didn't make a copy,' said Theo. 'And as for dumping it on the trainee, now that is kind of rough.'

It was meant as a joke, but Kumari could see the Abbot was not amused.

'By "trainee" I assume you mean Kumari. The gods did not "dump" this upon her. She was born to serve the Kingdom and I consider her more than up to the task.'

Kind, if not strictly accurate, thought Kumari. Fascinating how the Abbot's nostrils flared when he got angry. OK, maybe angry was the wrong word. When his calm was ruffled.

'Of course she is,' said Theo, without a trace of sarcasm. Doubly kind. It was eerie.

Although they were probably only being so nice on account of Papa. Kumari let out a shuddering sigh. 'Look,' she said. 'Can we just cut to the chase? I want to get back to Papa.'

'Cut to the . . .?' The Ancient Abbot looked perplexed.

'Just spit it out, honey,' said Ma.

'I . . . well, the Secrets are very real, to address your suspicions.' The Ancient Abbot glanced at Theo. 'It was deemed necessary to set them down in case the royal line ever died out. Of course,' he hurried on, seeing Kumari's face, 'that would be almost inconceivable. But it was felt that the Secrets should be kept in a safe place as a kind of safety net.'

'Not so safe, though,' said Theo.

'We thought so until tonight.' For a moment, the Ancient Abbot looked completely dejected. On an impulse, Kumari squeezed his hand.

'And you're saying the recipe, as you call it, for the fires is somewhere in these Secrets?' Theo looked at the Abbot, that scientist expression back on his face.

'There is a precise list of the eight ingredients needed to

57

create the holy fires of Happiness. It is assumed they are contained within the Secrets.'

'You assume that, but you cannot be sure?'

'We cannot be sure of anything.'

In the pause that followed, Papa's words echoed in Kumari's head. He had said something about Mamma guarding 'eight'. There were eight ingredients for the fires. Perhaps they were not with the other Secrets after all. She was about to open her mouth and speak out when she remembered Papa's admonition. She must tell no one of what he had said. Instead, she would act upon it.

'So it seems like we have to track these Secrets down,' said Theo. 'Send out search parties.'

'That is happening as we speak,' said the Abbot. 'So far we have found nothing.'

'But this is a small place. Almost impossible to penetrate. It has to be an inside job.'

Kumari looked into Theo's fervent face, alight with urgency. Everything she saw there mirrored how she felt. But what to do? The Ancient Abbot spread his hands.

'Believe me, we are doing our best. To lose the haze of Happiness would be a disaster. It's the protective shield that separates us from the World Beyond. Without it the Kingdom will die.'

The Abbot's words fell into a silence so deep Kumari thought she might drown in it. For the first time, it really hit home. This was truly life or death. Papa's life. Her people's lives. Kumari's own existence, come to that.

'Wow!' sighed Ma.

That about said it all.

CHAPTER 8

'Kumari, honey . . .'

It was Ma, peering round her bedroom door.

'Sweetie, in all the excitement I forgot to give you this.'

She was handing her a package.

Kumari stared at it, almost too tired to care. It had been one very long night. She had spent most of it staring out at the stars through the arched windows that lined the far wall of her room.

'Aren't you going to open it?'

Something in Ma's voice made her look up. On Ma's face was a mischievous smile. In her eye, the old glint. She was doing her best to cheer Kumari up.

'It's from your friends back home, Kumari. Your other

home, that is. I'll always think of you as belonging in the Bronx even if you can't come back there. LeeLee and CeeCee, they put something in there, along with all the ladies at the salon. And your schoolfriends, they sent you stuff too and so did your teachers. You might even find a letter from someone special. You know. Whatshisname.'

'Whatshisname? You mean Chico?'

Ma tried and failed to look innocent.

'That's the one. Chico.'

Tearing open the packet, Kumari shook it over her canopied bed. A mass of cards, letters, photographs and more packages tumbled out, the majority tiny and carefully wrapped. Kumari picked up a postcard at random. It was a picture of Manhattan. On the back:

Still shopping till we're dropping . . .

Love ya!

Charley & Hannah xxx

Along with the postcard, they had sent a bunch of photos, mostly of school and the neighbourhood. There was one of them gesturing to the school gates, pulling faces, *Rita Moreno Middle School* clearly visible above the entrance. Then there was another of the cafeteria, her entire class clustered around the Coke machine. Kumari sighed. What she would give for a can of Coke.

As she gazed at it longingly, Ma handed her one of the larger parcels.

'Go on, unwrap it,' she urged. 'It's from CeeCee and LeeLee.'

Kumari ripped off the gift-wrap. A shiny object tumbled out.

'Oh my god!' she cried. There it was, a can of the murky brew.

'They thought you might be needing that,' said Ma. 'I'd say they thought right.'

Greedily, Kumari popped the tab and took a long swig. Instantly she was transported in her mind back to the Bronx, to the corner shop where she used to grab a Coke, to the cafeteria machine she once attacked.

'That is so good,' said Kumari, carefully putting the Coke aside for now. There were so many photos still to look at, so many cards and letters to read. Here was one from Mrs Brinkman, a note written in a crabbed hand: *For darling Kumari*. Stuck next to it, a candy bar. First Coke, now a candy bar. This was too much to take in. Badmash eyed the shiny wrapper.

'Get off, you greedy bird,' said Kumari.

A leopard-print headband from Lola, a pair of skull earrings from Ms Martin. So many expressions of love from all her friends. The tears sprang to Kumari's eyes.

'Why don't you open this one?' said Ma, pressing a little box into Kumari's hands. Opening it, she extracted a tiny object, earphones dangling, ready.

'It's an iPod!' gasped Kumari.

'Go on. Have a listen.'

Ma was helping her insert the earphones, beaming all the while.

A momentary crackle and then Kumari's jaw dropped. She would know that voice anywhere. It was Chico talking to her.

'Hey there, Kumari. Thought you might like to hear some of your favourite songs. Miss you girl, so much.'

'We all do.' That was Hannah.

And then a chorus of *yeahs* and cheering. It sounded like the whole class was there.

'Hey Kumari, love you.'

Hannah again.

'Big kiss.'

And that was Charley.

'Hello, Kumari. Hope you're working hard.'

Ms Martin. *Amazing.* And then she added, 'Look after Theo.'

Double, double amazing.

'Kumari, we all miss you at Rita Moreno.' Oh my god, no way. Ms LaMotta! The principal, of all people. This was so great.

Kumari pulled one earphone out for Ma to hear. 'I can't believe they did this.'

'Why not? They love you,' smiled Ma.

'And now,' said Chico, 'some more friends want to say hello.'

A lull and then another chorus of voices:

'Hello, Kumari!'

It was the ladies from Hoodoo Hair. In the background, the hum of hairdryers. Ma still kept a couple of the old-fashioned ones in the salon for her elderly clients.

'I sent you some candy, honey.' That was Mrs Brinkman.

'Hi, sweetie. Don't be too good now.' A loud cackle from Lola.

'She should talk,' said Ma.

Then they were hearing Chico's voice again.

'OK, some sounds. You enjoy, Kumari.'

An intro blasted out. Deranged, her favourite band. And

they were playing 'Heaven Sent'. The best song ever. As they swung into the first chorus, she was right back there, on the stage at Madison Square Garden, singing along. In the audience, Chico, smiling up at her. They'd all been there: Ma. Charley, Hannah. CeeCee, LeeLee. Ms Martin, Theo.

Another song now, blasting away the sudden bleakness. 'Shoot Me Down in Flames'. Her second favourite song ever. Kumari warbled along, jigging about on her bed. 'Shoot me. Shoot me . . .'

Badmash glared at her from the pillow as she bounced him around but Kumari did not care. She was back with her friends, so happy she did not want it to end. Happier there than here, if only for a moment. The song ended and he was talking again. Chico. Her boy.

'Kumari, I wish you were here or I was there. You have no idea how much I miss you.'

'Me too,' she murmured. 'I miss you.'

And then he was gone.

Kumari listened to the yawning silence for a moment. Then she pulled the earphones from her ears and lay down on her bed. As her shoulders shook in silent sobs, Ma patted her like a child.

'It's OK, honey, you let it out,' she soothed. 'Have a good cry and you'll feel better.'

From the depths of her misery Kumari heard Ma's words. If only they were true.

KUMARI'S JOURNAL
(TOP SECRET. FOR MY EYES ONLY.
EVERYONE ELSE KEEP OUT!)
THIS MEANS YOU!

My bedroom (again)

First Dark Moon of the Year

I am so tired I can barely see to write this, but I also can't seem to sleep. I can't believe all those things from my friends. I mean, amazing!! It was such a sweet thought and I loved it, but it makes me miss them all more than ever. I wish I had them here now. It's good to have friends around when things are so bad. I know I have Ma and Theo and people like Cook and the Ancient Abbot, but it's not like they're my own age. They don't really understand.

Well, maybe Ma does. She is sitting with Papa tonight. Says she might as well seeing as jet lag keeps her up anyway. She promised to call me if he wakes up. And he is going to wake up. I don't care what anyone else thinks. He has to wake up. He's my Papa. I need him. I know the people need him too, but right now it's my heart that's hurting.

We simply have to find the Secrets of the Kingdom fast, and we only have one moon to do that. Any longer and the haze of Happiness will disappear and then everything will be lost. Tomorrow the New Moon will rise which means every second counts. Theo has his scientist head on – I just hope he thinks of something. I know the RHM is also working on it, but right now I feel so helpless.

Lucky old Badmash – he slept through the whole thing. Look at him dreaming now, his little feet twitching. I wish tonight had been just a dream, but it's not. It's real. Who could have stolen the Secrets? It's not like they're easy to take. The temple guardian could not believe it – the guy looked like he might cry. And the RHM – he was really angry, but in that way of his where he never says much, just looks really, really cold like he could turn you to ice.

Thing is, as the Ancient Abbot said, it's no use being angry now. We need to find the Secrets, not run around looking for someone to blame. Although, actually, if we knew who to blame, that might lead us to the Secrets. I mean, it could have been those people who chased us, me, Ma and Theo. I told the RHM about that but he just got all huffy at me. Said I should have told him before and I suppose I should, but there wasn't time. Aaargh – my mind is going round and round in circles. It really is hard to think.

And what about what Papa said? Something about Mamma guarding eight secrets. Could be eight secrets, eight ingredients . . . my brain doesn't seem to want to work any more . . .

CHAPTER 9

Theo's robes barely scraped his knees. The Ancient Abbot looked worried.

'You are somewhat taller than the average monk.'

'Story of my life,' said Theo.

'Are you ready, Brother Theo?'

'As ready I'll ever be. And please, it's just Theo.'

'While you stay with us, we consider you our brother. You are one of us now.'

The Ancient Abbot's gesture indicated Theo's garb and then swept open to take in his surroundings.

Casting one last glance round his cell, Theo reflected it was a little minimal. A low bed (far too short). A table. A chair. Nothing else. Nowhere to plug in his laptop. Thank god for his portable solar charger. Theo picked up his laptop and pulled the door to.

'How do I lock this?'

The Ancient Abbot looked shocked.

'There are no locks on the majority of doors in the Kingdom. We find such a notion offensive. There is no need to lock an ordinary door such as this. No one will take anything.'

No power and now no locks. There was something to be said for civilisation as he knew it. In any case, the Abbot was clearly wrong.

'But there were locks on those temple doors,' said Theo. 'And someone did get in to steal. The question is how they did it.'

The Ancient Abbot looked perturbed. 'That we don't know.'

Clearly this was a thorny issue. The Abbot looked almost shamefaced. Averting his eyes, he began to lead the way. Their discussion was evidently over.

'We monks move somewhat slowly,' advised the Ancient Abbot as they processed through the labyrinth of passageways. Theo gritted his teeth. The guy was practically sleepwalking. At this rate they would be in the laboratory just in time for lunch. Theo's stomach growled. He had not yet had breakfast.

'Say, is there any place I can get a coffee?' asked Theo.

'I will get someone to bring you tea,' said the Ancient Abbot. 'I'm afraid there is no coffee here.'

No coffee. Unreal. Theo was a New Yorker, after all. The city that ran on caffeine. Not some kind of weak, herbal tea. This was not a good start.

They came to an intersection. The Ancient Abbot turned right. Theo glanced over his shoulder. The other way, the corridor was in complete darkness.

'What's up there?' he asked, jerking his thumb.

'We call it the Forbidden Sanctuary. Those are the holy hermit's quarters.'

A holy hermit? Now the picture really was complete. Theo smiled to himself. And then the Ancient Abbot was opening yet another door, leading him into a light room lined with plain wooden benches. At these, several monks stood, dissecting medicinal plant specimens or grinding powders. The Ancient Abbot inclined his head and the monks bowed in return.

'Brother Theo,' he announced. 'He is here to help us.'

If the monks were surprised at Theo's appearance they were too polite to show it.

'Brother Lopsang here will show you what to do,' said the Abbot. There was a knowing gleam in the old man's eye.

Scarcely acknowledging his presence, Brother Lopsang led Theo to a bench. Theo could almost feel the tension rising from the young monk. There was obviously some issue here.

'Nice cup,' said Theo, indicating a vessel shaped like a silver frog, half hidden amongst a collection of stone jars and glass flasks.

The monk snatched it up and held it protectively to his chest.

'Hey, no problem,' said Theo easily.

Theo glanced at the other monks. It looked like they were painstakingly cataloguing every plant specimen. Except that they had nothing to compare them to, no way of gaining the bigger picture.

Theo pulled out his laptop. They could check everything against his exhaustive database. Anything not already there was guaranteed unique to this place.

'Waaaaaah!'

Theo looked up. One of the monks was staring at the laptop screen. The others dropped their specimens and flocked round. They had obviously never seen such a thing.

'This is a laptop,' explained Theo.

The monk stared back at him, bemused.

The Ancient Abbot placed a hand on Theo's arm. 'Only a very few of us speak your language, and none of the monks do. I learned it some hundred and fifty years ago from a gentleman explorer called Randolph Gillman, who was literally blown here in a great storm. Mr Gillman brought us two great gifts: your language and tiddlywinks. The language has been kept within the palace, but tiddlywinks became a national passion.'

'Tiddlywinks? Must have been quite a guy. So others have found your Kingdom before?'

'Only Mr Gillman and the RHM. In both cases, they were brought here through the compassion of the king. In Mr Gillman's case, the present king's father. You see, I am somewhat older than the majority of our people. That is why I am known as the Ancient Abbot. The RHM was found in the borderlands as a boy. Exceptionally, he was allowed to stay.'

'He is certainly exceptional,' said Theo. This was all so intriguing. How come the RHM had been allowed to stay? And what had happened to this Mr Gillman?

'It was I who taught English to the RHM,' went on the Ancient Abbot. 'When he came here he only spoke the language of the borderlands. Kumari was about to begin her studies in English when she was kidnapped. Of course, being a goddess means she has the Gift of Tongues anyway, but the RHM believes solid learning should underpin things more ethereal.'

There was a note in the Ancient Abbot's voice that sounded a warning to Theo. Things here were not as straightforward as they might at first appear. The Abbot and the RHM obviously held very different attitudes. Theo wanted to ask the Ancient Abbot more, but the old guy's attention kept wandering to the laptop. Like honey bees drawn to nectar, the monks were mesmerised by the screen and what was on it.

As Theo took them through the first few pages of his database, they watched in respectful silence. He pointed, mimed and said each name very loudly, not sure if any of this was going in. Not that it mattered; the laptop itself was what fascinated them. It was like watching a bunch of kids discover an amazing new toy, only twenty times better. Mindful of his battery, Theo waved his hands to indicate the show was over.

Obediently, the monks glided back to their benches. All this serenity was too much. Theo longed to crack a joke or make a clever comment. But what was the point when they did not understand him? All at once he understood how Kumari must have felt in the World Beyond, an exotic fish out of water. Except here he was hardly the exotic one. Or maybe he was to them.

In any case, he had to get to work – his primary task to find an antidote for the king. Whatever poison had been used was still paralysing his lower body. According to the Abbot, they had already tried everything they knew. It was time to come up with another formula. If only he could take a sample of the king's blood. But that was strictly forbidden – to spill the monarch's blood in any way was sacrilege. Theo would simply have to work without it. He would analyse each plant in turn, check its medicinal properties. Then start to combine them in different ways, using all his knowledge of science. Beside him, Brother Lopsang was hard at work, making notes in a neat hand. Theo peered over his shoulder, wishing he could understand what Lopsang had written.

'You're thorough, I'll give you that,' said Theo.

Lopsang glanced up and smiled briefly. *Strange*, thought Theo. *I could have sworn he understood me.* But the Abbot had said none of the monks spoke English. Theo filed away the thought for later.

At that very moment, a bell rang in the corridor. Instantly, the monks fell to the floor, prostrate in obeisance. The Ancient Abbot, too, was laid flat out. Theo was the last man standing. As he looked about, wondering what to do, the bell came closer then stopped. It was as if everyone was holding their breath. And then the bell began to move, dying away.

Slowly, everyone raised their heads.

'What was that?' Theo demanded.

'The holy hermit,' said the Abbot.

A hushed reverence hung in the air. Theo looked into the awestruck faces of the monks. This hermit was clearly someone very special indeed to leave such power lingering in his wake.

CHAPTER 10

'Hello, Mamma. How was your day? Mine was lousy, as it happens.'

Kumari rested her cheek on Mamma's throne, gazing up into her painted eyes. Of course, the portrait did not respond. It helped, though, to talk. It was what she and Mamma had always done at the end of each day, chatting about what was what, putting Kumari's world to rights, Mamma offering advice. Now Kumari came alone to the throne room. The portrait was all she had left.

It was hard to think how she might have handled today any differently. Or yesterday, or the day before. Papa still lay motionless, unaware of the world around him. The Secrets were still missing. Really, life completely sucked. As for

Palace School, forget it. Today had gone worse than ever. And yet the RHM insisted she must attend in order to keep up appearances.

As usual, they had all stared while Kumari made her way to her desk. You'd think they'd have got used to sitting next to the girl-goddess by now. Maybe even realised she was as normal as they were. There was one girl in particular, Asha, who specialised in evil stares. They glowered out from under a straight fringe that framed a thin, clever face, the poison dart of her glare directed straight at Kumari. Generally, Kumari glared right back, but today she could not be bothered. Dumping her books down on her desk, she had slumped behind it and dropped her head. There was so much to think about: Papa, the Secrets. The holy fires.

Almost immediately, there had been a discreet cough from the front. Oh great. The RHM. Sitting up straighter, Kumari had given normal her best shot. All through a particularly dull linguistics class she had kept her eyes wide open. Her lids had begun to droop, however, when the Ancient Abbot took over for metaphysics. By the time the RHM returned for calculus, Kumari had practically slid under her desk. It took a sharp prod in the back to bring her bolt upright.

She had looked over her shoulder to see Tenzin grinning at her. Then, out of the corner of her eye, she had caught Asha's hard stare. The girl's eyes darted to Tenzin and then back to her. Of course! That was it. Asha fancied Tenzin. Plain as day, in front of her face, *how could you be so dumb* blatant. Worse, Asha thought *she* fancied Tenzin too. Aaaargh – far, far too complicated.

'But it's not fair, Mamma,' said Kumari. 'It's not my fault she likes Tenzin.'

Mamma's painted eyes looked out at her, inscrutable. Kumari sighed. Of course she knew it was only a picture, but it really seemed Mamma's skin still glowed with life. Whoever had painted her portrait was evidently a great artist. He had captured Mamma's exact essence with brush-strokes that were so fine they appeared invisible. Although only Mamma's head and shoulders were depicted, it felt as if all of her were present. So much so that, for Kumari, it was entirely natural to carry on talking while Mamma listened.

'Thing is, now I know that, I think everything she says is meant to wind me up.'

One dig in particular still made Kumari mad. It had happened during linguistics.

'Give me an example of a simile,' the RHM had said.

'Like a goddess,' Asha had piped up.

'Very good. And another one?'

'As slow as a goddess?' Asha had smirked.

The RHM had frowned as the rest of the class fell about. Kumari had glanced at the blackboard behind him. Written on it, the daily quote: *The tongue like a sharp knife . . . Kills without drawing blood.*

Wincing at the memory, Kumari sighed again. Asha could be very sharp. Although when it came to Tenzin she was so embarrassingly *obvious*.

'It's funny, isn't it, Mamma, how clever people are often really dumb?'

Mamma stared back serenely. Who was being dumb now?

If anyone saw her talking to a portrait they would think she had lost her mind. But it made Kumari feel better and that was the main thing. After all, it was Mamma who had taught her she must do what felt right and always, always stay positive.

'But it's so hard, Mamma,' said Kumari. 'I'm sick with worry about Papa. I couldn't bear to lose him too. It's bad enough not having you. You know, I think I see you sometimes, out of the corner of my eye, and then I turn around and you're not there. It makes me feel emptier than ever. I've tried and tried to summon you up again, but I guess it only worked that one time. Oh Mamma, please, please come back. Just once more, that's all I need.'

It was like a tight band around her chest, the pain of loss gripping her in its vice. It never really let go, just loosened now and again. If she lost her Papa too, it would just get tighter, crushing her heart and her spirit. Fear dragged its cold claws down Kumari's spine. She felt so alone. Head bowed, she sat, oblivious to the cold stone beneath her, one hand stretched towards her Mamma's picture, reaching out for the impossible. If only Mamma were still alive. If only she were here now, holding her. Too desolate even to cry, Kumari sat, defeated.

She could hear Mamma's voice in her head, almost as if she were whispering in her ear.

'Never despair, Kumari. Where there is breath there is life and where there is life there is hope.'

Oh, how she wished it were so simple. Take Mamma's portrait, for instance. No matter what she said or did it would not live or breathe. The thing was just a picture. Hauling it from the throne in exasperation, Kumari held it up to the light.

'Doesn't work, Mamma, does it? As much as I hope, I can't give you life.'

For a second, she felt like smashing it to pieces. And then all the anger drained away. She balanced it on the floor at the base of the throne and gazed at it, half focusing. The portrait was unwieldy, coming up to waist-level. Still, she wanted to see it once more in full light. Heaving it up again, she held it out at arm's length. She could see the dust motes dancing in the watery sunlight filtering through the windows. Her arms ached, but she held on. Suddenly, she noticed something: a detail she had never seen before. The shadow of a form emerging from the background of the picture. Frustratingly, it would not take more solid shape, no matter how much she stared.

'What are you?' muttered Kumari. Her gut told her this was important. But however much she angled the heavy portrait this way and that, there was nothing more to see. Or at least, nothing to see in a conventional way.

'Of course,' said Kumari.

If there was something here to see, it might only be visible to another living goddess. Mamma was a living goddess, after all. Or she had been until the Ayah murdered her. Gathering all her concentration, Kumari tried to use Power No 2, the Power of Extraordinary Sight. It had worked pretty much to the max in the World Beyond. All she had to do was feel it from the heart. Let go, chant goddess stuff, believe . . . and see . . .

Nothing.

She tried again. And again. Still nothing, not a twitch. Her Power was firmly switched off at the divine plug. Now what to do? Absently, she glimpsed the amulet dangling around her wrist.

'What would you do, Mamma?'

The amulet. It had worked before. She jiggled her arm, sliding it against her flesh. *Hey, Mamma, I need you. There's something you want to show me.* The sunlight seemed to intensify and grow brighter. *Oh my god. It's working.* A definite shape, illuminated in a shaft of light that appeared to penetrate beneath the paint. As she gazed at it, details began to emerge, coalescing into the form of a slender stem. Smothering it like sprays of sunshine, sprigs of small, yellow flowers.

Kumari studied the image, nonplussed. Yellow flowers. So what?

Papa's words came back to her: 'The Secrets . . . your Mamma, she guards eight.'

Could it be that the eight Secrets that Mamma guarded were right here in her portrait? Ignoring her aching arms, Kumari angled the picture this way and that, trying to see if there were more. The light lent an iridescence to the colours. It was as if a layer had been peeled away. Slowly, more images started to emerge, at first barely discernible.

Another flower, this time purple, its stamens a vivid streak of orange. Beside that, a frog, its reptilian jaws agape. Above it, a crimson squiggle. Just beneath Mamma's throat, a crane in full flight, its feathers and even its feet shining gold. Almost hidden, a third flower, peeping out pink and shy. In the bottom right hand corner, a chrysanthemum looking oddly solid. Whoever had painted these could not be the same, great artist who had executed the portrait. Above the chrysanthemum, a red blob.

Kumari squinted at it. What on earth was a red blob supposed to mean? As she scrutinised it, she realised with a shiver that the images were slowly fading. Even now, they were merging once more with the background. Soon they would be all but invisible. Kumari had an idea. Grabbing her bag, she pulled out her notebook. Swiftly, she began to sketch, recording as much of each image as she could. Propping the portrait close to the window, she worked fast, aware that any minute now someone might come looking for her. That was fine if it was Ma, but it was just as likely to be the RHM.

Within minutes all eight sketches were done. Not perfect but they would have to do. She glanced at the portrait one last time to check. The images had disappeared.

'Just as well, Mamma,' said Kumari, placing the portrait gently back on the empty throne. 'We don't want the whole world discovering those, do we?'

There was no answer. Of course.

'I wonder where you are,' murmured Kumari. 'Still flying about on your lion?'

No, of course not. She was back in limbo, in the foothills of the Holy Mountain. Did they let lions into limbo? If only she could set Mamma free.

'I still have to make sure you're avenged,' whispered Kumari. 'I have to *know* the Ayah's soul has been obliterated. Oh, Mamma, there is so much to do. Find the Secrets. Help Papa. Find you. I don't know where to start. And I can't even begin to work out what these pictures mean. What am I supposed to do with them?'

A sudden thud made her jump. The portrait had fallen

from the throne, landing on the marble floor, centimetres from where Kumari knelt. Carefully, she picked it up. No damage done, thank goodness. She must have placed it carelessly. Story of her life. Then again, maybe not. She distinctly remembered making sure it was secure. Was this, then, a message? Kumari stared into her Mamma's eyes.

'What are you trying to tell me?' she murmured.

The portrait had fallen face up in a pool of shadow, its dark edges punctuated by silvered patches of light. Gently, Kumari placed it back on Mamma's empty throne. She had seen all there was to see in it for now. Tomorrow afternoon she would come back and try again. Satisfied that the portrait sat steady on the throne, Kumari glanced over her shoulder.

Her eyes fell once more on the pool of shadow. Why had Mamma's portrait fallen precisely there? From this angle, the shadow looked different – less elliptical, rounder. Kumari studied it for a moment then glanced up, her eyes sweeping the vast length of the throne room's outer wall. They settled on the great circular window, decorated with swirling twists of stone tracery. She looked back at the shadow. The silvered patches matched the patterns in the window. The new moon was casting its light through it, throwing pewter-coloured shapes upon the floor.

Unfiltered by pollution, moonlight in the hidden Kingdom was strong and pure. Especially now, just after the New Moon, when the skies were exceptionally clear. Kumari looked at the patterns this way and that, trying to work out their significance. Only a section of the window was reflected, the moon being in its first phase. As it climbed higher in its orbit later in the month, its light would hit the window full on. At the heart of the existing reflection was what looked to be a tangled mass. Protruding from the mass, a twisting column. Something about it struck a chord.

'The dragon tree,' whispered Kumari. The tree by the lake where she and Mamma had enjoyed so many picnics.

Like a photographic negative, its image lay before her, only discernible from this angle, viewed directly from Mamma's throne. Was this, then, another piece of the puzzle? And, if so, how to fit it all together? She had eight sketches and one shadow. Eight sketches. Eight ingredients. These had to be ingredients for the holy fires. But if this motley collection was really the ingredients then what was with the shadow? A clue, perhaps, to where she might find them? Kumari chewed her lip.

All at once, a scent began to fill the air, the perfume of a thousand roses. Rising through it, a powerful undertone of musk, followed by an afterthought of frangipani. The fragrance of her Mamma, unique and unforgettable. Tears filled Kumari's eyes. At that moment, the butter lamps surged, their flames casting long shadows. Eight sketches. One shadow. It was all Kumari had to go on. As the moon moved across the window, so more might be revealed. She could only wait and hope.

Leaning forward, she kissed her Mamma's painted cheek.

'I'll try, Mamma,' she murmured.

In her heart, a sinking feeling.

She might have got this horribly wrong.

KUMARI'S JOURNAL
(TOP SECRET. FOR MY EYES ONLY.
EVERYONE ELSE KEEP OUT!)
THIS MEANS YOU!

My bedroom(yet again)

The New Moon – 28 days to go until next New Moon

I have to make a plan. I mean, it's all very well having these sketches, but I know it's not going to be that easy. It never is. I need to take a closer look at the dragon tree. First chance I've got is tomorrow and I'm just going to have to skip school. The RHM will be furious, but finding those ingredients is far more important.

Thing is, I'll have to head off really early otherwise someone might spot me and ask why I'm not in class. I can't even let anyone know where I'm going or why – for one thing, they'd ask questions. And there's absolutely no way I can tell anyone about the pictures in Mamma's portrait. Papa asked me to tell no one about Mamma guarding secrets and I think it's better that way. If I'm the only one who knows about them then I'm the only one who can get hurt. Of course I can tell Badmash – he's hardly going to talk. But no one else, not even Ma and Theo. Especially not them –they're my friends.

As they are my friends, I have to protect them, even though they think they're protecting me. It's not like the World Beyond. They don't understand our ways. Take food, for instance. Ma freaked when she found out there are no fast-food places here. She kept muttering, 'Say what? No cof-

fee, and now no pizza?' like it was the end of the world. I suppose this is the end of the world to them, or at least the end of the world as they know it. Mind you, I agree with Ma. I think a few pizza places would add to the place.

OK, maybe just one, and a shop selling candy and Coke. I'm just going to nibble a tiny bit of this chocolate bar. Mmmmmm. That is SO nice. I've counted out a square or a piece of candy for each day of this moon cycle. I know it's silly, but it helps keep me going. Each day that passes is another less for the haze of Happiness. Another day less for Papa. I can't bear to think about it.

So I won't think about it. I'll think about something positive. Like having Ma and Theo here. Ma helps lighten things up so much. It makes me giggle the way she can't get her head around this Ayah thing. Today, she even put her feet up on the table at supper. Should have seen the RHM's face. And then Ma helped herself to holy nectar and that just about did it. The RHM snatched away the bottle like it was contaminated or something.

I think Theo's having a hard time in the monastery, although he doesn't say so. Only the Ancient Abbot speaks English, so I guess it's lonely up there. Theo does seem pretty excited about his plant specimens providing a cure for Papa, though. I mean, only Theo could get excited about a bunch of leaves and twigs. Which reminds me – the sketches. If I show those flowers to Theo he might know what they are and maybe even where they might grow. Urgh – I have to think about this tomorrow. My brain is all fuzzy. I'll just listen to my iPod for a minute. Then I can hear Chico's voice. He helps me think clearer. Well, as clear as I ever will.

CHAPTER 11

Very early the next morning, Kumari nudged Badmash awake.

'Hey, sleepy bird,' she murmured. 'Time to get up.'

She had made sure of waking early by leaving the curtains open, allowing the grey dawn light to infiltrate the room unimpeded by layers of silk. The moment the light stole across her face, Kumari's eyes were open. This was such an important day. The start of her new quest.

Sketches stuffed up the sleeves of her robe, Kumari crept from her bedroom. Badmash swayed on her shoulder, head drooping as he dozed. In Kumari's pocket, essential supplies of honey cakes purloined from Cook the night before.

'They're for Badmash,' Kumari had explained. 'I think he's a bit depressed.'

Kindly Cook always kept a supply in hand for just such emergencies.

They were sneaking past the kitchens now, en route to a back door. No delicious smells wafted from the stoves. It was far too early for breakfast. In an hour or so, though, Cook would be bustling about, whipping up pancakes and ladling yoghurt. Ma was now entrusted with delivery of the breakfast tray, but Kumari still had to make sure no alarm was raised. From her pocket she took a note, the exact same one she had left on her pillow for Ma. Cook and Ma had become such great friends that it was inevitable they would talk.

Gone for an early walk with Badmash, the note read. *Am collecting flowers for nature class. Please don't bother with breakfast. I have plenty of honey cakes. Will go straight to school from the fields. See you later! Kumari x*

Placing the note on Cook's chopping board, Kumari weighted it down with a pepper pot. That should just about cover it. Both women would think she was in school. All that remained was her third note, to be left on the teacher's desk. This one was written in a different hand, as close to Ma's flamboyant scrawl as she could muster.

Kumari will not be in school today, it read. *She is unwell and will remain in her room.*

So long as the Abbot did not check with Ma, Kumari was home and dry. Luckily for her, the RHM was absent today, pursuing his enquiries. There was no way the note would have fooled the RHM. In fact, there was a good chance it would not convince the Abbot. It was, however, the best she could manage: the only way she could buy time. Even if the alarm were raised it was unlikely they would look for her by the lake. Far more important was not to worry anyone. There was already enough anxiety in the palace.

Whatever happened, though, she knew she had to do this. It might be Papa's only chance. The Kingdom's only chance, come to that. Each day the haze grew thinner. As she slipped out the back door, Kumari glanced up at the morning sky. A shell-pink dawn caressed the clouds. There were far too few of them. Another phase of the moon and there might well be none at all.

As cover diminished, so danger grew. Pretty soon the Kingdom would be exposed to the World Beyond, to the warlords clamouring at its western frontier. Kumari shivered, and it was not because of the morning cool. Determinedly, she strode towards the lake, down through the meadows, across the orchards. Behind her, the town was waking up, the odd sound carried to her on the breeze. The palace, too, must be preparing for the day ahead. She could only hope her notes would work.

Surmounting the hillock that formed a natural ridge, Kumari could see the lake below, its surface satin-like in the morning light, its waters calm. Badmash nibbled her ear as they wound their way along the path, stones skittering from under Kumari's feet. Last time she had walked this way it had been with Ma and Theo, albeit in the opposite direction. A long time ago she had also walked this way with Mamma, picnic basket in hand. Kumari's eyes fixed on the dragon tree. This was where they had always sat.

First things first. She would scout around the dragon tree,

trying to find some or all of the objects in Mamma's portrait. Although, as she had sat here a hundred times before, it seemed pretty unlikely that she'd find any of them. She glanced across the lake. The waters were slowly coming to life. As the sun warmed the sky, ripples began to appear. Fish, perhaps, hunting for their breakfast. A curlew called out from the distant shore, its cry plaintive, haunting. The sound resonated through Kumari's bones, bringing a sudden chill. The bird's cry was full of such longing, it echoed the vacuum in her heart. Here, more than anywhere else, she missed her Mamma. It made the fear of losing Papa too so much worse.

For a long time after Mamma's death she could not bear to come to the lake. Since her return home, though, it had somehow called her. Maybe that, too, was Mamma's doing. Perhaps she had been trying to tell her something all along. Kumari pulled the sketches from her sleeve. She was no artist, but she had done her best. A yellow sprig. A purple flower.

There was nothing at the base of the tree save a few scrappy blades of grass.

'Gotcha!' A hand gripped her shoulder.

'Oh my god, you made me jump.'

Tenzin, of all people. Had he followed her from the palace? Suddenly, Kumari was furious.

'What are you doing here?'

'I came to fish.'

'Oh really? So where's your gear?'

'Over there, as it happens. What's wrong with you, Kumari?'

'What do you mean what's wrong with me? You came sneaking up on me, that's what.'

'I came to say hello, that was all. I'm sorry if I scared you.'

For a second, Kumari felt shamefaced.

'I'm sorry too. Forget it. But how come you're not in school?'

'I could ask you the same question.'

For a moment, their eyes met. Kumari's slid away first.

'What are you looking at down there?' asked Tenzin, following her gaze.

'Never you mind.'

Oops, once more she sounded a little snappy.

'I meant,' Kumari tried again, 'I'm looking at nothing.'

She began to ferret in the roots of the tree. Maybe he'd go away if she ignored him. It was not that she wasn't pleased to see him. She was – but not here, not now. She had ingredients to find, secret ingredients at that. Tenzin's presence was a hindrance.

'Oh come *on*, Kumari. It's obvious you're looking for something.'

'OK, I'll tell you,' said Kumari. 'I'm trying to find the spot where Mamma and I sat on our last picnic here. I was hoping she might have left something behind. You know a . . . well, anything really. Kind of silly, I know, but that's me all over.'

'You're not silly.' Oh no, his voice had softened. He was looking at her with *that* expression. The one that said *you poor thing*. Far too many people had looked at her like that since Mamma's death.

'Anyway,' Kumari went on, 'I'll just take a look around. See what I can see.'

87

'I'll help,' said Tenzin.

'But you don't know what you're looking for.'

'So? Nor do you.'

He was still smiling at her in that infuriating way.

'Well, yes, but at least I might know when I find it.'

'Skraaark.'

'Oh no, Badmash, I am sorry. I didn't mean to tread on you.' She had quite forgotten he was there, what with Tenzin appearing. Hopping around, looking aggrieved, Badmash pointedly held up a squashed foot.

'OK, I said I was sorry.'

Boy, he did like to milk a situation.

'What are these?' Tenzin was holding up her sketches. They must have slipped from under her arm as she reached for Badmash.

'Those? Um . . . they're nothing.'

Tenzin quirked one eyebrow.

Distract him, Kumari, distract him.

'Uh . . . I feel kind of weird.'

Clutching her head, Kumari did her best to sway swooningly. It was what princesses did in storybooks, after all, fainting prettily here and there.

'Quick, stick your head between your knees,' commanded Tenzin, helping her to the ground.

Hmmm. This hadn't been in the storybooks. Bent double was not a good look.

'That's better,' declared Kumari, getting up in a rush.

Instantly, the world really did begin to spin. She stumbled and Tenzin caught her by the arm.

'Steady now. You need to sit down again.'

'I'm fine, really,' said Kumari, seizing the opportunity to retrieve her sketches and stuff them hastily into her pocket.

He was holding her by the shoulders. She could see the few downy hairs above his upper lip. Up this close, his eyes were caramel. Funny, they had always looked brown before. But no, distinctly caramel, the colour of Cook's best toffee treats.

'Kumari?' He was looking at her strangely. Mind you, everything at this distance looked a bit strange. Experimentally, she half closed her own eyes. That was better, if a bit blurry.

'Kumari, are you OK?'

'Uh, yes, sorry, I was just . . .'

Oh no, how embarrassing. Caught staring into Tenzin's eyes like she was interested or something. And she certainly was not, not in that way at any rate. Boys were off the agenda. End of story . . . For now.

'You were just . . . ?'

Aaargh, help. He was smirking. *Backtrack, Kumari, quickly.* Don't let this boy think for one second that he has got the upper hand.

'I was just looking at that fluff above your mouth,' said Kumari.

Now it was his turn to look embarrassed. Instantly she felt mean.

'OK, look, I'll level with you. I'm trying to find some of the things I've drawn. They were all things Mamma liked to collect.'

'I see.' Tenzin's expression was frankly sceptical. And then a smile broke through that erased the doubt. 'Whatever you want, Kumari. Can I help?'

'Uh, sure. I mean, that would be nice.' He might as well help, now he was here. Besides, he couldn't possibly guess what she was really looking for, that these could be the ingredients for the fires of Happiness.

'You take the roots. I'll try the trunk. Mamma . . . always used to find things around this tree.'

If Tenzin thought this odd he did not say as much. Purposefully, Kumari began to inspect the trunk. All of a sudden, she remembered the canopies. Ma and Theo's parachutes were still stuffed up the tree. Kumari glanced anxiously at Tenzin. He seemed well and truly distracted, absently staring at the tangle of roots, twisted so tightly they resembled a coiled mass of intestines.

'Ark!'

'If one more person makes me jump . . .' Kumari glared at Badmash. OK, so he was a vulture and not a person, but her heart simply could not take any more surprises.

Badmash was clinging on to a branch, greedily inspecting the trunk. He particularly liked to suck the sap – rich, sticky and blood red. Occasionally a small wound would open up in the tree, allowing Badmash his special treat. Today, however, there were none visible. Badmash burrowed deeper between the grooves that cut, river-like, through the gnarled bark. A small squeak of triumph indicated he had spotted something. No doubt a glistening bead of sap.

It must be a rich seam, thought Kumari, for Badmash to work it that hard. He was digging away with his beak, tugging like a baby on a teat.

'Aark!' Now he was looking at her in annoyance.

'What is it, Badmash? Can't you get it?'

Funny – there was no sap on his beak. She peered into the groove. There was something there, gleaming red all right, but it looked too solid to be sap. Excitedly, Kumari inserted her slender hand. She could just about touch it with her fingertips.

'Badmash, get your beak around this.'

There was no way she could pull it out on her own. A combined effort, however, might just yield results. Holding his fat little belly, she waited until he had a good grip then, gently but firmly, she tried to help him pull it out.

'What's happening? You've found something?'

Tenzin was squinting over her shoulder.

'Hold on to me,' commanded Kumari. 'When I say, pull. One, two, three . . . pull!'

In a heap they fell, Badmash's wings flapping wildly. In his beak, a slim, red object, which he dropped at Kumari's side.

'A paintbrush. What on earth is this doing here?'

She stared at it, perplexed. The brush was covered in a red substance. Mamma had sometimes brought her easel down to paint the lake, but why stick a brush in the tree? Absently, she glanced at the trunk once more. Now there was sap pouring down it. Snaking its way through the whorls and grooves, a meandering, deep red streak. Narrowing her eyes, Kumari focused on the rivulet. It was exactly like the crimson squiggle in the portrait.

'This is it,' murmured Kumari. 'The first ingredient. I've found it.'

'First ingredient? What do you mean?'

'Uh . . . nothing.' Oh my god, she had nearly given it away. She had to be more careful.

'So nothing's going on, and we're looking at nothing here?' It was Tenzin's turn to sound angry.

'Do you have anything like a cup on you?'

'For what?'

'Obviously I can't tell you.'

She stared him out, daring him to insist. After a moment, he shrugged.

'OK, so don't tell me then. Seems like you don't need my help.'

Oh great. Now she felt bad again.

'It's not that,' said Kumari. 'It's just . . . I'm sorry, but I can't tell you. I would if I could, but I can't. Honestly, Tenzin.'

'So you don't trust me, is that it?'

'I do trust you. I just can't tell you.'

Miserably, Kumari met his scornful gaze. He *had* been really kind, helping her look.

'Fine. Well, I don't have a cup on me.'

Now what? Improvise. Come on, Kumari, there must be something lying around. Helplessly, she scanned the lakeshore. Nothing there or in the water. She glanced behind her, looking at the distant frangipani orchards, bringing her gaze back to the grassy scrub around the tree, then back again to the pebbly shore. Something on the water caught her eye. It began drifting closer. Hope rose once more, a bubble rising, bursting from her throat:

'There it is! That is perfect.'

Tenzin looked at her for a second and then he was rolling up his cotton trousers, hitching up his tunic, before plunging into the water. He had to wade out about five metres before he could finally grab it. And then he strode out of the water bearing it aloft.

'A banana leaf, your highness.'

He placed it at her feet, bowing low. Kumari could not help but giggle. She had never been able to stay cross with Tenzin for long and, in any case, he had done her a big favour. But for him the banana leaf would have floated off, costing her yet more time and effort. She had to get the sap to Theo, ask him to analyse it in secret. If the sap really was one of the ingredients, it might show some peculiar properties. There was nothing Theo loved more than peculiar properties. They made his scientist's heart sing.

Hastily, Kumari began to scoop up the sap into the folded leaf, batting away Badmash as he tried to steal it.

'So I guess I'm not allowed to ask why you're doing that either?'

Kumari smiled at Tenzin. 'You guessed right.'

At least he was smiling too. The tension between them had dissipated.

'You are one strange girl,' said Tenzin.

Funny, someone else had once said that. She could see Chico's face now, hear his voice say the words. For a second she was back in New York, and then the moment had passed.

'Get used to it,' said Kumari. 'There's plenty more strangeness where this came from.'

She was past fitting in or acting normal.

It was time to be herself.

CHAPTER 12

There was one thing more important than delivering the sap and that was checking on Papa. She could hear the school bell ring in the distance as she slipped up the stairs. The end of morning lessons. Excellent timing. As she put her hand on the handle, the door to Papa's room opened.

'Kumari,' said the RHM.

'RHM . . .' stuttered Kumari.

She did her best to look him innocently in the eye, wondering if he knew of her absence.

'I have just come from the monastery,' said the RHM. 'As yet we have discovered nothing.'

The RHM looked tired, Kumari noticed.

'And Papa?'

'His holy majesty is stable.'

She did not know if that was good or bad. At least he had not deteriorated.

'One small improvement,' said the RHM. 'We've managed to get a little soup down him.'

From behind the RHM, a kitchen maid emerged, carrying a tray.

'Oh good,' said Kumari. Soup would keep up Papa's strength. Although actually he only liked one kind of soup. She had better make sure they knew that.

'Is it Celestial Chicken?' she demanded. 'That's the one Papa likes.'

'It is, your holy highness,' smiled the kitchen maid. 'Cook made it specially.' Cook insisted on making Papa's food personally, pouring into it all her love and care. Now it was even more important she performed her sacred duty solo, ensuring no one could tamper with it. Even so, every morsel the king ate was now tasted a second time at his bedroom door. If his food had indeed been poisoned, it would be impossible to slip him another dose.

'Great,' mumbled Kumari. 'Um . . . can I see him now?'

For a second she thought the RHM might actually refuse, but then he stood aside.

'Of course. I'll wait outside.'

Beside Papa's bed the lamp burned low, just the way he liked it. Once upon a time, Mamma had slept here too. The room still smelled of her fragrance. Papa kept a bottle of her favourite scent beneath his pillow. It reminded him of her. Gently, Kumari slipped a hand under the silken pad. It was there – a small, silver flask. Drawing it out, she removed the

95

stopper and inhaled deeply. Roses, musk, frangipani and something else, something indefinable.

'Here, Papa,' Kumari whispered, holding it beneath his nostrils. Apparently the sense of smell was the last to leave a person. Not that Papa's senses were going anywhere.

Papa's face was waxy white. Was that a bead of sweat on his forehead? Carefully, Kumari wiped it away. He seemed hotter than usual.

'Can you smell it, Papa? It smells of Mamma.'

Was it her imagination or did his nostrils twitch? There it was, a definite movement. And then a tiny curl of his upper lip. Papa was smiling. He was actually smiling. Somewhere in there, he still lived and breathed. Underneath the colourless mask of his familiar face, Papa remained aware. The scent wafted round the room, filling it with Mamma's presence. It was as if she, too, sat here at Papa's side, willing him to get better.

'Come back, Papa,' Kumari whispered. 'Come back,' she said a little louder. 'Come back to me!' she cried, slamming her fist down on the bed, her sobs erupting. Her head dropped, the tears flowed free. It was useless. There was no hope. And then she felt it, a hand brushing her cheek, smoothing the sticky strands of hair from her face. The scent was so strong it caught at her throat.

'Mamma?' said Kumari.

For a brief moment she thought she saw her there, bending over Papa, dropping a kiss on his brow. Then, in the blink of a swollen eye, she was gone. Perhaps she had never even been there. It was enough, though, to galvanise Kumari. There was hope, after all. And if there was hope then she had to do her part, she had to follow the clues in the picture.

'I love you, Papa,' said Kumari, bending to kiss him too, placing her lips in exactly the same spot as Mamma. As they met Papa's skin, they seemed to tingle. She felt a rush of energy surge through her.

'You hang on in there, Papa,' Kumari said. 'We're going to help you.'

She daubed a couple of drops of perfume on each wrist.

Now Mamma walked with her.

CHAPTER 13

'Kumari! There you are!'
Ma's face was contorted with worry.

Kumari felt a flush of remorse stain her cheeks. Looked like her notes had not worked.

'Where you been, girl? I've been frantic ever since I spoke with the Abbot.'

The flaw in her plan had been exposed. There was always a chance they might confer.

'I've been . . . out,' said Kumari.

'Out, huh? Where "out"?'

'You know. Here, there and everywhere.'

'No, I don't know. Try me.'

Hands on hips, Ma faced her down. There was no wriggling out of this one.

'You forget I got two teenage daughters of my own, Kumari. I know the score, so save me the stories.'

Ah yes. CeeCee and LeeLee. But then, they were never much trouble. In fact, it had often seemed they were mothering Ma, such was their frightening maturity.

'OK, OK,' said Kumari. 'Come in my room. I can't talk out here.'

Ma's eyes bulged and then flicked up and down the corridor.

'You think there might be someone listening in this here corridor?'

'Who knows?' said Kumari. 'It's better to be safe than sorry.'

Besides, Ma's voice carried for miles. It was easier to contain it behind her bedroom door. The moment she shut it behind them, Kumari noticed the tray set beside her bed. Badmash saw it too, a split second after she did. With a delighted cry, he pulled aside the cloth that covered it. On the tray, a plate of momos and a bowl of sliced mango.

'Cook left it there for you,' said Ma. 'Didn't take us long to figure out those notes you left us were baloney. She thought you might be hungry when you came back from wherever you had been, bless her heart. So come on, Kumari, 'fess up.'

'I went to the lake,' said Kumari. Sometimes the best lies were those closest to the truth. 'I like to go there to think of Mamma. It's where we used to go for picnics.'

'You were at the lake for all that time?' Ma's tone was far gentler.

'It's a long way and I wanted to have a Think. You know I need to do that sometimes.'

Ma heaved a husky sigh. 'I do, child. Oh boy, I do. But, honey, you go disappearing like that again, you gonna give me a heart attack.'

'I'm sorry,' said Kumari. 'I didn't mean to worry you. That's why I left the notes. I thought it was better like that.'

'Telling the truth is better,' said Ma. 'How come you couldn't just come right out and tell me? You know you can trust your Ma. You didn't need to go scaring me. Cook too, she was beside herself. Anything could have happened.'

Kumari felt her heart contract. Ma was right, of course.

'Aw, honey, don't look like that. Your Papa's going to be all right.'

Was he, though? Kumari was not so sure, despite Ma's comforting arms around her. All at once, she could contain herself no longer. She simply had to tell someone.

'There is something else . . . ' she muttered into Ma's chest.

'What did you say, sweetie?'

'I said there's something else you need to know. I think I might be able to find the ingredients. You know, for the holy fires. To relight them so we can restore the haze. I think my Mamma has told me what to find and where to look. I can't tell you any more. I'm sorry.'

'You think your Mamma told you that?'

Ma's face was troubled. 'Kumari, honey, your Mamma's dead.'

'I know that,' said Kumari. All of a sudden, something snapped. 'I thought you of all people would understand. I mean, you believe in hoodoo and all. You were there when Mamma appeared on her lion.'

'Of course I was,' soothed Ma. 'And it's not that I don't believe you. It's just that when times are tough we all cling on to things. Sometimes our minds make up stuff.'

'My mind is not making up stuff. I saw them with my own eyes.'

Now she had gone and said too much. Trembling, Kumari dropped her gaze.

'You saw what? OK, so you won't tell me. That's fine, Kumari. Just promise me one thing. Promise me you'll always tell me where you are going. If you'll let me, I'll even come along so I can watch your back.'

'Thanks, but I need to do this alone.' Kumari felt all the stubborn fire drain from her. 'But I really appreciate you saying that. And, Ma, thanks for being here.'

'Aw shucks, you know I'd do anything to help you out.'

Ma's eyes were all wet and shiny. They looked at each other for a long moment.

'What's that noise?' said Ma suddenly, looking towards the windows. From somewhere, a rising rumble.

'It's from the town,' said Kumari, sticking her head out. 'I can see people marching up the hill.'

A clamour could clearly be heard from the direction of the main palace doors.

'We'd better go see what's going on,' said Kumari. 'Let's take the back stairs.'

In the grand entrance hall, a phalanx of guards struggled to hold back a surging crowd. Someone spotted Kumari and cried out:

'There's the girl-goddess! Let's ask her.'

'Ask me? Ask me what?' Kumari looked at the seething throng, bewildered. There were thirty, perhaps forty people actually inside the doors, hundreds more trying to get in. Men and women, mostly townsfolk, their faces contorted with anxiety.

'We need to talk to the king,' cried out another voice. 'He'll tell us what's happening.'

'The king! The king!' More people took up the chant. It looked like things were getting out of hand.

And then another voice, cutting through the rising cacophony.

'What exactly is going on here?'

It was the RHM, thank goodness.

'We want to see the king,' shouted an angry man.

'Yes, bring us the king. We need him.'

'His majesty is busy tending the holy fires. Perhaps I can help you?'

Kumari marvelled at how calm the RHM remained. He seemed unfazed by the jostling rabble.

'If you're so clever tell us why there's a giant bird in the sky.'

'A giant bird?'

'Made of metal.'

All at once, the RHM went very still. Kumari could almost see him thinking. A giant bird made of metal in the sky. It could only mean one thing. The haze of Happiness was now so thin that aeroplanes could be seen high above the Kingdom. And if planes could be seen it stood to reason that the Kingdom was no longer hidden. Eventually someone would spot it. Then they would descend, curious to explore this hitherto hidden valley, an oasis set deep in a distant mountain range. Kumari shuddered at the thought. It must never, ever happen.

'There is no such thing as a bird made of metal,' said the RHM. 'What you saw was probably a cloud formation. In certain conditions clouds take on unusual shapes. The current weather system would support this.'

'A cloud formation?' The murmur ran through the crowd. 'A cloud. He says it's a cloud.'

'I've never seen a cloud like that,' said a man at the front. 'This thing gleamed, like gold or bronze.'

'That would be the sun reflected off the water droplets. All clouds are, in fact, composed of water.'

'This was no cloud,' insisted the same man. 'It moved across the sky like a giant bird.'

'The westerly winds are very strong right now,' said the RHM, 'giving rise to this formation. I can assure you, that's all it is. Now may I suggest you return to your homes?'

The RHM's tone brooked no further argument. Cowed, the majority turned and began to trudge off. The man at the front, however, remained. He stared straight at Kumari.

'And what do you think, girl-goddess?' he sneered. 'Do you agree with the king's Right Hand Man here? Come to that, where is your father now? I don't see much evidence of his efforts with the holy fires.'

'I . . . I . . . ' Kumari stuttered. Ma thrust herself between Kumari and the man.

'You leave the kid alone,' she cried. 'Go bully someone your own size.' Although the man could not have understood what she was saying, Ma's tone was all too clear.

Sarcastically, the man bowed low, then turned and followed his fellow citizens.

'Well,' said Ma as the heavy doors were bolted firmly behind him. 'Things sure have turned ugly.'

And if the sinking feeling in Kumari's stomach was right, they would only get worse.

CHAPTER 14

'So, all you have to do is fly up to the window and tap on it until Theo comes. I know you can do that.'

Kumari earned a baleful look from Badmash. All he wanted was the honey cake in her hand.

'You can have this once Theo appears,' she said, dangling it in front of his beak. Badmash tried to lunge for it, but Kumari was too quick.

She looked up at the lab window. The monastery walls rose, forbiddingly, in front of them. It was not that easy to get something to Theo when he was cloistered in there with all the other monks. Not even the girl-goddess could just stride into the monastery. It simply was not done. On top of everything else that had happened that evening, she was faced with this headache. The remnants of the mob had finally dispersed about an hour before, although Kumari could still hear their voices ringing in her head. Especially the voice of the man in front. He had seemed to despise her with a special passion.

Beside her, Ma craned her neck.

'This place is really spooky.'

'Don't say that. You'll put him off.'

With one last longing glance at the honey cake, Badmash took to his wings, flying gracefully towards the lab window. Watching him, Kumari marvelled. Not so long ago, he could barely hop fifteen centimetres in the air. Landing safely on the sill, Badmash once more looked back. Kumari waved the honey cake and pointed meaningfully. If a bird could have sighed he would. Realising there was nothing else for it, Badmash began to tap on the window, rapping with his beak, a staccato call for attention.

'What if he's not in there?' said Ma. 'They might have him doing some kinda monk thing. You know, meditation. Levitation. Whatever it is that monks do.'

At that very moment, the window was flung wide, sending Badmash into a fury of flapping feathers, feet bicycling, wings beating as he was knocked spinning from his perch. For what felt like a few very long seconds, Kumari's heart was in her mouth. And then he was back on the windowsill, beak poised to peck.

'Whoa, Badmash, I'm sorry. Didn't see you out there.'

Peering beyond Badmash, Theo spotted them standing below.

'Kumari! Ma!' he called.

'Shhhhh,' gestured Kumari, one finger to her lips, the other making a cutting throat signal.

'Oh, OK,' stage-whispered Theo. 'But there's no one else in here.'

Pointing at the low arch that formed the old layman's entrance to the monastery, Kumari made a beckoning gesture. Almost immediately, Theo disappeared back inside the lab. Deciding that the deed was done, Badmash swooped, snatching the honey cake from Kumari's fingers. He landed just a couple of metres from the archway and immediately began to munch.

'*Manners,*' Kumari hissed as she dragged Ma over to join him. Badmash simply buried his beak deeper in the honey cake, a look of ecstasy on his face.

Within a few moments, Theo was opening the door within the archway.

'We have to be quick,' said Kumari, bundling Ma inside. Theo shut the door behind them, glancing round to make sure the coast was clear.

'We've got so much to tell you,' whispered Kumari.

'Why don't we sneak upstairs?' suggested Theo. 'Don't worry. There's no one about. They're all at evening prayers. The Abbot gave me dispensation not to go. I think he realised I'm a lost cause.'

As quietly as they could, they scurried up the spiral staircase that took them to the first floor. At the top, Theo scouted ahead, beckoning them forward when he was sure the coast was clear. Once safely inside the lab, he wedged a chair under the latch.

'So, what's up?' he asked.

'First of all,' said Kumari, 'I have this sap here for you to analyse and second of all there was a crowd came to the palace. They said they'd seen a metal bird in the sky.'

'Whoa, slow down,' said Theo. 'A metal bird? You mean a plane?'

'It has to have been,' said Kumari. 'Although the RHM convinced them it was a cloud formation.'

'I don't think some of them were so convinced,' said Ma. 'There was one guy, he got really mean.'

'I see,' said Theo. 'Doesn't sound too good to me.'

'It's not,' said Kumari. 'It means the haze of Happiness is all but gone.'

'Right,' said Theo. 'And how's your dad? Is he holding up?'

'The same,' said Kumari. Her head, her heart, felt numb.

'And this sap?' said Theo. 'What's that all about?'

'Here,' said Kumari. 'I got it from the dragon tree.'

Theo took the folded banana leaf from Kumari. Carefully unwrapping it, he inspected the blood-red contents.

'*Sangre de drago*,' said Theo. 'Blood of the dragon. Comes from a tree known as *Dracaena Draco*. It's been highly prized for centuries.'

'I think you need to analyse it,' said Kumari. 'It could be one of the ingredients for the holy fires.'

'Why would you think that?' said Theo. 'All right, so it's long been considered to have magical properties. Of course, that is not the scientific view. There are other, more practical uses. Violin makers, for instance, use it in varnish. The ancient Guanche people of the Canary Islands used to mummify their dead with it.'

'It's a good colour,' said Ma. 'I could use some in my hair.'

'The Romans thought so too,' said Theo. 'Although they confined its use to paintings.'

'Yes, well that's all very interesting,' said Kumari. 'But what about its magical properties? There has to be some reason why Mamma led me to this stuff. I mean, what exactly can it do?'

'Your Mamma led you to this? Kumari, your Mamma is dead.'

'She's not dead. She's stuck,' snapped Kumari, irritated by the concern visible in Theo's eyes. The minute she spoke, she felt bad. Theo only meant well.

'Dead, stuck, whatever you want to call it. You have to face scientific fact.'

'Oh yeah?' said Kumari. 'Well here's a fact for you. My Mamma is a goddess. She can do what she likes. Or she will be able to when she's free.'

'Point well made and taken.'

Theo was placing a tiny drop of sap on a slide.

'Let's just see what you've got here.'

He inserted the slide under his microscope.

'Interesting,' murmured Theo. 'Not what I would expect to see.'

Finally, he looked up. 'A most unusual cell structure.'

'So what does that mean?' said Kumari.

'It means I need to look at it some more. Make some comparisons with my database. But I'd say we definitely have something.'

'So you think it could be an ingredient?'

'It's impossible to say, Kumari. There are, what, eight ingredients? I can't identify one by itself.'

'OK. So what if I bring you some more?'

'Then that would make things a whole lot easier. But where are you going to find these ingredients? Don't tell me . . . your Mamma.'

'That's right,' muttered Kumari. She would love to tell them about the picture clues, the shadow. It would make her life so much easier. But it was too great a risk to take. Such knowledge could place both Ma and Theo in danger. It was better she kept it to herself.

Luckily, Theo did not press her further.

'OK,' he said. 'You bring me some more I'll see what I can do. Meantime, I'm working on that cure for your Papa. We all are, real hard.'

All at once a bell rang out from the corridor. The three of them froze on the spot.

'What was that?' whispered Ma.

It rang again, coming closer.

'You know,' murmured Theo, 'I think I've heard that one before. They ring bells all the time, but that one sounds different.'

Suddenly, Kumari darted to the door and eased it open a crack.

Ding, ding, ding, the bell rang out, louder and louder, singing out what sounded like a warning note, at once terrible and beautiful. She could see someone approaching, a figure swathed in white clothing. Could it be? Yes, it was. Only the holy hermit would be afforded such ceremony just to walk along the monastery corridors. Not even Papa would have his way cleared by the sacred bell, his approach so extraordinarily signalled. The hermit was the holiest of holy sages, the spiritual fountainhead of truth, the only other person in the Kingdom accorded the right to enter the innermost sanctum of the temple.

Walking in front of the holy hermit, a monk, his gaze fixed straight ahead. No one was permitted to look upon the hermit or address him directly. Even Kumari felt the force of his presence. He truly was a saintly figure. Despite herself, though, she could not help but peer at him through her lashes. It felt forbidden, sacrilegious, but something compelled her to stare.

There was something about him that unsettled her. Maybe it was just all the stuff she had heard. How if you actually looked upon the hermit's face you would be eternally cursed. Well, Kumari did not believe in curses. Or rather, she did not believe in curses as far as she was concerned. She was a trainee-goddess, after all. Curses could not affect her, right?

The hermit's face was totally concealed, covered in an all-enveloping white shawl. His head was bowed, his eyes cast down. Even his feet were covered. It was like looking at a walking shroud. And then, just as he drew level with the door, the shawl slipped a fraction. Instantly, the hermit drew it forward once more, his hand reaching out from under the white layers. Kumari breathed out slowly. She had almost seen his face.

Another monk brought up the rear. His gaze, too, was fixed downward. Just as he passed the door, however, it slid sideways. It felt like he was looking straight at her. And then the little entourage was gone, the bell sounding fainter and fainter. Kumari waited a good minute before she gently closed the door. Someone else might yet appear.

'What was *that*?'

Ma had crept up behind her. Kumari spun round.

'Don't *do* that!'

She was as jumpy as a cricket on hot coals. The holy hermit was the icing on the freaked-out cake.

'That was the holy hermit,' she said.

'The man himself?' said Theo. 'The Ancient Abbot told me to keep out of his way. Some mumbo-jumbo about curses.'

'Yes, well,' said Kumari, 'it probably is better to keep clear.'

In the distance, another bell rang, deeper and more sonorous.

'That's the end of evening prayers,' said Theo. 'You guys had better get going.'

'We'll leave you to it,' said Kumari. 'And remember, listen out for Badmash. If you hear him tapping on the window it means we've brought you something else.'

'Can't wait,' said Theo. 'What will it be next time? A whole tree?'

Kumari shot him a look.

'You never know your luck.'

KUMARI'S JOURNAL
(TOP SECRET. FOR MY EYES ONLY.
EVERYONE ELSE KEEP OUT!)
THIS MEANS YOU!

My bedroom

First Quarter Moon – 20 days to go to next New Moon

The moon has just entered its First Quarter which means

there are only two more phases before our time is up. Even so, the haze is disappearing faster than anyone thought it would. And Papa grows weaker as each day passes. Our beautiful moon has become a time-bomb, ticking away the days we have left. I can see it now, a silver semi-circle in the sky. Tomorrow it will look a little rounder still and then in a few more days it will be full.

Normally, I love to watch the moon fatten up. Right now, though, it seems like one of those clocks they have in the World Beyond. Those things that tick away people's lives and hope. A circular death sentence. Poor Papa, I cannot bear to see him fade. I have already lost Mamma - I can't stand to lose him as well. I need him so much and I think he needs me. Sometimes it even seems he knows I'm there when I sit beside him.

The only good thing about the waxing moon is that it means the shadow in the throne room must be expanding too. On the one hand I dread the moon's progress and yet I need it to reveal the truth. The shadow of the dragon tree led me to the sap – what ingredient will the second shadow help me find? Last night I could almost make it out. Not enough to know what's there, but enough to see there is something. Another night or so and the next clue should be revealed. I'll be sitting by Mamma's throne, waiting . . .

CHAPTER 15

It was dark in the throne room now, too dark to make out any images. No sunlight streamed through the window. Instead, there was the faint glow of the growing moon, still too weak to cast any shadows. Kumari would simply have to wait until it struck the circular window. It was no hardship waiting with Mamma. She would never tire of gazing upon her face.

'I'm doing my best, Mamma,' murmured Kumari. 'But it's hard keeping your secrets to myself.'

The flames flickered once more. Mamma's mouth appeared to smile. Kumari looked over her shoulder. There must be a draught coming from somewhere. Normally, the lamps did not dance this much. Perhaps there was a window open. No, not at this time of the evening. Security had been stepped up even more since Papa's collapse. The RHM insisted on hourly patrols of the palace perimeter.

On her lap, Badmash dozed, exhausted from the day's excitement. Kumari, too, was bone-weary, but her mind refused to slow. All the time it raced, so fast she felt dizzy. It was as if she was being sucked into some kind of mental vortex, caught in a whirlwind of thought. The ingredients were an odd collection. Dragon's blood sap she had already. But these flowers. Where to find them? As for the red blob, she was stumped. Which image to follow first? She glanced at the floor and her heart leapt. There it was, the moonshadow.

Springing to her feet, she stared down as the strengthening moonlight etched in the final edges, the once nebulous mass now crisp and clear, a perfect semi-circle. Two sections of the window reflected side by side, the dragon tree and now this new shape. Kumari narrowed her eyes and opened her mind. It looked for all the world like a waterfall. She could see the rocky ridge over which a fountain of water gushed, make out foliage all around. But where to find it was another matter. She had never seen such a waterfall in the Kingdom.

There were mountain streams that trickled down from melting snows but nothing on this scale. Even in shadow she could see that the water spurted high before dropping into a pool below. To the left of the pool stood a sapling, its slender branches tipped with broad leaves. Where the shadow blurred it looked like there could be other trees. She had to record this, too, before it disappeared. Whipping out her pad, Kumari began to sketch. Tongue between teeth she concentrated, getting every detail just right.

A sudden flash across the sheet of paper as the lamps flared high then guttered. Cold air blasted across her forearms, bringing them out in goosebumps. Startled, Kumari's eyes flicked to the outer door. It was standing wide open. In the moonlit rectangle, no one. It was the wind, she told herself. Strange, when the door was always kept locked. Must have been one strong gust. Kumari stifled a sudden gasp.

Silhouetted against the moonlight, stood a figure, blocking the outside door of the throne room. There was nowhere to run, nowhere to hide. All Kumari could try and do was shrink into the shadows. The moments ticked by. And then, finally, the figure moved. Kumari felt rather than saw its eyes boring into her. Judging by its height and breadth, it was male. Could it be Razzle's henchmen come to get her? The hairs stood up on the back of her neck.

All at once, Badmash raised his head, a noise coming from deep in his throat. It sounded almost like a growl, a rumble of pure hatred. A thrust of his feet and he was flying straight at the figure, talons extended, beak open, emitting squawks of rage. Just as he dived to strike, the door slammed shut. Somewhere from outside, shouts could be heard. Infuriated, Badmash shrieked at the door, daring the figure to come back.

Kumari stood rooted to the spot, her heart beating so fast she thought she might pass out. But for Badmash, she might have thought it some sort of vision, an apparition maybe. This, however, was all too real.

Thud, thud, thud!

Kumari stifled a scream.

Someone hammering at the outer door. There was no way she was going to open it.

Another thud. And then a shout.

'Palace guards! Open up!'

More thuds. They were not going to go away.

And then the other throne room door burst open. A contingent of guards poured into the room with the RHM at their head.

'Kumari, are you all right? We've had reports of an intruder.'

'I'm fine,' she said, although in truth she was not. Under her robes, her legs were shaking. 'I saw someone, standing at the outer door. Somehow they managed to get it open.'

'The patrol spotted them too.' The RHM's voice was grim. 'They gave chase, but the person disappeared. What are you doing here on your own? This incident only illustrates that it's not safe.'

Kumari's eyes slid to the floor. The shadow had all but faded. The moon had mounted higher in the sky, taking its silver beam with it.

'I was talking to Mamma,' she murmured. 'I was saying goodnight.'

'I see.' Sadness flitted across the RHM's face. And then his sterner self returned.

'It's best you go to your room now.'

'Here, Badmash,' Kumari called. 'Let's go to bed, my little friend.'

With a soft coo he landed in her outstretched arms. Sweet Badmash, who had done his best to protect her.

'Goodnight, then, RHM.'

'Goodnight, Kumari.'

Wearily, she trudged to her room, her newest sketch

tucked away in her sleeve. In the morning she would try and work it out, think about possible locations. Right now she had had enough. It seemed she was not safe anywhere. Of course she was not safe. No one was safe. Look at Mamma and now Papa. Even in the palace they had not been protected, so what hope was there for her? About as much hope as there was for the Kingdom now the haze was steadily vanishing.

Beside her bed she found a glass of milk, propped against it a note:

Sitting with your Pops.
Sweet dreams.
Ma x

It brought a tiny smile to Kumari's face. She tried to sit with Papa as often as she could, but tonight she simply did not have the strength. It tore her heart to sit and watch him sleep. He looked so vulnerable as he lay there. Sometimes she would think he had simply slipped away, so still did he appear. And then he would sigh or move a fraction and she would breathe easy once more.

Sleep would heal him, or so the Ancient Abbot said. Kumari did not believe him. She knew he was trying to be kind, but it was so obvious Papa was fading. Every time she dared to face that fact, fear dug deeper in her gut. It sat silent there, like a snake, just waiting to be stirred up. Then something would happen like the incident tonight and, coldly, it would strike.

What would she do if she was all alone? How could she go on without her family? There had always been the three of them. Now it was two – or perhaps just one. If she failed to relight the fires then Papa would die and she would be for ever apart from the two people she loved most. Loved them in the present tense. *Come on Kumari, you have to be strong. You know love never dies, and nor will Papa.*

She would close her eyes and go to sleep. Get the early night she needed. Although sleep, when it came, was no respite. The nightmares had returned. The fears that dogged her waking hours lay in wait in her dreams, magnified. Demons and ghouls haunted her nights. She was afraid to succumb to them. And so she lay, wide-eyed, until, at last, exhaustion overtook. But a short while later she woke, screaming, tears running down her face.

'Mamma, Papa,' she sobbed. 'Help me.'

But no one heard, no one came.

Kumari lay staring out at the waxing moon, praying for the dawn to come.

KUMARI'S JOURNAL
(TOP SECRET. FOR MY EYES ONLY.
EVERYONE ELSE KEEP OUT!)
THIS MEANS YOU!

My bedroom

First Quarter Moon – 18 days to go until next New Moon

I can't sleep so I might as well write – it stops my imagination working overtime. If I write things down they don't seem so

119

bad, or at least I can sometimes make sense of them. Take tonight in the throne room. I mean, it's just impossible to believe what happened. No one can open that door unless they know the combination and there are only about three people who do. Of them, Papa is out so that leaves the RHM and the Abbot. It was obviously neither of them, so who does that leave? No one.

Badmash was incredibly brave. I've never seen him so angry. It was like he really hated whoever it was. He's sleeping peacefully, the lucky thing. At least his dreams are only about food – OMG, what was that noise? I really have to stop being so jumpy. It was probably only the wind. But then I thought that about the throne-room door. It came from over there by the window. There it is again, like a scraping. I'm not going to look. I'll just sit tight . . .

CHAPTER 16

A hand was clutching on to Kumari's windowsill, the fingers turning white with pressure. And then another hand appeared beside it. Any minute now the rest of the person would appear. Whoever it was, they were heaving themselves up, intending to climb into her room. Seizing a book from her bedside table, Kumari tiptoed over to the window. Keeping low, she raised the book, ready to strike. It was a big, heavy volume: *The Anatomy of Ancient Rites*. That could really do some damage if she whacked it on the intruder's fingers.

'Hey, Kumari.'

'Theo!'

Just in time, Kumari dropped the book to the floor.

'Give me a hand, will you? This wall is kind of tricky.'

'Uh, sure,' said Kumari, grabbing hold of his outstretched arm and pulling hard. With a grunt and a heave, Theo fell into her room.

'Phew. Thought I was a goner there. Ran into some guards below but I hid before they could see me. There are guards all over the place. Something is definitely going on.'

'There was an intruder,' said Kumari. 'Earlier this evening. I saw them, by the throne room. Whoever it was opened the outer door.'

'An intruder? And you saw them? Was anyone else with you?'

'Um . . . no,' said Kumari. 'Save it. The RHM already said his piece.'

Badmash lifted his head from the pillow and glared at Theo.

'Hey, fella,' said Theo.

Sticking his beak in the air, Badmash turned his head away.

'He's still sulking,' said Kumari. 'He hasn't forgiven you yet for the windowsill thing.'

'I brought this for your Papa,' said Theo, pulling a sealed flask from his backpack. 'It's the best we've come up with so far. A kind of restorative tonic. I need to administer it and evaluate the result so I can work on it some more.'

Kumari examined the flask, carefully removing the stopper.

'Eugh!' she said. 'That smells really bad.'

'It does, but it might just work.'

'You want to give it to him now?' Kumari was still looking at it dubiously. The potion was a kind of murky green and looked distinctly unappetising.

'Uh, yeah,' said Theo. 'I kind of wanted to try this one out on my own.'

'Why's that?'

'No reason. Kumari, don't look at me like that. It's just the monks and I . . . we do things differently, and it's not just the language problem. This mixture is not necessarily what they would try. But that doesn't mean it won't work.'

'OK,' said Kumari. 'But we have to be careful. If anyone sees you, there will be trouble. You're not supposed to be here.'

Kumari poked her head out of her bedroom door. She could see one guard along the corridor, standing duty outside Papa's room, looking distinctly bored.

'Hey,' she called out softly. 'Yes, you. I heard a noise. It came from that direction. I think it might be the intruder.'

At this, the guard perked up.

'You say from over there, your holy highness?' He looked about, knowing he should not leave his post.

'Quick! I heard it again!' said Kumari.

At that, the guard was off, sprinting in the opposite direction. She gave him fifteen seconds and then gave Theo the nod. They made it unscathed across the corridor and into Papa's bedroom.

'He looks so peaceful,' Kumari whispered. 'Are you sure this is a good idea?'

'We have to try everything,' said Theo. 'This is the one chance I get with this.'

Kumari looked again at the flask. It really did smell foul.

'And that stuff won't hurt him more?'

'No way. See, I'll try some.'

And with that, Theo tipped it to his lips and gulped some down.

'Disgusting. But harmless.'

'All right then. But be quick. That guard will be back in a minute.'

Cradling Papa's head in her hand, she watched as Theo held it to his mouth.

'Theo made this, Papa,' she crooned. 'It's going to make you better.'

As the potion passed through Papa's lips, he choked a little and spluttered. She gave Theo an anxious glance. He answered it with a nod of reassurance.

'All done,' he said. 'Now we simply have to wait and see.'

A few minutes passed with no other sign from Papa.

'No improvement,' said Theo. 'But no deterioration either. I guess I'll have to tweak this some more. We had better get out of here.'

Kumari dropped a kiss on Papa's forehead. 'Sleep well. Sweet dreams.'

They could hear footsteps approaching as they scurried back, diving behind Kumari's door.

'Phew! That was close,' Kumari gasped.

Someone rapped on the door behind her.

Gesturing to Theo to stay back, Kumari opened it a fraction.

'Kumari, honey, are you OK?' It was Ma.

'Quick, inside,' said Kumari. Pulling Ma into her bedroom, Kumari shut the door tight.

'Hello, Ma,' said Theo.

'Oh my lord, you made me jump!'

'Keep it down,' hissed Kumari. 'Or they'll come looking.'

'Sorry,' whispered Theo.

'It was his fault,' muttered Ma. 'Anyway, what are you doing here? If someone catches you there'll be trouble.'

'There's already trouble from what I hear,' said Theo. 'Kumari saw an intruder by the throne room.'

'An intruder? Oh my lord! Do you think it could be Razzle's heavies?'

'I don't know,' said Kumari. 'I only saw one person in the doorway.'

'Do you mean to tell me you were on your own?'

'Don't start,' said Kumari. 'I've already heard it from the RHM.'

Ma was giving her that look she knew only too well, the one that included the pursed lips and the slow shake of the head.

'I had to go alone,' said Kumari. 'I needed to visit Mamma. I like to go there and look at her portrait. It makes me feel like she's close by.'

'You don't need to look at her picture to feel that. You carry your Mamma in your heart. Unless there's some other reason you go to that throne room. Well, is there, Kumari?'

Kumari stared numbly at the floor, avoiding Ma's astute eyes. She so wanted to tell them everything. They might even be able to help. Maybe she could at least show them her latest sketch, without mentioning the rest. The shadow and the images could remain a secret. She wouldn't be giving it all away.

'Look,' said Kumari. 'I do go there to see Mamma. That's when she tells me where to find the ingredients. I can't tell you more than that. But I promise from the bottom of my heart I'm telling you all I can. Here, I have something to show you.'

With that, she pulled out her drawing of the waterfall and held them it up so that they could see.

'What's that?' asked Ma, peering at it.

'I think it's a waterfall,' said Kumari. 'See here, the rocks and the water gushing over them. Wherever it is, it's pretty big.'

'And you don't know where this is?'

'Not yet but I will. I think it's another clue.'

'Another clue from your Mamma?'

There was a hint of wariness in Ma's voice.

'Yes, another clue from my Mamma. You know I can't tell you any more than that.'

Kumari glanced at Theo. He was not even looking at the sketch.

'Look,' he said abruptly. 'I have a confession to make. I've been keeping something back as well. But only because I didn't want to alarm you. At least, not until I figured it out. But now I have, it's what I came to tell you.'

'Wonderful,' said Ma. 'More secrets. Seems like I'm the only one round here ain't got none.'

'Something has disappeared from the lab,' Theo went on. 'A sample of sap. Only it wasn't the *real* sample I left out – the one that you gave me. I kind of suspected something was going on. So I prepared a little trap and left out a fake sample. I'm pretty sure the monastery has been compromised and I'm also sure there must be a secret passage. There is someone in there who is up to no good. I think they are trying to sabotage us. Someone does not want those fires relit.'

'A secret passage? But why? To where?'

'Maybe out into the hillside. I hid just around the corner from the lab and no one came down that corridor. Beyond the lab it's a dead-end. A secret passage would be the only way to get in and out. All I know is that sample disappeared and it was while I was hiding. Someone came in and out of that lab without walking past me.'

'Do you think it's Razzle's men?'

Theo met Kumari's troubled gaze.

'It could be. It could be someone else. Don't forget the warlords and the rebel citizens.'

Suddenly, Kumari's mouth felt like chalk. It was all closing in on them.

If someone did not want the fires relit it meant they knew they had gone out. Which also meant this must be someone very close. Someone who wanted to destroy the Kingdom. Dread set up its slow drumbeat in her mind.

Who could hate the Kingdom that much?

KUMARI'S JOURNAL
(TOP SECRET. FOR MY EYES ONLY.
EVERYONE ELSE KEEP OUT!)
THIS MEANS YOU!

My bedroom (once more)

Full Moon – 14 days to go to next New Moon

It's been four nights now and I haven't slept. I was so scared after what Theo said that I asked Ma if she would sleep over in my room. Big mistake. Now she's snoring so loudly I can't hear myself think, never mind hear anyone trying to creep in. Although actually her snores might help keep people out – she does sound like a sleeping warthog. Like a louder version of Badmash's demon pigs. And if anyone thinks I have a giant demon guard-pig in my room they are far less likely to want to come in. Demon guard-pigs can be very fierce – how are they to know it's only Ma?

I asked Ma to come sit with me tonight and Papa was just the same. I sprinkled some more of Mamma's scent on the pillow, but this time he didn't seem to notice. Maybe I'll bring him something she used to wear so he can smell that too. I mean, I like to hold Mamma's clothes to my face sometimes. Then I breathe in and it's like breathing her in and it makes me feel like she's still here.

I so wish she was here, like really here. Mamma would find those ingredients in a flash. Although if Mamma were here, none of this would be happening. If only I could go back in time. Even if I went back just a little way I could see my friends, see Chico. Chico would help me find the ingredients if he was here. I just know he would never tell anyone. Nor would Ma and Theo of course. But I feel like I have to protect them. With Chico, it always feels like he's protecting me. Or rather that we're protecting each other.

We make a good team. Made a good team, that is. It's not like I'm ever going to see him again. I'm here and he's there and there's no way we can meet. I keep my iPod hidden beside the necklace he gave me – it's like my secret Chico stash. I look at the K&C all intertwined and I think it must mean we are supposed to be together. Maybe I'll just listen to my iPod one more time. I mean, it's not like I'm ever going to get any sleep. I've got to be careful about the batteries, but I so want to hear his voice. And it might help drown out the snorty demon pig chorus.

CHAPTER 17

Kumari scrabbled about for her iPod, trying not to wake Ma or Badmash. Really, it was like Grand Central Station in her bedroom what with all her extra visitors.

Aha, here it was beside the necklace, secreted under her stack of letters. She re-read them most nights, picking one or two from the pile. They were like a note of sanity in a world gone mad, which was weird when you considered they came from the World Beyond. Once she had thought the World Beyond was bizarre. Now, from a distance, she missed so much about it.

The World Beyond might be manic, but at least it did not need a big old bonfire to make it work. OK, so that was a bit harsh. The holy fires were Papa's sacred duty. It did seem really stupid, though, that the Kingdom needed them so much. But that was just the way things were and had always been and still would be if only she could follow Mamma's leads. Of course, Theo and the monks were hard at work in the lab, but Kumari knew it was Mamma's clues that would ultimately save them.

Plugging her earpieces in, Kumari clicked the button. Only she must have hit it wrong because there was nothing to be heard. She waited for quite some time. Still nothing but silence. She had obviously gone too far forward. Her finger was already on the button when suddenly the iPod sprang to life. First a cough, then a clearing of the throat and then a longed-for voice.

'Hey, Kumari.'

Chico! She had never heard this bit before. He'd obviously recorded it way after the rest.

'I . . . ah . . . I wrote you something.'

Ohmigosh what was coming next?

'So, ah, OK here we go. It's a, uh, it's a song. Well, kind of like a song. Maybe a song without music. So maybe, uh, more like a poem. Anyways, it goes like this . . . '

A poem. He'd written a poem. He'd written a poem for her?

'I . . . ' Another cough. Then silence. *Oh no, please say it.* She was clenching a fist, willing him on. This was so important.

'Walking the streets
And I'm thinking of you
A million faces pass by

But it's your face I see
'Cos I miss you
My goddess girl
Miss you more than I dreamed.
I put my hand to my face
But it's your skin I'm touching
And it's my eyes are weeping
Those are real tears
'Cos I miss you
My goddess girl
Miss you more than I dreamed
I miss you, my goddess girl
I'll see you in my dreams.'

Oh my god!! He'd written that. For her. She brushed the back of her hand across her eyes. Her tears were real, too.

'I miss you,' she whispered. 'Hey, Chico, I'll see you in my dreams. We could meet up there, whaddya say?'

Beside her, Ma thrashed about.

'Wha . . . ?' she mumbled, then fell back again, snoring. Badmash grumbled and shoved his beak in Kumari's shoulder where a small pool of bird dribble began to form.

'Great,' Kumari sighed.

Fat chance she had of meeting up with Chico like this. Even if she managed to fall asleep her dreams would be full of snorty demon pigs. She would just play her poem one more time. It might even drown out her bedmates. And maybe just one more time after that . . . and another . . . and another . . .

CHAPTER 18

'Kumari, wake up! Kumari, they've found him.'
'Gnf . . . ?'

Her eyelids were glued together. There were things stuck in her ears, wire tangled round her neck. Somewhere in her dreams, a voice faded.

'Kumari, they've got him.'

'Got who? Chico?'

'*Chico?* What you talking about girl? They've found him, they got the intruder.'

Ma's words dowsed her brain like a bucket of iced water. Instantly, Kumari's eyes snapped open.

'They got him? Who is it?'

She was scrambling for her clothes.

'Let me see him. I want to talk to him. We've got to get answers.'

She was gabbling now, mind racing, desperate to find out who it was. Would it be one of Razzle's heavies, or someone from the Kingdom?

'Where is he?' she demanded.

'Hey, now, just wait a minute.'

Ma was standing in front of the door, arms folded. 'Is this such a good idea, Kumari? Why don't you let the RHM deal with it?'

'*Of course* it's a good idea. This is the person who scared me stupid. The person who stalked me to the throne room. Possibly even the person who poisoned Papa. You have to let me go see him. I want *answers*, for heaven's sake. I need them.'

Ma did not budge one inch. 'And will that make you happy?'

Kumari hesitated. 'Maybe not. But I have to do it.'

'Then I'll come with you, honey. Even though I think it's a bad idea.'

They looked at one another. A wave of understanding flowed between them.

'I thought I was stubborn,' smiled Ma. 'But girl, you take some beating.'

'You taught me all I know.'

'I don't think so.'

Arms linked, they hurried along, Kumari's heart beating fast. At last, a chance to face down the enemy.

A small group was milling round outside the palace cell as they approached, Theo's head towering above all the others.

'Let me talk to him,' he was shouting. 'I need to see the RHM.'

The crowd parted at Kumari's approach. She could see several monks, a couple of guards and, beside Theo, the Ancient Abbot.

'What's going on?' she demanded. 'Why won't you let Theo in?'

'The RHM's orders, holy highness,' said a guard. 'He is not to be disturbed during the questioning process.'

'But he's got the wrong man!' snapped Theo. 'This is all such a waste of time. And while you've got the wrong guy in there, the real one is somewhere out there, free.'

'What do you mean the wrong man?' Kumari had never seen Theo so agitated. Even his curls seemed to bristle with anger. The Abbot was scarcely less annoyed.

'You cannot hold one of my monks,' he said. 'It is unthinkable. How can you accuse him of such a thing? He has taken vows, for heaven's sake.'

At that moment, the cell doors were flung open. On the threshold, the RHM.

'Silence!' he murmured and instantly a hush fell.

Behind him, Kumari caught a glimpse of a man sitting at a table, dressed in monks' robes. His head was bowed, his hands in his lap but there was nothing about him that looked defeated. On the contrary, he looked like a man who knew he was in the right. His spine was still erect, his shoulders set square. And then his eyes slid towards the door and Kumari frowned in recognition. She had seen that face somewhere before.

'There he is,' said Theo. 'Hey, Lopsang, look at me.'

135

At the sound of his name, the monk turned to Theo.

As he did so, Kumari realised where she had seen the monk before. He had been in the holy hermit's retinue.

'Is there some kind of problem?' The RHM addressed Theo.

'You bet there is. You've got the wrong man.'

'Indeed?' The RHM's expression barely altered as he eyed Theo, the Abbot, Kumari and Ma. 'You four had better come in.'

Inside, Lopsang sat motionless, eyes fixed on the table in front of him. The cell was small and forbidding, its walls plain, the single window barred. It smelled musty, dank with neglect. Kumari could not remember it ever having been used before. But then, this was the first intruder they had ever apprehended. And if Theo was to be believed, the monk was no such thing. Kumari looked at Ma and the Abbot. Their faces echoed her confusion. Only Theo seemed absolutely clear as to what was going on, his voice once more vehement.

'RHM, this is a terrible mistake. You have to let this man go at once.'

The RHM pressed his lips together. Not a good sign, in Kumari's experience.

'And why should I do that?' he enquired softly. 'What proof do you have that we are wrong? This man was found near the royal wing with a rope and a medicinal bottle. We have not yet analysed the substance inside, but I think I can safely say it will turn out to be harmful.'

A medicinal bottle? An image flashed through Kumari's mind. The flask Theo had brought to Papa. That flask had also contained a potion, although it had not appeared to affect Papa.

'You think wrong and I can prove it,' said Theo. 'That bottle contains nothing but preservative solution.'

At this, the monk's eyes once more flicked sideways. This time, he was staring at Theo. In them, an expression Kumari could not fathom. Another second later, the expression was gone, to be replaced by a careful blankness. It was the posture all the monks adopted, lids lowered in respect.

'How can you be so sure of that?'

There was an edge now to the RHM's voice.

'Because it was I who gave it to him.' Theo's tone was equally full of grit. 'I asked Lopsang here to collect a sample of a particular plant I'd seen growing high up on the palace wall. The best examples are to be found on the royal wing.'

'I see.'

Plainly, the RHM did not.

'I, too, can vouch for Brother Lopsang,' said the Ancient Abbot. 'I translated for him when Brother Theo made his request. Brother Lopsang is our most gifted young herbalist. It was only natural he should be granted this exacting task.'

The RHM looked from Theo to the monk and back to the Ancient Abbot. He appeared to be calculating something, weighing up the evidence. All at once, he made up his mind, inclining his head towards Brother Lopsang.

'It seems we have indeed made a mistake. You may go now. I am sorry.'

Unbelievable.

The RHM admitting to a mistake. And then actually apologising for it.

'But before you do, you will be searched one more time.

137

Mere procedure, I can assure you.' The RHM's tone brooked no argument. 'Abbot, would you take him to the Head Guardsman?'

Without a word, Lopsang rose from his chair and offered the RHM a deep bow. He then followed the Ancient Abbot from the room, walking the requisite three steps behind him. As he passed Theo, their hands touched briefly. Kumari blinked in astonishment. It looked as if Lopsang had passed something to Theo. No one else appeared to have noticed.

'I saw that,' Kumari murmured in English as Lopsang drew level, just loud enough so that only he could hear. She watched his shoulders stiffen. It was all the confirmation she needed.

The gentle click of the door sounded unnaturally loud in the silence that followed. And then the RHM looked straight at Theo.

'I hope you know what you're doing,' he said.

With that, he too swept from the room. Kumari, Ma and Theo let out a collective sigh.

'So they didn't get him after all,' said Kumari.

She could taste the disappointment in her mouth. It was like biting down on a grape pip. A bitter surprise hidden in the sweet flesh of anticipation.

'Don't you worry, Kumari. We'll find him,' said Theo.

She looked at his hands. Nothing there. She might have been mistaken. But there was something in his gaze that disturbed her. She had seen that selfsame glint in Lopsang's eyes. It was the gleam of secrets unshared, of knowledge kept hidden. Theo was working with the monk.

For a second the room seemed to spin, the floor tilting

under her feet. It was impossible that Theo could or would do anything so wrong. She heard Mamma's words in her mind:

'*Nothing is impossible, Kumari.*'

But not Theo, not her friend. He would never betray her.

Then again, the Ayah had betrayed her.

So anything was possible.

KUMARI'S JOURNAL
(TOP SECRET. FOR MY EYES ONLY.
EVERYONE ELSE KEEP OUT!)
THIS MEANS YOU!

My bedroom

Waning Moon – 13 days to go to next New Moon

I can't, won't believe it. I mean, Theo has always protected me. He's always been on my side. Why would he want to hurt me or my family, when he came here in the first place to warn me? But maybe that was not the real reason he came here. Maybe it was all a front. I mean, he could be pretending to warn me when in fact he's the one after me. It's the kind of thing villains do, after all. At least, they do in the World Beyond.

I remember seeing it on TV. It even happened in CSI. You think someone is the good guy and they turn out to be the baddie all along. Theo did climb into my room, after all.

That's a rather weird thing to do. OK, so he wanted to deliver a secret message, but he could have made up all that stuff about the sap. And anyway, how do we know he ever even laid a trap? Maybe he really came to harm me. If I hadn't been awake I would never have heard him. Why come sneaking in like that? Then there's the thing about Lopsang speaking English – what reason has Theo got to keep that to himself? How on earth did Lopsang learn it? Did Theo start to teach him?

Whoa. Wait a minute. This is Theo I'm writing about. Theo, Ms Martin's boyfriend. Oof – that looks really strange. OK, Theo who saved my life in the World Beyond. Theo who has never been anything but nice to me. Who is doing his best to help Papa. But the Ayah was nice to me too and look how that turned out.

Theo is a scientist, after all. Maybe he just can't resist something like this. With the Secrets you could do all kinds of stuff they've never even seen in the World Beyond. The knowledge in them is priceless. Perhaps that's his reason – money, plain and simple. I'd never have thought Theo would be so materialistic. Then again, do you ever really know other people?

I just don't know what to do. Nothing, for the moment. It's not like I have proof or anything. I'll simply have to watch and wait. Oh great – more watching and waiting. Like I really need that. Soon, though, the next bit of the shadow will be clear. Maybe another day or two. In the meantime, I've got to find that waterfall. It has to be out there somewhere.

I hate this. It feels so strange. I don't know who to trust any more.

CHAPTER 19

Kumari and Ma set out early the following morning. The plan was to climb the slopes to the west of the monastery and follow the stream, in the hope of finding the waterfall. In all her years of wandering near the palace compound, Kumari had yet to explore its wooded terraces. The proximity of the forbidding monastery walls had been enough to put her off. They rose, stark white, impenetrable apart from narrow slits of windows set high above the ground. Even the main door was narrow and unwelcoming. Kumari much preferred the palace grounds.

Fortified by Cook's splendid breakfast, they strode through the sunlit courtyard. From the gates came the sound of chatter. The kids were arriving for Palace School. Kumari suppressed a sudden twinge. It was not that she wanted to join them. But it would be nice to have nothing more to worry about than getting your homework in on time. It was the RHM who insisted the kids keep coming, although he had finally agreed to tell them Kumari was unwell. Stop Palace School and it might spread unease. One more thing to disturb the people. Although frankly there were more important things to worry about. Like the haze of Happiness for instance.

Kumari glanced at the sky as they slipped through the side door. Clear – too clear. A cerulean blue. With the palace behind them, she began to stride faster. The moon might be invisible now, but nothing stopped its passage across the heavens. Each night it claimed its place among the stars; each night brought the next New Moon closer and with it the threat of disaster if the fires were not re-lit.

They simply had to find the waterfall. But there were so many possibilities. She could see the wooded slopes now, beyond the monastery walls. Would they yield the answer she needed?

'Will you look at that,' said Ma.

'At what?'

Kumari tore her gaze from the hillside.

'That there. That field. Why, it's chock-full of tomatoes!'

'What? Oh, yes, the monks grow them. They grow all the palace fruit and vegetables. But why are we talking tomatoes when we've got a mission to accomplish?'

'Because with tomatoes I can make Hoodoo Soup.'

'So?'

'So, Hoodoo Soup is the most nourishing thing known to

142

man or woman. It can bring a blush to a nun's cheeks. Why, I reckon it might even work on old stiff-lips RHM. But the person I want to make it for is your Pops.'

'Papa likes his Celestial Chicken.'

'And he'll like Hoodoo Soup even more. It's not just any old soup, Kumari. This stuff can raise the dead.'

Kumari stopped in her tracks.

'My Papa is not dead.'

'Of course he's not, honey. What I'm trying to say in my clumsy way is that it's very powerful. Maybe enough to wake him up. Certainly to bring colour to his cheeks.'

'So why didn't you mention it before? You should have told Theo.'

Or maybe not.

'Those there are the first tomatoes I've seen in this place. How was I supposed to know you grew them here?'

A fair point, and at least Ma now had a chance to make her soup. Kumari's heart quickened. It just might even work.

'Anyways, you want me to tell Theo – he's right over there. Yoo hoo, Theo! He ain't seen us. Hey, Theo!'

Kumari looked where Ma was pointing. Sure enough, a lanky figure had stood up, slap bang in the middle of the tomato patch.

'Hey!' He was waving now. 'What are you two doing out here?'

I could ask the same, thought Kumari. There was a strange, rectangular object just visible by Theo's feet.

As they approached she could see something attached to it. It turned out to be Theo's laptop.

'So what are you up to?' Kumari kept her voice casual.

'Me? I'm setting up my solar charger. Need to keep this computer going if I'm to check all those samples against my database.'

He proudly indicated the panels on the black rectangle.

'Lightest one you can get. Folds up real small. Means I can recharge my laptop battery anywhere. Deserts, mountains, you name it. And now a tomato field. Just happens this one faces east. Perfect to catch the sun as it rises in the sky, and get this thing all powered up.'

'That's incredible,' said Kumari. 'You mean you can get power with this thing?'

'You bet I can,' said Theo. 'You folks could do the same. Got all this sunshine and no form of electricity, when the stuff is there for the taking. Bring a whole bunch of these in and you've got it on tap.'

'But that is brilliant,' breathed Kumari. Electricity in the Kingdom! It could open the way to so many things. No more butter lamps. All right, maybe a few butter lamps. She rather liked the soft light they cast. But just think of every-thing else they could have, like . . . refrigerators . . . the Internet . . .

OK, maybe not the Internet. How would they hook it up? Maybe Theo had found some way. Maybe he was really sending a covert message. *Oh come on, Kumari. He couldn't do that. Or could he?*

'So.' Kumari cleared her throat, aiming for that casual tone again. 'Is there any way you could, say, send an email?'

'From here? No way.'

Theo was looking at her now like she was a little crazy, which was not so far from the truth given that her head was full of bizarre thoughts. Like, maybe Theo was some kind of spy. Perhaps he was even now sending out coded messages. There were satellites in space after all, and the haze was very thin. His laptop could be a homing device, pinpointing the Kingdom. He might even have a cell phone on him. They could use those to track you down. She had seen it on *CSI*, when they found a body in the desert. The Kingdom was not so different to a desert, being so remote.

'Ah, Theo, did you bring your cell phone with you by any chance?'

Now he really was looking at her strangely.

'It's back in the monastery. Not much use out here, Kumari.'

'No, no, of course not.'

But then he would say that, wouldn't he?

'Why, did you want to make a call?'

Now he was laughing at her.

'Don't be ridiculous! It wouldn't work here.'

'Are you OK, Kumari?'

'Yes, of course. Why?'

'You seem a little tense, that's all.'

'Well of course I'm a little tense. My Papa's lying in a coma. The haze of Happiness has all but gone and the Secrets have been stolen. And now it's up to me to find the ingredients for the holy fires except I can't even find the stupid waterfall, never mind the other stuff.' She could hear her own voice rising, feel the pressure behind her eyeballs. Oh no, not tears again. She was totally sick of crying.

'Hey, hey,' soothed Ma. 'Cool it, will you? We'll find the waterfall. We haven't even really started looking yet.'

'Right. Yes. OK. Let's get going. We've already wasted loads of time.'

And with that Kumari strode off through the tomato field, not caring how many she squashed underfoot. She could hear Theo say something and then Ma calling after her:

'Hey, wait up, Kumari! Slow down, for heaven's sakes.'

Not once did she slacken. In fact, she marched all the faster. Trying to outrun the thoughts racing through her mind. The suspicion lurking in her gut.

KUMARI'S JOURNAL
(TOP SECRET. FOR MY EYES ONLY. EVERYONE ELSE KEEP OUT!) THIS MEANS YOU!

My bedroom

Waning Moon - 12 days to go until next New Moon

OK, so no waterfall. Ma and I followed the stream for hours, but it just kept on being a stream. I'm not giving up on it. It's out there, somewhere in the Kingdom. Next time I'll try and give Ma the slip. It's not that it's not nice to have her along and I really appreciate her trying to help, but she keeps crashing into things and having to stop for a rest. And that thing with Theo – I just don't know what to believe. I mean, it's amazing to think we might make our own electricity, but was that really what he was doing?

Of course it was. It must have been. Why would Theo lie about something like that? Because he's a spy maybe . . . spies lie all the time. That's their job, isn't it, pretending to be something else? But I can't really see Theo as a spy. Apart from anything else, he's too tall. Spies can only really be good spies if they're not that noticeable, surely. But then James Bond is pretty noticeable. He certainly was in the movies.

Anyway, I have to keep an open mind. That's what Mamma would have told me. I'm almost certain I saw that in her eyes tonight: Keep an Open Mind, Kumari. I need to keep an open mind about the waterfall – try less obvious places. But it's going to be hard getting out of here on my own. I need to think of a way to distract Ma.

She's already started on her Hoodoo Soup – she's soaking the tomatoes overnight in something or other. Maybe if she gets busy with it again tomorrow I can sneak away without her knowing. That feels mean, but, then again, she needs to concentrate on her hoodoo. I almost don't dare hope that it will work – nothing has so far. I know Theo says he's working as fast as he can on a cure for Papa, but it's not happening fast enough for me.

But is he – working on a cure? Aaaargh – I don't know what to think any more. And the moon seems to move so slowly. I wish it would hurry up and reveal the third segment. Then at least I'd have something else to work on, somewhere else to try. Then again, the faster it goes the less time there is left to relight the holy fires. The less time for Papa and the Kingdom.

CHAPTER 20

Kumari found the folded scrap of paper on the pillow beside her when she awoke the next morning. She reached out for it, bleary-eyed. Ma must be already up and about. She had probably left her a note, no doubt some missive instructing Kumari on her whereabouts. Badmash had obviously gone with her, eager for his honey cakes.

Kumari peered at it, puzzled. There was something not quite right about this message. The paper curled at the edges as if it had once been wrapped into a cylinder. In one corner, there was an indent where it had been clasped tight by something. Unfolding it, she scanned the contents then sat bolt upright, rigid with shock. This note was from the RHM. She knew each spiky letter all too well. And she was obviously not the intended recipient.

Kumari read it again, digesting each word with a mounting sense of alarm:

My Esteemed Colleague,

Regrettably, I write to ask for your assistance once more and hope that this letter finds you in good health and prospering as ever.

It seems we are facing a grave situation which can only be resolved with the aid of outside intervention. It would be wise to meet rather than correspond and I suggest the usual venue as being most suitable. I will make all the arrangements and will send word once these are in place. Please do not plan your departure until I have confirmed the details, although I anticipate that this will be in the near future as the situation is, indeed, quite desperate.

I must impress upon you once more the need for absolute discretion. It would, indeed, be fatal if our relationship were to be revealed. Naturally, you will be well rewarded for your services and can count on my continued friendship at all times. I trust you are of like mind and understand our compact.

Please do not avail of the pigeon post unless absolutely necessary. Instead, wait until I write again, as I fear I must.

With all good wishes,
Your Comrade

Absolute discretion. A grave situation. Who on earth was the RHM writing to and, more important, why? And what was with this 'pigeon post'? It would seem that he was inviting someone from the World Beyond to interfere with matters of the Kingdom. That was a treasonable offence in itself, which must be why any revelation would be 'fatal'. Of course, people were not killed for treason in the Kingdom. They were not killed for anything. But the punishment was immediate banishment to the World Beyond, which more or less amounted to the same thing in the end.

Even if he were convinced it was the best thing for the Kingdom, the RHM was simply not allowed to share its secrets with outsiders. And the current situation was most certainly a big secret, especially from the very people it could affect the most. But how had this note found its way to her pillow, when it was supposed to be attached to a carrier pigeon? Kumari's eyes fell on the dent in the pillow, the hollow left by the small, fluffy body of its usual occupant.

'Badmash,' she whispered. 'Was it you that brought this to me?'

Unusual for him not to be there when breakfast was due. But then he was obviously busy intercepting carrier pigeons.

'Kumari, honey, you look like you've seen a ghost.' It was Ma, bustling through the door with her breakfast tray, red splatters lurid against her work-worn hands. Kumari shoved the note inside her pillowcase. Best not to involve Ma.

'What have you done? Have you cut yourself?' Kumari looked at Ma's hands in concern.

'What, these? Heavens, no. I been tending my Hoodoo Soup. Now you get yourself up and dressed, girl. I could do with some assistance. I need you to help me stir in the mojo. It's real important we get that right. That's the bag of magical ingredients.'

Shovelling her breakfast in with one hand, Kumari pulled on random garments with the other. A minute or so later she was dressed. Ten minutes later they were in the kitchen. The kitchens sat in the heart of the palace, as they did in every house in the Kingdom. Food and warmth were the stuff of life. Everything revolved around them.

'My darlings!' cried Cook the moment she saw them. Kumari caught a flash of a pink streak in her hair. It looked like Ma's handiwork.

'Hey honey,' smiled Ma. 'Mind if I cook up a little hoodoo?'

'You two do what you like. Don't mind me. I'm going to market.' And with that Cook bustled off, basket over her arm.

While Kumari grasped a wooden spoon, Ma measured out her mojo. A pinch of this, a sniff of that, all bound up in a scrap of cloth. As she tied the tiny bag, Ma muttered, endowing her mojo with magic. Then, with a nod to Kumari, she dropped it. It hit the soup with a resounding *plop*. At once, Kumari began stirring, just as Ma had instructed, once, twice, three times anticlockwise, keeping in time with Ma's keening. As the last of Ma's high-pitched notes faded, Kumari could hear other voices rising and falling. It was time for Palace School and the kids were filing right past the kitchens. Without thinking, Kumari ran out. She might just catch a glimpse of Tenzin. Of course, he was a friend, and nothing more. But still, it would be good to see him.

One or two of the kids glanced her way, quickly averting their eyes the moment they met hers. Great. More of a pariah than ever. Defiantly, Kumari lifted her chin. And then

Asha came round the corner. This time, when their eyes met, they locked.

'Thought you were sick,' said Asha.

Then Asha's eyes travelled down to Kumari's neck.

'What's that?' she demanded, pulling at the wire protruding from Kumari's top.

Too late, Kumari realised that her iPod was still around her neck from the night before. She had dressed so quickly she had forgotten to remove it. Ordinarily, it sat hidden in her bedside bureau. Only now it was in Asha's grasp.

Asha's fingers were moving quickly, clicking away at the wheel. All at once, music blasted, tinny, from the headphones. Asha leaped about a foot.

'Aaargh, this thing is bewitched! There are people in here playing music. But how could there be? Unless you've somehow shrunk them? Is this some kind of goddess trick?'

Asha peered down the earpiece, trying to see what was in there.

'Helloooo? Anybody in there? Can you hear me? Hello?'

Now all the other kids were crowding round. Desperately, Kumari tried to grab the iPod back. Asha was having none of it.

'Hey, you know, this music isn't bad. Really weird, but I like it.'

She was dancing away from her, the headphones held to her ears.

'Give that to me now!' shrieked Kumari, finally getting close enough to snatch it back.

'What on earth is going on?'

Wonderful. The RHM arriving for class.

'Uh, nothing,' said Kumari.

'It doesn't look like "nothing" to me. Asha?'

'Like she says, it's nothing.'

'Very well. Then carry on.'

The RHM pressed his lips together. It was clear he did not believe a word. He waited until all the kids had filed past. Disappointingly, Tenzin did not appear. He must already have gone in. Unusual for Tenzin to be so keen.

'Kumari.'

'Yes, RHM?'

She waited. The RHM sighed and ran a hand through his hair. The gesture was so out of character Kumari stared. And then she remembered. The note.

'You really must be more careful. It's bad enough that you are not attending school – although, in the circumstances, it's understandable. We had told the other children you were sick. This kind of thing makes us all look untrustworthy. We also agreed you would not speak of the things you saw out in the World Beyond. It would only create a disturbance. Especially right now, when matters are so uncertain.'

'Do you believe that, RHM?'

In the face of her direct gaze, she saw him waver.

'Some things . . . the Kingdom is simply not ready for. It is what your Papa wishes.'

Wishes. At least he was talking about him in the present tense. All of a sudden, Kumari's eyes welled up.

'Oh good heavens . . . Kumari, child, please don't cry.'

'I can't help it,' she sobbed. 'Papa is so sick and there's nothing I can do to help him except try and find the Secrets

153

and there are so many weird things going on and I don't know what to think. I found a note you had written to someone. How can you talk to me about not corrupting people when you're obviously sending messages to the World Beyond?'

She stopped on a gulp. Oh my god, now she had really done it. She never meant to say all that. It just somehow spilled out of her mouth. She braced herself waiting for the RHM to shout or scream. Instead, he went very still. After a moment, she dared to look up from under her tear-spiked lashes. Unbelievable. The RHM's eyes were pink.

The RHM crying? Unheard of. His lips worked as he tried to find the words.

'My message was a desperate plea for help, Kumari. I thought in the circumstances it was justified.'

What, no demanding to know how she had seen it? No inquisition on the whys and wherefores? Kumari gaped at him, open-mouthed. This was a turn-up for the books.

'You see,' the RHM went on, 'I have a . . . friend in the World Beyond. An eminent physician. I felt it was the only thing I could do. I would do anything to try to save his majesty.'

Every seam in his stricken face said he was telling the truth. Each crack in his voice spoke volumes.

'Um . . . OK,' said Kumari at length. 'So what did you ask him?'

Now this would be the real test. Would he lie about the contents of his message? If he did, she was not sure she could stand it. Another person who had betrayed her trust.

'I asked him to meet with me so I could describe the king's

symptoms. Naturally, we must aim for absolute discretion.'

The very words he had used in his letter. All at once, Kumari felt very mean. He had only been trying to help. The RHM was unshakeably loyal. Another thought occurred to her.

'So how did you meet this friend?'

'He is in fact my cousin.'

Of course. The RHM originally came from the World Beyond. It still did not excuse the forbidden contact. Then again, who was she to talk? She would do anything to be able to communicate with Chico and her friends back in the Bronx.

'Can we keep this our secret?' said the RHM.

'Absolutely,' said Kumari.

Fantastic. Another secret. As if she didn't have enough already.

CHAPTER 21

Ma's soup had to simmer until nightfall. Which meant she had to watch it all day. The perfect opportunity for Kumari to go waterfall hunting. But as she walked away from the kitchen, she realised someone was on her tail. She took a few more steps then stopped dead. The person ran straight into her back.

'Ow! Oh, it's you.'

'Sorry,' said Tenzin sheepishly.

Her back was still tingling, perhaps more than strictly necessary.

'Can I walk with you?' he asked.

'What, and have Asha stab me round the next corner?'

'Sorry?'

'Oh nothing. And will you stop saying sorry.'

'Sorry.'

'For goodness' sake!'

'Just kidding,' he grinned.

His smile had always been irresistible. Still, she had a mission to carry out.

'Look, I meant it. I have to go now. Alone.'

'You're always rushing off somewhere. Is it something to do with that stuff by the dragon tree? Come on, Kumari. You can trust me.'

'I know I can, but I can't tell you. Nothing personal, I just can't. Anyway, shouldn't you be in class now? Asha will be missing you, apart from anything else.'

'All right. If you won't tell me, you won't. But what is it with this Asha stuff? It's not like she's anyone special. You've got it all wrong, Kumari.'

'Have I?'

Kumari looked straight into his eyes. Not a flicker. Except in her stomach. Oh no, that was a mistake. There was a definite, confusing fluttering.

'I . . .'

'Yeah, I know. You've got to go. See you later.'

And then he leaned forward and dropped a kiss on her lips. The lightest of brushes that reverberated all the way to her little toe. He pulled back and they gazed at one another. Their faces were centimetres apart. If she didn't move now he would do it again. If he did she was not sure she would ever want him to stop. Oh no, this could not be happening. Two guys laying claim to her heart. Chico was still very much in residence. She had no room in her life for this now.

157

Kumari took a step back and then another, one hand raised as if to stave him off.

'Look, I'm not interested, right? This is never going to work.'

Tenzin stared at her, bewildered, and in that instant she turned on her heels. *Quick, march. Get away, Kumari.* Before he could read the confusion in her eyes. Before he could work out what his kiss had meant. Kumari let out a heartfelt sigh as she stepped through the archway into the courtyard. The one man who truly had her heart was still lying helpless in the royal bedchamber. Pulling her sketches from her pocket, Kumari held them up. As she did so, the amulet on her wrist glinted.

'Mamma,' she whispered, her fingers stroking the silver band.

'What's up?' she heard someone say. She spun round, heart thumping once more.

It was Asha, loitering by the fragrant trumpet-shaped flowers that sprang from a giant lily stem. Fantastic. The last person she wanted to see. Unconsciously, Kumari raised a finger to her lips, as if to conceal Tenzin's kiss.

'What do you care?' asked Kumari. 'And how come you're not in class?'

What was with everyone today? First Tenzin, and now *her.*

'Why aren't *you*?' asked Asha.

'Yes, well, I have my reasons.'

'And so do I,' said Asha. 'I wanted to talk to you. Alone.' Asha's thin face was pale and set. She actually looked slightly nervous.

'Look, I don't have time for this,' said Kumari. 'There's

158

something I need to do for my Papa.'

She almost choked over that last word. Saying his name tripped her up.

Asha looked at her for a moment.

'Do you want some help?' she asked finally.

'I'm fine,' muttered Kumari.

'You don't look fine.'

'Oh, thanks.'

'I didn't mean it that way. And I'm sorry about your music thing.'

Asha, sorry? Yeah, right. Although she did look pretty sincere.

'You nearly broke it,' said Kumari.

'I didn't mean to. I said I was sorry.'

As if to prove it, she glanced helpfully at the sketches clutched in Kumari's hand.

'Hey, I recognise that,' she said.

'You do?'

'Well of course. That's the Peach Stone Waterfall.'

'The *what*?'

'See that boulder at the top. You've drawn it slightly wrong. It's really shaped like a peach stone. That's why the waterfall has its name. Or so my grandmother told me. She lives in the village another hour distant.'

'What village would that be?' asked Kumari, an idea forming.

'The Village of the Chrysanthemums. Close to the western borderlands.'

The Village of the Chrysanthemums. Mamma's home village. The second time chrysanthemums had cropped up recently. There had been a chrysanthemum depicted in

Mamma's portrait. Could there be a connection? And how amazing Asha's family should also come from there. They might even be related. It was not a comfortable thought, having an enemy as some sort of cousin. Although this enemy was now looking at her rather kindly. Double, double confusion.

'I could take you to the waterfall,' offered Asha. 'If we left now we could just be back before dark. We would not have time to get to the village and back as well. That would mean an overnight stay.'

'But what about this afternoon's lessons?'

'What about them?'

The two looked at one another. Kumari's face was the first to break into a smile.

It made sense to take Asha up on her offer. Besides, two heads were better than one according to the Ancient Abbot. OK, so she had turned Tenzin down. He would be nothing but a distraction. An even bigger one than ever, thanks to that kiss. A flush of guilt crept up Kumari's neck. *Don't be silly*, she told herself. It was not like he and Asha were together. Besides, Asha actually knew where the waterfall was, or so she claimed. And, in any case, Kumari remembered something else her Mamma had taught her:

'Keep your friends close, Kumari, and your enemies even closer.'

This way she could keep an eye on Asha and find her next ingredient into the bargain. She did not need to tell her too much, after all, just that it was something Papa needed.

'You can't come dressed like that, though,' said Asha. 'The quickest way is through the town. If the people see you in your imperial robes, they will report you to the RHM at once.'

160

Kumari looked down at her red robes. She *was* rather conspicuous. The girl-goddess was not supposed to walk through the town just like that. But there was yet another tiny problem.

'I have nothing else to wear,' she said. 'Except maybe my plainest cloak.'

'Nuh uh.' Asha shook her head. 'They'll spot you a mile off. Look, you'd better come with me. It's not far to my place. My father is one of the guardsmen. We live in the quarters just beyond the palace gates. We're about the same size. You can borrow something of mine if you like.'

Oh my god. Asha was actually offering to lend her own clothes. Kumari's day was getting weirder by the minute. First the RHM crying and now Asha being *nice*.

'Um . . . thanks,' muttered Kumari. 'That would be great. I'd better just call Badmash. He likes to come everywhere with me, or he sulks.'

'But don't you think he'd be a dead giveaway?' said Asha. 'Everyone knows about your pet vulture.'

Good point. Kumari had not thought of that. But there was no way she was leaving Badmash behind. His feelings would be irreparably hurt. And he wouldn't let her forget it for ages.

'How about I get him to fly on ahead? I'll bribe him or something.'

'Fine, but whatever you do we have to hurry. It's quite a long way to the waterfall.'

'Here, Badmash. Come here, boy.'

A sleepy head popped out from between the branches of a small mango tree. Having whispered vague promises in his ear of distant doughnut bushes beyond the town, Kumari watched as he flapped off, feeling only the slightest twinge of guilt. He should know better than to believe in doughnut bushes. Besides, it really was time he cut down on the treats. His belly had begun to scrape the ground. It was hardly aerodynamic.

'Let's go out the southern side door,' said Kumari. 'It's pretty easy to avoid the guards if you time it right.'

'I know a better way,' said Asha. 'Follow me.'

She had already set off across the courtyard. Kumari had no choice but to follow. It was a novelty, not being the one in charge.

'Quick, in here,' said Asha.

'But that's the guard room.'

'I know, but they're all out on patrol. Are you coming or not?'

This could be a trap designed to get her into big trouble. The RHM would not take kindly to Kumari being caught in the guard room. Then again, why would Asha bother? There were better ways to catch Kumari out.

'Hurry up,' said Asha. 'They'll be back any minute.'

With that, Kumari followed her through the door into a dingy room, a few chairs scattered here and there about the place. On the bare wooden table, some dirty cups. No servants to clear up here. Kumari stared at the cups. This was a side of the palace she had never seen. Never even thought about, come to that. It was a revelation.

Asha was wrestling with the bolt on the door, muttering under her breath. Finally, it gave with a squeak and a judder. They were stepping out into fresh air.

'Did you hear about the intruder the other night?' Kumari whispered as they slipped through the jacaranda groves.

'My dad did mention something,' said Asha. 'Apparently they never caught the guy.'

At the edge of the lawn, Asha veered right, heading downhill towards the guards' quarters. Over a low wall, and they were facing a small white house identical to those on either side of it. Kumari scarcely had time to take it in before Asha was bundling her and Badmash inside.

'Quick, before anyone sees us.'

And then she was eyeball to eyeball with a yak, its eyes surveying her with curiosity.

'This one's not too well,' said Asha. 'So we haven't turned her out today.'

Kumari looked about her. She was standing in what seemed to be the yak's living quarters, the floor laid with straw, a feeding trough in the corner. Badmash immediately went to investigate the trough, but Kumari had no time to linger. Asha was leading her up a flight of stairs to the floor above where, thankfully, no more animals lurked.

Instead, low divans were set around a central hearth, the chimney a hole in the roof. Although the room was simple, she rather liked it. It made a change from the ornate palace. Everything in the palace was so grand, designed to dignify the gods painted on every surface. Each table was gilt-edged, every chair lined with brocade. Sumptuous though it was, Kumari often felt she might suffocate. Here, you could be yourself, put your own stamp on the place.

'What are you looking at?' asked Asha. 'Haven't you ever been in a normal house before?'

'Yes. I mean, no.'

Mindful of the RHM, she did not want to mention Ma's apartment. In any case, this place was entirely different to Ma's apartment. There was no TV eternally blaring for one thing.

'That is so bizarre,' said Asha.

'I guess it is,' said Kumari.

Asha was rummaging in a chest in one corner, pulling out some items of clothing.

'Try these,' she said. 'You can change in the bathroom.'

At least they had a bathroom. It must be strange to have a home like this. Even stranger to come to the palace every day for school and see the difference in the way they lived. Suddenly, Kumari felt a bit uncomfortable. No wonder the other kids acted the way they did. They must think of her as the hoity-toity girl-goddess, when really she was just Kumari.

'They fit,' said Kumari, emerging from the bathroom. Asha's tunic and trousers felt rough against her skin, unlike her customary silks.

'Great. Then let's get going.'

'I-I like your house,' said Kumari shyly.

'You do?'

'Yes. It feels like a home.'

It was true. Although the house was simple, Kumari liked it for that very reason. The first floor was cosy and welcoming. Wood smoke lingered in the air from the hearth. Kumari loved that smell. Even the divans looked inviting. How nice it must be to sit and gaze into the flames. She even liked the fact that it was topsy turvy, although Asha snorted when she said as much.

'Well, where do you expect the animals to live?' said Asha.

'They're not so good at climbing stairs, although the chickens try all the time.'

Chickens, too. Amazing. In the palace, food just appeared. She supposed they must have chickens running around somewhere, perhaps near the grazing yaks. Funny how she had never really stopped to think about how the ordinary people lived in the Kingdom. This was turning out to be a very interesting expedition.

Hauling Badmash, protesting, from the trough, they headed out of the palace compound and down towards the town. As they came to its outskirts, Asha nudged Kumari.

'Act confident. Don't be nervous. Pretend you come here every day.'

'Go, Badmash, fly!' Kumari watched him soar up over the buildings, skimming rooftops from which smoky spirals rose, each signalling a hearth below. Every person in the Kingdom had a home to call their own. There was enough food and clothing for all and more besides. Houses and shops shone with a quiet prosperity. A constant procession of folk went about their business.

It was odd, seeing the streets from this perspective. Usually, she was carried through them in a palanquin, the people bowing low, eyes averted, not daring to look upon the girl-goddess. Well, that was a blessing at least. It meant no one would recognise her, unless they were unlucky enough to run into someone who worked at the palace or one of the other kids. But the other kids were at class right now which was, of course, where they should also be. Which meant they only had to keep an eye out for a palace employee, or one of the RHM's spies.

Kumari did not officially know about the spies, but she had always suspected. How else did the RHM know the things he knew? How had he found her in New York? It was not something she ever discussed with Papa. Not until she acquired all her Powers would he even begin to teach her about affairs of state. As things stood, that might never happen. *Of course it will. Don't be silly.* There was just so much going on in her life right now. Powers were not exactly the priority.

Fiercely, Kumari brushed away the tear that sprang, unbidden, threatening to spill and give her away.

'No tears, Kumari.'

It was what Mamma had always said. Papa would get better. She would acquire all her Powers. In fact, she would redouble her efforts, just so he could be proud of her when he woke up.

'Are you OK?'

Asha was looking at her with concern.

'It's just that you were pulling this weird face.'

'I'm fine,' said Kumari. 'Just a little worried someone might recognise me.'

'They're not going to if you pull a face like that,' retorted Asha.

Kumari could not help but smile. She was the only one doing so, however. All around her, faces were glum. Every single person they passed looked downtrodden, defeated. It was as if someone had thrown the Happiness switch. *But they can't know*, thought Kumari. *They can't have heard about the Secrets or Papa.* In a way, that was worse. The disappearing haze was having a profound effect.

They wove their way through narrow lanes, passing white houses with overhanging roofs. Although far less elaborate than the palace, each house was nevertheless beautifully constructed. Doors and windows were intricately carved then painted in perfect detail. Plants adorned sills and steps. Everywhere there was evidence of bounty. *But for how long?* thought Kumari. *No, she must not think like that. Keep marching. Find the next ingredient. You can still save these people.*

In the centre of the town they reached the market place, where goods were brought for barter. On one side were stalls piled high with silks and woven cloth, on another, glistening fruit and vegetables. The people called out, advertising their wares, extolling their virtues. But their voices sounded muted, unenthusiastic. Or was it her imagination? A dog trotted past, tail held low, ears drooping. Even the animals were depressed, the yak-mules standing listless. Kumari marched even faster. Beside her, Asha kept pace.

And then they were through the town, leaving the outskirts behind them. Ahead lay a wide track that led to the outlying villages. They took the left fork. All at once, they spotted a black speck ahead in the sky. Kumari's heart soared with pride. It was Badmash, flying magnificently, banking and turning as he spotted them. With a squawk of delight, he landed on her shoulder. Only a telltale dusting of cane sugar down his front revealed he'd stopped for a snack on the way. A few metres further on, a man carrying a sack of rice came towards them, heading for the town.

'Good day,' said Asha brightly.

The man barely nodded, his eyes averted.

'What's up with him?' said Kumari.

A bell of recognition chimed in her head. She had seen that face somewhere. She remembered frightened eyes, voices raised. The day the aeroplane was sighted. It was the same man who had refused to leave, stoking the people's panic. And now he was heading once more for the town, perhaps to incite more insurrection.

'I don't know,' said Asha, breaking into her thoughts. 'Everyone seems grumpy lately. My father says there's a lot of crazy talk. That there are warlords waiting to attack in the western borderlands. That people have seen strange things in the sky. But you know what people are like.'

Her worst suspicions confirmed, Kumari kept her mouth shut. They walked companionably enough, saving their breath for their efforts. Which was why, when Asha suddenly spoke, it sounded all the more startling.

'I heard you,' said Asha. 'Earlier. Talking to Tenzin.'

Her voice had changed. It sounded harsher.

'You did?' Kumari played for time. There was a strange look on Asha's face. Oh great – the girl had led her out here to this lonely spot to attack her. Aside from that man, they had seen no one else for miles. Even the landscape seemed more barren. Boulders littered the scrubby ground, twisted trees fought the elements. Away from the palace and its guards, Kumari was easy prey.

'Kumari.'

All of a sudden, Asha stopped. Kumari braced herself. Would she have to fend her off physically? She hoped not. Asha was school Karali champion. Kumari, though, was a master of the martial art. Why oh why had she come out here?

168

She should have known Asha was up to no good.

Preparing for the inevitable, Kumari dropped into a Karali crouch.

CHAPTER 22

'Kumari, why are you standing like that?'

'Like what?'

'Like you're about to aim a Karali kick.'

'I am not.'

'Yes you are.'

'I'm just . . . '

'Worried I'm going to attack you?'

Asha's face broke into a broad smile.

'Kumari, that is ridiculous. If I wanted to attack you, I'd do it close to home. I wouldn't bother coming all the way out here. Anyway, I don't want to attack you. I want to thank you.'

'Thank me?' Ah, now she got it. Asha had lost her mind.

'For telling the truth to Tenzin.'

'Oh. That. Um . . . no problem. Shouldn't we be heading back now? I think it might be getting dark.'

'Heading back? What are you talking about? We haven't got to the waterfall yet. Kumari, just let me say my piece and then we can carry on.'

'OK. If you insist.'

Come to think of it, there was a wild look in Asha's eye. Kumari had put it down to super intelligence when it was, in fact, insanity. Why on earth would Asha want to thank her? She had kissed him, for heaven's sake.

'I know you don't care one way or the other,' said Asha. 'But it meant a lot that you told him. And I know now you really are not interested in him. I could hear it in your voice. It's for that I want to thank you. I know you've guessed that I *do* care.'

'Uh . . . sure. I mean, of course I was telling him the truth. I'm not interested. You can have him.'

'Gosh. Thanks.'

'Why so sarcastic?'

'Well, it's not like he's yours to give.'

Kumari looked at Asha. The girl really was sparky. She liked her for that. It made a change from all the fawning.

'Sorry. That was a bit girl-goddess, wasn't it?'

'Just a bit.'

'I didn't mean it. I don't think like that really.'

'I know you don't, Kumari, but some of the other kids think you do.'

'Really? Is that why they hate me?'

'They don't hate you. They're in awe of you. Think about it, Kumari. We've all been trained to revere you from birth. It's kind of hard to suddenly be in class with someone you are supposed to worship. It's no wonder they don't know what to say to you sometimes. You have this aura.'

'*Aura?* Me?'

Now this was definitely a first. So taken aback was Kumari, she slumped down on the nearest boulder. Funny – the rock felt familiar. It was particularly smooth, black obsidian. An image flashed through her mind, a tiny hand stroking its cool surface. *Her hand.* A voice in the background:

'Come along, Kumari.'

Mamma's voice. Had she been here before? If she had, it must have been when she was very small. She could not recall coming to this part of the Kingdom with anyone. She had never even visited Mamma's village.

The closest she had been with Mamma was the rock face that marked the western frontier, beyond which towered the distant peak of Eagle Beak Mountain. Even then they had gone there under guise of a berry-picking expedition. Mamma had told her how she used to come and play in the labyrinth within the rock face, the secret she shared with her sister, Kumari's Ayah. Their village was perhaps two kilometres from there but it might as well have been on the moon. Once elevated to royal holiness, you were not supposed to return to your former life. Of course, Papa had been born royal but Mamma had married into it. It must have been strange living so close to her former haunts and yet forbidden to visit them.

'Kumari?'

She looked up at Asha.

'Sorry, I was a million miles away.'

'It looked like it. Shall we carry on? The waterfall is not far.'

Asha led them up the forested slope. The vegetation was lush and thick. Here, trees soared above fern fronds and wildflowers. Orchids clung to moss-clad trunks.

'I wonder what sort of trees these are?' said Kumari, glancing up at the branches that formed a canopy over their heads.

'The tallest ones are eaglewood. My grandmother taught me all about the trees and flowers. She's a respected herbalist in her village. We still come here for picnics, whenever my father and I visit my grandparents.'

Kumari wondered what could have happened to Asha's mother. Almost everyone in the Kingdom had two parents. Longevity and good health were a given. In fact, the only other person she knew of with just one parent was herself. And that was only thanks to the most unusual circumstances. It was not every day a queen was murdered in a Kingdom where crime was non-existent.

'I can hear something,' said Kumari. It sounded like torrential rain. The vegetation here was so dense they had to push their way through it, Badmash hopping from branch to branch. It was impossible to fly at this height. From far above, in the tree canopy, they could hear innumerable birds singing.

'What was that?' gasped Kumari as a creature darted from a bush in front of her.

'That was a monkey,' said Asha. 'They like to forage on the forest floor.'

All at once, they emerged into a glade carpeted with flowers, the tree canopy punctuated by glimpses of an ominously clear sky. At the far side of the glade was the waterfall, its waters rushing and bouncing over a large rock, shaped like a giant peach stone. To the left of it, a tree with broad leaves tipping its branches. It was exactly like the image in the moonshadow, a facsimile of the sketch she carried.

The waters fell into a small, deep pool from which a narrow stream meandered through the trees across the glade. It was an idyllic scene. Kumari could imagine people here, picnicking. Could see it so clearly she wondered if, in fact, it was another half-forgotten memory.

Asha pulled a small lump of bread from her pocket and crumbled it into the water.

'What are you doing?' asked Kumari.

'Appeasing the water spirit.'

Of course. The people had to appease the spirits of any living thing before they tried to use it. Water counted as a living thing. Just about everything in the Kingdom did. Mountains, trees, flowers, the earth itself. All were believed to have a spirit. Being a goddess, Kumari was exempt from appeasement. Goddesses took precedence over spirits. In fact, they even got to command them once they had mastered Power No 8, which was pretty cool. She was very nearly there on that one, the Power to have Command over the Elements.

Satisfied the water spirit was now appeased, Asha bent and scooped some water to her mouth.

'Mmmm – that tastes good. Try it, Kumari. Best water you will ever drink. At least, that's what my grandmother says.'

Kumari took a gulp. It was, indeed, wonderful. Better even

than the water that ran down from the mountains to fill the river, and that was saying something. They were truly blessed in the Kingdom. Everything tasted so good. The fruit, the vegetables, even the sweet air itself. All of it made your tongue sing. It was one thing she had noticed in the World Beyond, how everything made your mouth feel like it was full of cotton. Oh sure, junk food was gorgealicious, but it left you wanting more and more. Here, the taste was so intense, you could feel it fill you up with goodness as you ate.

Of course, she could not tell Asha that. She was absolutely forbidden to talk about the World Beyond, as the RHM had so recently reminded her. Instead, she looked casually about, hoping to spot some kind of clue to the next ingredient.

'Oh look. A rock primula.' Asha plucked a small, pink flower from the rocks. 'It's always been one of my favourites. Ever since my grandmother made some into an essence for me. You see, my mother disappeared when I was very young. As I got older, her loss began to get to me. The essence my grandmother made is supposed to help bring peace and acceptance.'

Kumari stared at the flower in Asha's hand. It was the pink flower she had seen in Mamma's portrait. Relief swelled within her chest. This was the right place after all.

'And did it work?' she stammered, eyes fixed on the flower. Carefully, she extracted it from Asha's hand and discreetly wrapped it in her scarf.

'I think so,' Asha smiled.

'But how could your mother just disappear?'

'That was what used to upset me the most, the fact no one

knew what had happened. She just vanished one day when out collecting plants, not too far from here. My grandmother was minding me. My mother was doing her a favour. Grandma, well she's not very tall. She found it hard to reach this particular plant she needed. So my mother went for her, and it was as if someone had wiped her from the earth. No trace of her, or her basket.'

'That's so awful,' Kumari breathed. 'How terrible for you and your father.'

'My father cannot speak of my mother still. If he hears her name, he starts to cry.'

Poor him. Poor Asha. At least Kumari knew what had happened to her Mamma, still had some way to reach her. Or she would have once the fires were relit and the haze of Happiness restored.

'I'm sorry,' said Kumari, squeezing Asha's arm.

'Don't be. I've come to terms with it. Or as much as I ever will.'

This must be what made Asha so strong, the suffering that lay behind that cool exterior.

'Your grandmother,' said Kumari carefully. 'Does she make many of these essences?'

'Oh yes. There are essences for every emotional state. She uses them alongside her herbal medicine. She says that even though this is such a joyous Kingdom, people sometimes need rebalancing.'

'Rebalancing? Like a set of alchemy scales?'

'Exactly like that. And the essences help.'

'So what would you take if, say, you were feeling kind of glum?'

'It depends on why you feel that way.'

'Well, suppose there is no special reason. You're just feeling sort of miserable.'

'Kumari, if there's something you want to know why don't you just ask me straight? I know we have to be here for a reason. You could at least tell me what it is.'

Kumari hesitated then made her decision. Pulling her sketches from the pocket of her tunic she held them out.

'I need to find these. I can't tell you why.'

Asha stared hard at the sketches then smiled up at Kumari.

'All right. I'll help as much as I can. I think I recognise some of the flowers.'

Kumari smiled at her gratefully. 'You're a true friend, Asha. Thank you.'

'Well, what are you waiting for? Let's get hunting.'

Together they began scouring the clearing inch by inch. It was a slow, frustrating task. Kumari could not see anything that resembled the images. No tiny purple flower. Not a glimpse of yellow petals. Perhaps she needed to call upon her Powers. Try some Extraordinary Sight. Turning her back, she lowered her eyelids, falling down, down into her centre, all the while chanting in her head, feeling the energy begin to whirl. Opening her eyes, she looked about. Still nothing. *Look harder*. It was not working. There were no ingredients. All at once, Asha called out.

'I think I've found something. Over here.'

She was staring at a small flower. In its centre, orange and yellow threads curled, almost iridescent against pale purple petals. The purple flower she had seen in Mamma's portrait.

'What is it?' Kumari asked.

'It's a saffron crocus,' explained Asha. 'It stands for love, healing and happiness. My grandmother uses it to flavour dishes that bring extra joy to the home.'

Carefully, Kumari picked one and placed it with the pink flower in her scarf, wrapping the edges over to protect it. Asha glanced at them side by side, but refrained from comment. Gratefully, Kumari watched as she resumed her search. Asha was clever in more ways than one. Her heart leaped as she saw her pause.

'Wait a minute. This looks like another one.'

Asha was bending over a small plant, its yellow petals sprouting like a firework from the top of a slender stem. The third flower from the portrait. Kumari could not believe her eyes.

'Mustard flower,' Asha explained. 'That's also associated with happiness and peace of mind.'

'Fantastic,' said Kumari. 'I'll pick a couple of these.'

'Take the root as well,' said Asha. 'It might help. For whatever you're doing with them.'

They looked at one another and smiled. *I've found a friend*, thought Kumari. Only this morning she had thought they were enemies. It was funny how things turned out. Funnier still that Asha could spot things where she could not. It just proved Powers were not everything. Sometimes all you needed was a friend. Kumari glanced down at the plant in her hand. The amulet on her wrist glinted. Her amulet. She'd stroked it just before she bumped into Asha. Kumari smiled to herself. It felt as if they had Mamma's blessing.

My bedroom

Waning Moon – 9 days to go until next New Moon

It's a cave. At least, I think it is. I mean, the new shadow looked just like one. A dark hole, rock all around. But what are these weird things dangling down from the top? They look like a row of tiger teeth. In fact, my sketch looks like an open mouth, like a wild animal yawning. And there's that thing that looks like a bush across the entrance – that could be its fur. At least now I have somewhere else to look for ingredients. Only the last quarter of the moon to go. Then hopefully the moonshadow will give me the final clue.

But if the shadow gives me the final clue then it also means time is running out. I just can't wait until I have all four. I mean, it's hard enough getting time on my own, never mind sneaking into the throne room alone at night. Especially with the intruder still at large. Everyone's keeping a really close eye on me. When I bumped into the RHM outside Papa's room I really thought I might not make it at all. Thank the gods for Ma showing up with her Hoodoo Soup. That was exactly the distraction I needed.

Anyway, I miss going to see my Mamma. It wouldn't be the same if someone else came along. I know people are only trying to protect me, but some things are private, aren't they?

I couldn't talk to Mamma in front of another person, even if that person was only Ma. When I talk to Mamma it's between her and me. Anyone listening would think I was crazy. And I couldn't do my sketches if someone else was there or I'd give away the moonshadow. I'm the only one who knows you can see it from that particular spot. It looked so beautiful tonight.

CHAPTER 23

Papa's chest barely moved as he breathed. Kumari was watching it like a hawk. A slight rise, an almost imperceptible fall. She willed him to keep going.

'That's it, Papa, in and out. You know, I found some more ingredients the other day. It was Asha who helped me out. She's good at flowers and that sort of thing. Theo's looking at them right now, trying all different combinations to see if they make a spark. I did wonder if I should hand them over to him, but then I decided it was the best thing to do. Theo is a scientist, after all. I'll use his knowledge as long as I need to.'

Not a flicker from Papa. She expected nothing else. Still, it was good to talk to him. She did so every chance she could. She was certain Papa could hear her, in spite of his deep sleep.

Anyway, it was kind of nice to sit and talk to him, just the two of them. She had never really had the opportunity before. Papa was always so busy with affairs of state or making sure the fires of Happiness were tended. And after Mamma's death he retreated like a wounded tortoise into his shell. Funny how the fires going out finally gave her the chance to see more of him.

Badmash poked his beak into the empty bowl by Papa's bed. Someone must have forgotten to remove it after they last fed him. Papa's soup was brought to his room every few hours and painstakingly spooned into his mouth, most often by a maid, although both Kumari and Ma liked to take their turns.

'Leave it, Badmash,' scolded Kumari, shooing him off. In response, Badmash hopped on to the bed and perched beside Papa. She was about to shoo him again when Badmash did the most extraordinary thing, extending one wing to softly stroke Papa's face, all the while making cooing sounds.

'Oh Badmash,' said Kumari. 'You're trying to make him better.'

Her eyes welled up as they so often did these days. Angrily, she brushed away a tear. She was not going to give in to despair. They already had plenty of potential ingredients. Theo was working as fast as he could, analysing anything and everything. Seeing if two or three combined would combust, checking for unusual properties. At the same time, working so hard on a cure for Papa that it sometimes made Kumari stop and think. Would someone do all that and still turn out to be a traitor? Of course they would. Look at the Ayah. No, her plan of action was the best course to take. She would use Theo just as he had used her.

Absently, Kumari stroked her amulet. She still found it hard to believe that Mamma and the Ayah were actually sisters. Why was it that one sibling could be so very good and the other fuelled by hatred? She could understand why Mamma had never mentioned it. If you married royalty, all ties were severed. But Mamma had smuggled her sister into the palace, doing her best to keep her close. And look how the Ayah had repaid her love. With murderous disloyalty.

Kumari would never forget the look on Papa's face when he learned it was the Ayah who had betrayed them.

'I trusted that woman,' he had said in a strange, quiet voice. 'I talked to her constantly while you were gone. I told her how afraid I was I might never see you again. And she knew where you were all the time. Not content with kidnapping you, she tried to kill you too. It would be unforgivable from anyone, but from someone you say was your Mamma's *sister*?'

With that, Papa had shaken his head, unable to continue. His jaw was clenched, his face set rigid, eyes wide with disbelief.

Luckily for her, the Ayah had been taken by Mamma and her lion, or who knew what Papa might have done. Papa was a peace-loving ruler, wise and fair, but, as a god-king, capable of fearsome wrath. Although looking at him now you would never guess, so weak and wan was his face. Kumari gently stroked his cheek. There was a tap at the door.

It was the kitchen maid, bearing a tray on which sat one, solitary bowl and a pepper pot.

'It is time for his holy majesty's soup,' whispered the girl, eyes cast down.

Kumari sighed. He was hardly eating. Papa had managed

perhaps two spoons of Ma's Hoodoo soup. Not enough to make a difference. Might as well see if this one would slip down any easier. Celestial Chicken was his favourite.

'It's all right. I'll feed him,' smiled Kumari.

'Of course, your holy highness,' said the girl, placing the tray beside Kumari.

Carefully, Kumari scooped out a spoonful of soup and blew on it gently. It smelled mouth-wateringly of herbs and spices, just the way Papa liked it. She held the spoon to Papa's lips, propping his head up with her other hand.

'Come on, Papa, it's your favourite.'

Resolutely, his lips refused to part.

'Just a tiny drop, Papa,' she tried again, coaxing him as best she could. Not even the wheedling tone in her voice, however, would entice Papa to eat.

'Try adding some pepper,' said the girl. 'Cook says he prefers it that way.'

Replacing the spoon, Kumari ground the pepper pot once, twice, scattering its speckles across the soup. It smelled fresh, aromatic. This time, when she lifted the spoon to Papa's lips, they parted enough for him to sip some. Ecstatic, Kumari kept on scooping it up from the bowl, one nourishing spoonful at a time.

'I'll leave you to it,' smiled the girl. She could not have been much older than Kumari.

'Thank you,' said Kumari. 'He really seems to be enjoying it.'

Once the girl had gone, though, Papa appeared to lose interest. Perhaps he had had enough. Or maybe she should add a touch more pepper. That seemed to revive his appetite for a couple more spoonfuls. This pepper must be particularly pungent for it to affect his taste buds so. Experimentally, Kumari tried a sip. It tasted pleasantly spicy and warming. There was a subtle aftertaste, one she could not identify. Really quite delicious.

Papa appeared to be sinking into an even deeper sleep, his arms a deadweight on top of the sheets. Theo had explained he would probably follow a cycle, at times more alert than others. This must be his dream time. Kumari could see his eyelids twitching. Was he dreaming of her, of Mamma? Looking at him made her feel tired too. In fact, she was suddenly exhausted. Her limbs felt heavy, her mind spinning with drowsiness. It had been another long day.

As she stood up, Kumari lurched to one side. My goodness, she was even more tired than she had thought.

'Come on, Badmash,' she slurred. It came out sounding like 'shumonbamsh'.

She really must go to bed. Even getting to the door felt like an effort. Somehow she made it along the corridor and to her room.

She flopped down on her bed and slept like a baby.

CHAPTER 24

'So you see here, this looks like the entrance to a cave.'
Kumari's tongue felt too thick for her mouth. She had
woken that morning with a pounding head and limbs that
felt as if she'd run several marathons. She could recall nothing except staggering off to bed. All this stress must be
really getting to her. Her hand shook as she smoothed out
her sketch. Ma shot her a worried look.

'I see what you mean,' murmured Theo. Kumari watched
his face closely. For a guilty man he remained remarkably
cool. All of a sudden, his eyes lit up.

'Wait a minute,' he murmured. 'I knew I'd seen this before.
That's the big cave up behind the monastery. You can only
see it if you climb the slopes to the rear. That's where the

holy hermit hangs out. I know because the Abbot told me. We were out the back collecting plants a few days back. I looked up and I saw it.'

'The hermit's cave,' said Kumari. 'That cave is the most demon-infested in the Kingdom. That's why the holy hermit goes there. He's the only one that can tame them.'

'Do you believe that?' asked Theo. 'About the demons and everything?'

'I don't know. All the caves in the Kingdom have demons. At least, that's what the Abbot taught me.'

Theo shrugged his shoulders.

'Demons or not, it's impossible to get to. The rock face beneath it is practically sheer.'

'So how does the holy hermit get there?'

'Good question,' said Theo. 'Maybe through a secret passageway? The same passage someone used to steal the sap sample. Think about it, it makes sense.'

'That's all very well,' said Kumari. 'But we have no idea where this passage is. You said you went over every inch of that corridor.'

'And there was nothing,' said Theo.

Kumari could hear the silence that fell. It buzzed with possibilities. Huddled together in the gloom of the old layman's entrance, they were safe from any eavesdroppers. No one used the spiral staircase any more. No one except Theo. The monks were busy in the lab above. Still, they had kept their voices low. When Theo next spoke it was almost in a whisper.

'There might be a way,' he said. 'There's a ledge runs along each side of the building below the roof. Trouble is, they don't connect up. We'd need to take you through the Forbidden Sanctuary.'

The Forbidden Sanctuary, holy of holies. Closed to all but the hermit and his acolytes.

'Darn fool idea if you ask me,' muttered Ma.

'Do you have a better one?' asked Theo. 'I'll be there to make sure she's safe. It's the only way I can think of to find out how to reach the cave. Even then, it's a long shot. What do you say, Kumari? It's your choice, your decision.'

They looked at one another. There was no hint of malice in his eyes. Besides, she did not actually have a choice. She would do anything to save Papa and the Kingdom.

'I'll do it,' said Kumari.

'I thought you might,' murmured Ma.

'Good for you,' said Theo. 'Now all we need to do is get you in.'

***

It was hard to look like a monk when you kept tripping over the hem of your robes. Then again, it was hard not to trip when there was a shawl over your head. How did the hermit do it? Maybe he had X-ray vision. Perhaps she should try and call up Power No 2. No, her chanting would attract too much attention. She could chant in her head, but it was hard enough just to put one foot in front of the other. The only thing to do was keep a close eye on Theo's heels, just visible ahead.

'You OK back there?' Theo murmured.

'Yup. Ow! Why did you stop?'

Rubbing her stubbed toe, Kumari hopped about. Theo's heels were very hard.

'Shhhh! Stay still,' he whispered. Then, in a louder voice: 'Good evening.'

From beneath her shawl, Kumari caught a glimpse of a monk. Theo dropped him a courteous bow. The monk inclined his head in return, but not before casting Kumari a suspicious look. She stayed stock still under her robes, head huddled low. OK, so it was odd, yet another new monk appearing, especially a very small one covered from head to toe. But it was the only way they could think of to get Kumari to the Forbidden Sanctuary and from there to the cave. Smuggling her in had been the easy part. Proceeding this far, not too difficult. But from hereon in things got harder. None but the hermit was permitted any further.

As they passed under a low arch, Theo had to duck his head. The light grew dimmer and dimmer until they were practically walking in darkness.

'This is where the hermit lives,' muttered Theo. 'The Abbot pointed it out my first day here.'

An involuntary shudder passed through Kumari. There was something sinister about the holy hermit. Now they were travelling blind, neither of them sure where they were going. The plan was to find their way out on to the parapet that ran both sides of the monastery and from there find some way up to the cave above. As plans went it was pretty basic, but it was the best they could come up with on the spot. Every moment wasted not trying to find the other ingredients was another few seconds of Papa's life lost.

'This is it,' she heard Theo say as he paused by an open window. 'Give me your hand,' he commanded. 'Take it slow.'

His outstretched fingers reached for hers, beckoning.

Kumari hesitated, staring at his hand, wondering where it might lead her. There was no one around, no witnesses.

'It's OK, Kumari. I'll hold you tight.'

She took a tiny step forward. She had to trust him. There was no other way. She flung her shawl to the floor. And then she was crawling out on to the parapet, unable to stop herself looking down. The ground swam dizzyingly towards them. The parapet was perhaps a metre deep. A few paces separated her from the abyss.

'Keep your eyes on me,' said Theo.

Easier said than done. It was an awfully long way down. A mesmerisingly deep drop. At the bottom, a treacherous outcrop of thrusting rocks that looked as if they had been deliberately sharpened. Ahead of her, a man who could be leading her to her doom. Nausea churned up her stomach. All right, so she would not die if she somehow fell. But it would hurt. A lot.

'There's the cave,' said Theo. 'Look, up there, Kumari.'

Look up. Good idea.

'But how do we get there?' she murmured.

They both stared at the cave set into sheer rock, hundreds of metres above their heads. There was no way up and no way down. Across the cave entrance, a row of firethorn. Long, sharp spikes jutted from its branches, deterring all but the most determined intruder. To get to and from the monastery appeared impossible. Perhaps the hermit had magical powers after all.

But when she said as much, Theo snorted in that scientist way of his.

'No chance. There has to be another way. I tell you, there is a passage.'

'You don't believe in magical powers?' said Kumari. 'That means you don't believe in mine?'

'Of course I believe in yours, Kumari. You're different. You're special.'

Yeah, right. Easy to say. His smile shone with sincerity. Then again, the Ayah had smiled even as she raised the sacred sword. And it was in that moment that Kumari had cried out to the heavens for help. She was, after all, a trainee goddess. *So act like one now*, she told herself. *What was it the Ancient Abbot once said?*

'No, no!'

That wasn't what he'd said at all but it *was* his voice shouting out. Theo and she looked at one another. They must have edged along so they were right above the Abbot's room. Directly below them, the Abbot's balcony.

'No!' the Abbot cried again. Then a kind of sick, solid sound, like a sack of sand hitting the ground. In the immediate silence that fell they heard a groan, then a soft, low moaning.

'Someone's hurt the Abbot,' Kumari gasped. 'We have to go help him.'

But if they went to help the Abbot they would lose precious time. Already night was drawing in.

'I'll go,' said Theo. 'His attacker might still be there.'

Kumari looked at him a moment. Could this be a trick?

'I'll carry on round and try to find another way to reach the cave,' she said.

'Don't be silly. You stay right here.'

'But we have to get to the cave. The next ingredients are in there. Trust me, Theo, I just know it.'

191

'Kumari, it's too dangerous for you to go alone.'

'Theo, just go. I'll stay here, I promise. But you must go and help the Abbot. Right now. He's in trouble.'

She glanced up at the cave high above their heads. She could have sworn she saw a light flicker. There it was again, the glow of a lantern moving. Someone was definitely up there. Hastily averting her eyes so as not to alert Theo, she settled herself against the wall and smiled.

'See? I'll sit right here until you get back. Go on Theo, please hurry.'

'OK, but you'd better be here,' said Theo sternly. She gave him her most innocent look.

She watched as he swung over the parapet, dropping to the Abbot's balcony below. A few seconds later she heard him call out:

'It's OK. He's alive.'

That was all Kumari needed to know. That light in the cave was still flickering. Whatever Theo said, she had to get up there and find the next ingredient for the fires. She knew in her gut she was right. Mamma had led her to them and Mamma would never let her down. Flickering light or no, part of the holy fires lay up there. She stared once more at the unbridgeable gap, the gulf that separated her from the rock face.

'What shall I do, Mamma?' she murmured under her breath, touching her amulet for comfort.

The answer to her question was already there. *You're a goddess. So act like one.* A goddess takes risks mere mortals never would. A goddess leaps into the unknown. She had access to all her Powers, if only she could learn to harness them. The first and greatest lesson of all: *Believe in yourself, Kumari*. She could hear Mamma say it now, knew in her heart it was the truth. And yet fear rose up in her throat. She fought to ignore it.

Raising her arms, Kumari gathered her energy. *Magic is in the mind and in the heart.* She closed her eyes and began to chant.

'OM BEMA TARE SENDARA
HRI SARVA LOKA KURU SOHA . . .'

Softly, beneath her breath, aware that sound carried on the clear air. Over and over, focusing all her strength. And then she threw herself upon the mercy of the heavens.

Flinging herself upon the winds, she leapt into thin air.

'OM TARE TUTTARE TURE
DZALA BHAYA SHINDHAM KURU SOHA . . .'

Opening her eyes. The ground rushing up. Lethal spikes about to pierce her belly and her heart. *Oh my god, no. Close your eyes again. Keep chanting. I'm falling. I'm going to hit the rocks. No you're not. You're floating. You're flying!* And so she was, hovering above the ground, lifting higher and higher. Soaring towards the cave, buoyed up by her own belief. She'd done it. She'd faced her fear. She'd found the Sixth Power.

Power No 6, the Power to Levitate or Fly Through the Sky. And it felt amazing. Confident now, she risked a look down and instantly started dropping. She'd lost it. Her Power had gone. Her throat was dry. She could not chant.

'DZALA BHAYA SHINDAM . . .'

The rocks were inches from her spine. *Shut your eyes, Kumari!*

193

'KURU SOHA . . .'

Somehow she croaked it out.

That's it. Keep your eyes shut. Keep chanting. I'm rising! The next moment, she was landing on the ledge, her outstretched arms grabbing firethorn.

'Ouch!' she squeaked before she could stop herself. *Shhh, Kumari. It's only a prickle. You're alive and that's the main thing.* The pain actually proved it. No time to catch her breath even though every limb was trembling. She had to get inside that cave. Ouch, ouch. These were big thorns. Prising the branches apart as best she could, she finally managed to squeeze through. Scratched, torn, but nevertheless triumphant. She had made it inside.

There was no sign of the flickering light. As her eyes adjusted, she could see rocks strewn about the cave floor. The further from the entrance she moved, the darker it grew. All of a sudden, she spotted it, a tiny pinprick. Only this one was static, unlike the earlier light she had seen. Holding on to the cave walls, she stumbled towards it, her fingers scraping across slime.

The light was growing brighter all the while. A noise filled her ears, like low humming. Or perhaps the croon of a demonic chant. And she was heading straight for it. The breath died in Kumari's throat. Demons could see in the dark. She swore she could see them now, red eyes seeking her out. Glowing like the coals of hell, they glared at her from all around. Don't be silly, she told herself. Those are not eyes. They're gemstones.

Demons did not live within cave walls. These were crimson crystals set into limestone. Such riches were often found.

And besides, demons did not carry lanterns. Whoever or whatever was ahead had need of artificial light. Demons had no need of anything save themselves and the occasional meal of human flesh. Her fingers slithered over an oozing mass. A lump of moss. At least, she hoped so. Her heart pounded in her ears. *Keep going, Kumari. Find the ingredients.*

The cave walls began to close in, narrowing down to a jagged aperture. Beyond it, a sliver of light. Kumari held her breath as she squeezed through. The jutting rocks scraped at her ribs and thighs, but still she forced herself to go slowly. There could be anything or anyone on the other side. Suddenly, she was standing at the edge of a small, dimly-lit cave chamber. On the other side of the chamber, another opening, framed by stalactites and stalagmites, their crystalline points shining crisply.

Picking her way to the opening, Kumari peered through. It was hard to see beyond the pillars that blocked her line of sight. All of a sudden, she felt something brush across her shoulders. The hairs on the back of her neck began to prickle. There was something breathing in her ear. Something, not someone. The pants were animal, hot and fierce. *Oh my god*, it must be a demon.

Leave me alone, she wanted to scream but her vocal cords seemed paralysed.

It was snuffling closer. She could feel it. The fetid blast of its breath scorched her skin. Any minute now it would be upon her. *No, no, please no*, she prayed, squeezing her eyes tight shut. Demons did things to you so terrible that no one ever talked about them. She was on its territory, with nowhere to hide.

195

It was right behind her now, centimetres from her back. She waited, bracing herself for what was to come. A moment passed like an eternity and then, all of a sudden, it had gone. Disappeared just like that, its panting breath silenced. Upon her neck, nothing more than the cool touch of cave air.

Kumari opened her eyes.

Light blazed forth, brighter than before, blinding her momentarily. She put up one hand to shield her gaze. And then something fell across her face. She was being dragged back into darkness once more, her screams smothered, choking. The demon had her in its grasp. This time there was no escape.

CHAPTER 25

'**D**on't panic, Kumari, it's me.'

Don't panic? What a stupid suggestion! Squirming and wriggling beneath the heavy cloth across her face, Kumari lashed out with every limb.

'Stop it, Kumari. Be quiet. They'll hear you, child. Be still.'

The voice kept up its soothing murmur. Dimly, she began to realise it was a voice she knew.

'RHM? Is that you?'

At last the cloth was pulled away from her face and Kumari blinked into the semi-darkness. They were crouching behind a boulder to one side of the stalactites and stalagmites. The RHM's breath floated, cool, across her cheek. It could not have been he who first sneaked up on her. In which case it must have been a demon that, for some reason, had let her be. Was it because she was a goddess? Dazed, Kumari stared at the RHM. She could scarcely believe he was here. He had saved her from something, that much was clear. But from what, she could only wonder.

'I'm sorry I had to do that, child. But it was the only way to stop you.'

'What are you doing here?'

'Hush, Kumari,' hissed the RHM. 'This is no time for us to talk. I have seen what I came to see. We need to get back to the palace.'

'But who are those people?' Kumari whispered.

'All in good time, child. Now please, we must go.'

'Just tell me what they are doing.'

'I believe they stole the Secrets, amongst other things. Kumari, these people are dangerous. Theo and I have been on their trail for some time now. We think they are the ones who have been poisoning his holy majesty.'

'*We* think? You mean you and Theo . . . '

'I will explain everything later. Right now we need to go and get help. We cannot tackle them by ourselves.'

'But how can we get back to the palace?'

The RHM could not, after all, use Power No 6.

'There's a secret passage. It runs between here and the Forbidden Sanctuary.'

So Theo had been right. And he had been working with the RHM all along. Dismay washed over Kumari.

'So that's how the hermit gets here,' she said. 'But he can't have anything to do with this.'

'Oh can't he?' said another familiar voice.

Kumari blinked as a flaming torch was thrust into their faces.

She stared at the man before them. It was the holy hermit, his shawl thrown back. Only this was no holy hermit. Kumari's whole body shuddered as she recognised Simon Razzle, the crazed cosmetic surgeon, the man who had once threatened to cut off her face. He was stroking it now with those fingers, the ones that had weighed up her flesh.

'Still so pretty, Kumari.'

She turned her head and sank her teeth into his hand.

'Ow! You little . . . '

Snatching his hand back, Razzle composed himself.

'And still as feisty I see.'

She stared at him with hatred. She should have known. He would not leave this pleasure to a couple of heavies. Trust Razzle to sneak into the Kingdom disguised as something he so wasn't. Of all things, a holy man. The man was such a hypocrite. But then what could you expect from a Park Avenue cosmetic surgeon? Especially one who kidnapped young girls so he could slice them up.

'Stand up. Both of you,' Razzle commanded.

Reluctantly, Kumari and the RHM got to their feet. In Razzle's hand, something glinted. The RHM squeezed Kumari's hand. The message was clear: do nothing. The enemy was armed.

'Now walk,' said Razzle, shoving them ahead, into the cave chamber. Three people were busily packing, stuffing items into bags, their faces sallow in the light. Horrified, Kumari recognised priceless palace treasures being manhandled by a monk, another man – and – no, it couldn't be.

199

Kumari stared open-mouthed as she took in the fact that the third traitor was Cook. At that moment Cook glanced up and saw Kumari. She had the grace to look embarrassed.

The monk beside her had no such compunction. She recognised him at once. It was the monk the RHM had arrested. Lopsang, the one who spoke English. He must have been one of the people Theo and the RHM had been following. She thought back to the time Lopsang had been arrested. Had that all been part of the RHM and Theo's plan? Lopsang slid his gaze away as she looked at him with contempt, a smirk playing round his mouth. Kumari glanced at the third man, dressed in rough country clothes, a scrubby beard covering half his face.

'How could you?' said Kumari, glaring at Cook. 'Why are you doing this?'

No answer.

'My father has always looked after you. You let me play in the kitchen when I was small.'

Cook looked at the ground, but Lopsang's eyes shone with a wild light. He glanced at Cook then spoke in rapid-fire English:

'Yes, well, she has better places to be now than a kitchen. We are going to the World Beyond. Out there we will be rich and free. We will have access to all the modern marvels. I will be revered as the great alchemist I am, far greater than the Abbot. That old man thinks he knows everything. Well, I've dealt with him, nosy old fool. With my knowledge, I'll make a fortune.'

Kumari could not believe her ears.

'It was you attacked the Abbot!'

'Silly old man heard me coming past his room. I was on my way to the lab.'

'You attacked the Ancient Abbot?' said the RHM.

'He's all right,' said Kumari. 'Although no thanks to you, you sick bully.'

'How is it you speak English?' the RHM demanded, fixing Lopsang with an appraising look.

'I learned from your books, master,' Lopsang sneered. 'The ones you keep hidden in your room.'

'It was as Theo guessed,' said the RHM.

So Theo had known and had confided in the RHM. It was all beginning to make sense. Kumari looked at Lopsang's smug smile and felt a surge of fury.

'You're the idiot, for believing Razzle's promises. You'll die out in the World Beyond. RHM, you tell them. Tell them what Time will do to them.'

Beside her, the RHM was silent. After a lengthy pause, he spoke.

'She's right. You will die out there. But I consider it your choice.'

'No!' cried Kumari. 'Razzle's lied to them. He's promised them all kinds of things. Listen to me, Cook, he's tricked you. I know. He tried to kill me in the World Beyond.'

A sudden, shocked silence. The RHM let out a soft, low sigh as Lopsang rapidly translated what she'd said for Razzle. Great. Now she'd gone and done it. No one was supposed to know she'd been to the World Beyond. But this was life and death. All right, so Cook was a thief. She was still the woman who had baked cakes for Kumari and allowed her to lick the bowl. Ma had become her bosom

201

buddy, for heaven's sake. She must have been hoodwinked into this by Razzle.

'I . . . ' Cook looked from Kumari to Simon Razzle. Her eyes were clouded with confusion. The torchlight caught the pink streak in her hair. Ma's unmistakable handiwork. They had all trusted her.

'She's just trying to stop you taking the treasure,' said Razzle to Lopsang. 'Besides, I guarantee that neither of you will die.'

'So how are you going to keep them alive?' Kumari demanded.

Infuriatingly, she could feel her knees begin to shake. Every time she looked at Razzle she was right back there in his surgery, bound, gagged and drugged. Kumari could still remember her sense of utter helplessness. It made her all the more determined not to give in now. The man was a bully and a coward. He always got others to do his dirty work for him. First Sonny and now these three. She would *not* be cowed by him. She stared straight into his cold, hard eyes.

'Simple. I have the Secrets of the Kingdom.' Razzle grinned as Kumari gasped.

'I don't believe you,' said the RHM. 'Only a person of holy blood could have entered the innermost sanctum of the temple. You may be wearing the correct costume but that's about as close as you will get.'

'Oh it wasn't me,' said Razzle. 'I got the original to do that bit. You know, it was easier than I thought. All we had to do was slip a little something into the guards' tea. Bet they didn't tell you that bit, did they? How they all fell asleep on the job? Your hermit was kind of reluctant to go in there at first, but I can be very persuasive.'

The RHM closed his eyes as if in pain. 'What have you done with the holy hermit?'

Razzle's eyes flicked to a corner of the cave, a discoloured patch on the wall evidence of recent disturbance.

'You put him in there . . . ?' the RHM croaked.

'Hey, he loved this cave,' said Razzle. 'I did the guy a favour. Now he's holed up here, literally. It's not like he was doing anything apart from sitting here.'

'You murdered the holy hermit?' gasped Kumari.

'Murder's a little strong. I prefer to think of it as profound meditation.'

'May the gods forgive you,' said the RHM. 'Although I sincerely doubt they will.'

'Gods, schmods,' said Razzle. 'Who cares when I have the Secrets? Once my young friend here has translated them, I am confident they'll be worth billions.'

'Show me the Secrets then,' said Kumari, recovering a little. 'See, he hasn't got them. He's lying to you.'

She threw Razzle a look of triumph, although she felt sick to her stomach.

'I assure you that the Secrets are in a very safe place. As you will shortly see,' smiled Razzle.

'There's no way I'm going with you.'

'Oh but Kumari you are.'

The RHM shoved away Razzle's reaching hands.

'Don't you dare touch the girl-goddess. You take your treasures and go. Take the Secrets too, for all I care, but you do not harm a hair on her head.'

'Very noble,' sneered Simon Razzle. 'And what are you going to do to stop me?'

And with that, he brought his torch down on the RHM's head, the heavy handle contacting with a sickening crunch.

Instinctively, Kumari tried to grab the RHM and break his fall, but Razzle seized her by the arms. His touch felt horribly familiar. Those cool fingers, smooth like polished stone. It made her skin crawl.

'Tie her up,' he said to the monk.

'Don't you dare touch me,' snarled Kumari, but it was no use. The monk smiled as he expertly strapped up her hands and feet with his sash, securing it to a column of rock. Up this close, she could see what lay behind those eyes: pure, undiluted resentment. For some reason, this guy really hated her.

'I wish those yaks had gored you and your friends,' he said. 'It would have saved me some trouble.'

'It was you,' she gasped. 'You who chased us that night.'

Her eyes flicked to the other man. Suddenly, Kumari remembered where she knew him from. It was the man with the sack of rice, the one who had passed her and Asha that day. The one who had led the people to the palace and done his best to incite rebellion.

'What have I ever done to you?' said Kumari.

'Nothing,' said Lopsang. 'That is the problem.'

She puzzled over this as she watched them heave the RHM out of the way. That blow had been really hard.

'Is he breathing?' she demanded.

'He'll live,' said Simon Razzle. 'At least, until we have no further use for him.'

The monk found this so funny he actually sniggered.

'Come on,' said Razzle. 'We have an appointment to keep.'

Lopsang turned to Cook and barked out orders. With that, they carried on cramming stuff in boxes, Razzle pointing and shouting, the monk translating for the other man and poor old Cook. OK, so she was a traitor and a turncoat, but Kumari still felt sorry for her. She looked worn down, hot and bothered.

'You don't have to do this,' Kumari called out to her.

'Shut up,' snapped Simon Razzle.

Actually, that might be a good idea, otherwise they would only gag her. In any case, there seemed nothing she could say or do; no way she could stop this outrage. These people had attacked the RHM and were even now robbing the Kingdom of its treasures. Heaven only knew what they would do to her. She had to get away somehow. But how, with her hands and feet securely bound? *Get a grip, Kumari. You're supposed to be a goddess.* Oh yeah, goddess, right. A goddess with three Powers. Even then, they were intermittent. But three Powers were better than none at all. It could be worse. She could be mortal.

As she stared at Razzle, her heart began to race, hammering with such ferocity it rattled her ribcage. He wanted her back in the World Beyond, where she was condemned to mortality. Back on his butcher's slab, where he could slice open her veins. Where he could sell her face for a pretty price and make billions out of blood her heart was now pumping.

Except that once she left the Kingdom, its regular motion would cease. The clock had been ticking even as she made it back from the World Beyond. Spend even a few minutes out there now and she would surely perish. Not that it mattered to Razzle. She was as good to him freshly dead as alive. She could still recall the way he had said it, with a cold, clinical precision. She was no more than a profitable animal to dissect. Panic swept over her then in a frantic, nauseating rush.

I don't want to die, thought Kumari. *I have to save Papa and the Kingdom. I want to become a real goddess and make everyone proud of me.* So be a real goddess. You have Powers, use them. *Come on, Kumari, think.* Which one should you choose? Power No 6? Useless. What was the point of flying through the sky when you were tied to solid rock? Power No 4, the Power to Become Invisible? Pointless. Besides, they'd still see the bindings round her hands and feet. Invisibility only extended to personal belongings such as clothing.

OK, what about Power No 8, the Power to Have Command Over the Elements? She could whip up a storm or something to distract them. But then what would she do? How about one she could do really well, like Power No 2? She had used the Power of Extraordinary Sight only recently. Maybe there was something vital she could see. Something not ordinarily visible, like a hidden exit. Unlikely in a cave carved into a rock face hundreds of metres above the ground. Sure, there was a passageway between here and the monastery, but Razzle would have that covered. There had to be something else. Hopelessly, she looked around.

If that something were obvious, she would have found it by now. The chamber extended no further. This had to be the limit of the cave. OK, so Power No 2 was a good choice. She'd have to really, really concentrate, chanting entirely in her head, focusing without moving a muscle. If they found out what she was doing they might knock her out like they had the RHM. If they did that, there was no hope. She would never find what she had come for. Dropping her head forward and closing her eyes, Kumari tried to gather her strength.

The trick was to both relax and focus, letting the Power flow freely. *Relax.* Not so easy when your hands and feet are tied and the guy not three metres away wants you dead. *Relax. Let go. Forget about him. I can't. It won't work. These bindings feel so tight. It feels like they're burning my wrists. No, that's not the bindings. That's my amulet. It's getting warmer. Weird. Mamma, is that you? Are you out there somewhere?*

It was working, she could feel it, her stomach growing liquid. The Power spreading through her limbs as she kept chanting in her head. *That's it, pull it up, chant, chant, focus.* With a whoosh, it was there. Kumari opened her eyes. Slowly raising her head, she cautiously looked about, seeing now with a goddess's gaze. At first, nothing leaped out at her and then she noticed a small shard of stone in the cave wall.

Regular in shape, slightly smoother than the rock, it fitted so perfectly it would not be visible to the naked eye. With Extraordinary Sight, however, she could see at once that it was different. She scanned the rest of the chamber. Nothing. This had to be a clue. Then she stared at the aperture through which she'd squeezed, seeing through solid rock, back to the entrance. Wow, this was really good. She could even make out the individual prickles on the firethorn and then, beyond that, the night sky. So it was dark outside. How long had she been here?

'OK, we're done. Let's get moving.'

Razzle's voice snapped her back. Her concentration was broken. Power No 2 was gone for now, but each time it got better and better. Next time she would be able to sustain it. At least she had seen what she came to see. The problem now was to get her hands on the shard of stone.

'I need the bathroom,' she called out.

Razzle flicked her a glance.

'I need it right now,' she insisted.

He hesitated then waved at Cook.

'Tell her to take her over behind that rock,' he ordered Lopsang.

Phew. Her plan had worked. She had been afraid he would tell her to do it right where she sat, bound to the boulder. It was what she had been banking on, a last vestige of Park Avenue manners. Simon might be a murdering lunatic, but he was still squeamish about some things. And letting ladies pee their pants was simply not done.

The monk undid the rope that held her to the boulder. Together with Cook, he helped her shuffle across the cave chamber. She kept her eyes down, trying not to so much as glance at the shard in the wall. She knew exactly where it was, had marked it in her mind as precisely as she could. It was to the left of the rock Razzle had indicated, just about level with her waist.

Squatting down behind the rock, Kumari glanced up, trying to estimate how far she would have to reach to grab the shard. Mercifully, Cook remained on the other side of the rock. At least she still had some level of respect. Kumari hummed softly. Well, it was good to provide a few sound effects. How to reach the shard without alerting them she was up to anything? A diversion was what was required.

As she came out from behind the rock, Kumari deliberately stumbled. Cook reached out to right her.

'Get your hands off me!' shouted Kumari, pretending to stagger back from her reach.

In the few seconds that followed, she scrabbled for the shard stuck in the wall. Where was it? Was she in the right place? And then she felt it, like an electric shock. It was right beneath her fingertips, silently crackling with energy. Her fingers closed around it, easing it from the wall. Safely tucked in her pocket, she could still feel it tingling through to her skin.

'You won't be so uppity where you're going,' muttered Cook.

'What do you mean?' snapped Kumari. She could hear the resentment that lay behind Cook's words. Any vestige of shame had disappeared.

'Be quiet, woman!' snarled the monk to Cook but the damage was done.

'What does she mean, "where you're going"?' said Kumari to Razzle. 'I'm not going anywhere with you lot.'

She was acting a lot braver than she felt. Underneath her robes, her knees were still quaking.

'Most impressive,' said Simon Razzle. 'But I'm afraid you have no choice. You're coming with us, Kumari, whether you like it or not.'

'So where are you taking me?' she demanded.

'That you will find out in good time.'

Rats. Her plan had failed. Still, it had been worth a try. She might just have goaded him into giving her some information. Information she could have put to good use. If she could find out where they were taking her, she might work out some way to escape. OK, it was a long shot. Right now, she had to try anything she could.

'When are we leaving?' she tried again.

'Too many questions, Kumari.' Razzle snapped his fingers at the monk. 'As it happens, it's time to go.'

With that, Lopsang threw a cloak over Kumari's head. Instantly, she began to kick out. Not again. She could not see. She could not breathe. She was suffocating under here. And then a dull crack that sent judders of pain shooting through her skull. She scarcely had time to cry out before oblivion once more swallowed her whole.

CHAPTER 26

For a few seconds, she thought she was back in a Manhattan taxi, being thrown from side to side, at the mercy of a lawless bunch of men. And then Kumari realised that history had indeed repeated itself, only this was no taxi. It was a palanquin, a covered litter in which a person could be carried. The Ayah's lawless men had been replaced by the equally ruthless Razzle and his cronies. Even so, one set of kidnappers was much the same as another. She was still helpless in their hands.

Maybe not so helpless. Experimentally, she kicked against the side of the palanquin. Sealed. Not so much as a centimetre gave way. They had made sure of that. The movement made her skull ache. Even so, it could not match the pain in her chest. Her heart truly felt it might break. She had failed utterly and miserably. She would never save Papa and the Kingdom.

She should have told someone about the moonshadow. The moon was entering its last quarter. Perhaps even tonight the shadow would give up its final secret, but she would not be there to see what the last quarter would reveal. She would never find out where to find the remaining ingredients. If only she had told someone else. Asha, say, or Ma. Maybe even the Ancient Abbot. She dared not think of the RHM. That blow couldn't have killed him, could it?

He was the only other person who knew that the hermit was, in fact, Razzle. Except of course, for Razzle's partners in crime. The ones who had helped him murder the real hermit. It was Cook she found hardest to understand. The woman who lovingly made Papa's nourishing soups. The dull thud of realisation. Those soups. Of course. It had been Cook poisoning Papa all along. But how had she done it? The king's food was tasted before it passed his lips. No one else had become ill. And then she remembered.

'The pepper,' she whispered.

That time she had added it to Papa's soup and then drunk it, she had barely been able to stagger to her bed. There was something in that pepper that was slowly killing her Papa. She wanted to scream, to kick her way out of the palanquin. She had to break free and tell someone. But her hands and feet were tied, the palanquin a prison. Desperately she tried to think, but her mind no longer seemed to work.

Her brain was probably bruised. It certainly felt extra slow. Or perhaps even now she was in the World Beyond, her cells starting to decay and die. Yes, that could be it. Maybe her mind went first. She might even be dead now, although, if she was dead, would her head hurt quite so much? Well, there was one way to find out. She pinched herself hard. Yup. Definitely still flesh and blood. Now her leg hurt as well as her head. Her wrists hurt, too, come to think of it, secured tightly behind her back.

If she was still alive then she was still within the Kingdom, which meant there was a chance she could escape. Not easy, with her hands and feet bound so tight she felt like a trussed pig. But if she managed to wriggle her hands to the front there was a chance she could gnaw off her bindings. She had seen it once on *Scooby-Doo*. It hadn't looked so hard. But it took an age, her muscles shrieking, arm sockets tearing before, with a final, painful jerk, she managed to loop her hands under her feet. She had to be careful not to wriggle too violently or they might suspect she was not only conscious but up to something.

She waited a moment, but the regular motion of the palanquin continued. OK, time to free up her hands and feet. She would start with the bindings on her wrists. They proved pretty hard to chew. It looked so easy on TV. Gnaw, gnaw. *Eugh.* Spit out a hairy mass. Chomp, chomp. Nothing doing. Scarcely a thread had given way. OK, try something else. There was the shard of stone in her pocket. That had looked pretty sharp. But there was no way to reach her hands inside and no amount of squirming would get it out. Back to her bindings, then. She would work them loose by wriggling. Pulling, jerking, twisting this way and that, biting her lip at the pain.

All of a sudden, they were stopping. The palanquin was set down with a bump. One last desperate wrench of her wrists only made the ropes dig in all the more. They were red raw, the skin peeling. And then the sides of the palanquin were released and she was being pulled roughly from it by the monk. If only she could kick him hard and make a run for it, but with her ankles still so tightly bound, she could barely stand upright.

Besides, she was outnumbered three to one. Next to the palanquin stood Cook. A few metres away, Razzle and the bearded man. All three looked pale and ghostly in the moonlight. As Lopsang steadied her, Kumari looked about, trying to work out where she was. A vast rock wall loomed about a metre ahead. Beyond it in the borderlands, just visible, a peak she recognised. The moonlight outlined it to perfection, silhouetting the craggy shape that resembled a bird's head.

'Eagle Beak Mountain,' she murmured to herself. This was the rock wall where Mamma had once played as a child. Within it, the labyrinth which led to the World Beyond. Kumari's heart contracted as she remembered her Mamma leading her gently between the high granite walls, sheer on either side. Mamma had not known who had carved out the labyrinth and built the door. All she could tell Kumari was that it had been there as long as she and the Ayah could remember. Kumari shivered at the thought. The Ayah had once played here too.

'Hello, Kumari.'

Kumari's whole body went rigid and a chill sent its icy fingers crawling up her spine. That voice – it was the Ayah's.

No, it couldn't be. Her mind was playing tricks. The Ayah was dead.

But the voice was unmistakable. Surely a spirit could not sound so real.

From the shadows, a figure emerged.

'You thought I was dead, didn't you?'

'I . . . ' Kumari could only stand and stare. It was as if she had been punched in the gut, the air sucked from her body. The Ayah. Alive. Impossible. She was awake in her own worst nightmare.

In the Ayah's hand a flaming torch cast its pitiless light upon her face. As its flames flickered, Kumari could not help but gasp. One side of the woman's face looked as if it had been torn away. Pockmarking the skin, deep puncture marks. A livid scar ran from cheek to cheek. The marks of Mamma's lion. But why hadn't it torn her limb from limb? The Ayah's cloak fell back, revealing her other arm, bent at a hideous angle, its flesh a withered patchwork, the hand crabbed and twisted.

'Not a pretty sight, am I?' said the Ayah. 'But then I never was as pretty as your Mamma.'

Her Mamma. Whom the Ayah had murdered. At last it all made sense. No wonder Kumari's Banishment Rite had not worked. The Ayah was still alive. A hot rush of nausea burned Kumari's throat. Cold sweat prickled upon her brow. This could not be happening. The Ayah could not be here. How had she escaped?

'It wasn't easy,' smiled the Ayah, as if reading Kumari's thoughts.

She had always been able to tell what Kumari was thinking. But then, she had known the girl-goddess since the day she was born, had tended and nurtured her. Which made it all the harder to understand her betrayal.

'You see,' the Ayah went on, 'your Mamma was always soft. So I appealed to her better nature. We were sisters, after all. I begged her to leave me in the World Beyond so I could die in my own time. I pleaded with her that it would be more dignified that way. She believed me, the fool. She left me out there in the most desolate place she could. She must have thought I would never find my way back. But I did. All the way to New York.'

Here, the Ayah smiled again. The effect was grotesque. Hatred glinted insanely in her eyes. The same hatred that fuelled her strength.

'I persuaded Mr Razzle here we should collaborate once more. He was only too happy to agree. Your mother had foolishly told me about the Secrets of the Kingdom and what they were reputed to contain. Once I had explained this to Mr Razzle, he was most eager to accompany me. The information in them will make us millions. As, of course, will you. Come, Kumari, you didn't think that I would leave you here? You are priceless to me, alive or dead. The blood in your veins acts as proof. It is tangible evidence the Secrets work, especially those that concern eternal life.'

So it had been the Ayah who brought Razzle here, who had helped him get into the Kingdom. For a few seconds Kumari could not speak, and then the words stumbled out.

'B-but you can't take the Secrets. We need them. Papa needs them . . .'

'Stupid girl. Of course I can. And you're coming with me.'

With that, she seized Kumari by the wrists. Involuntarily, Kumari cried out. Then, to her surprise, the Ayah turned to the monk.

'Untie her,' she commanded.

The Ayah showing compassion? Surely not.

'There is no way I can take her through the labyrinth like this. The walls are too narrow. What do you expect me to do, carry the girl on my own?'

'But we're coming with you . . . ' said Razzle.

A crafty look flashed across the Ayah's face. Kumari was not even sure Razzle had noticed. She had, however, and it made her think. What was the Ayah up to now? Razzle had the money and skills the Ayah needed to carry out her ghastly plans. He had not yet served his purpose.

'Of course you are,' said the Ayah.

'Of course we are,' echoed Razzle.

Two sets of cold eyes met mistrustfully. They were perfectly matched.

The monk stepped forward, a blade upraised. Involuntarily, Kumari flinched. With a couple of swift movements, he sliced her bindings. Shaking her stiff wrists and ankles, Kumari felt the shard of stone slide down her sleeve into her palm. Tightening her fingers around it she wondered if there was any way to use it as a weapon. *Don't be silly. There are four of them.*

'Time to go,' said the Ayah, seizing her by the wrist.

Kumari winced and bit her lip once more. The rope marks stood out livid against her skin.

The Ayah glanced down and smiled.

'Poor little Kumari,' she cooed. 'Not so perfect now, are you?'

Kumari turned her head away to hide the tears that sprang to her eyes. *I'm not going to cry*, she told herself. *I will not give her that satisfaction. No tears, Mamma said. I am Mamma's daughter. Which means I am also a goddess. And goddesses don't cry.* Except for that one time. The tear on Mamma's portrait – so long ago, it seemed now. But that had been a message. A sign of things to come.

She gazed at the rock face, seemingly impenetrable. Only it wasn't. It was an optical illusion, a cunning arrangement of overlapping folds that concealed a hidden stone door. Mamma had shown her young daughter where to press – then, to Kumari's astonishment, the labyrinth had opened up before them, a winding maze through granite that led to the World Beyond.

The Ayah was feeling for the door now behind the fold of rock, locating it with a grunt of satisfaction. She pressed and the stone door swivelled out, revealing a narrow, rock-strewn passage ahead. Grabbing Kumari by the arm, she dragged her roughly into the maze. The walls closed in on them from either side, illuminated by the flickering flame of the Ayah's torch. Ahead, the labyrinth was pitch black, its airless gloom suffocating.

Behind them, Kumari could hear the laboured panting of Razzle and his crew. The Ayah thrust onwards soundlessly, her bony fingers digging into Kumari's wrist as she hauled her towards certain death. Kumari kept her eyes fixed on the Ayah's torch as she stumbled on, trying to ignore the grotesque shadows it cast. There had to be some way to

218

escape. But how, when there was no way forward or back and when she was so heavily outnumbered?

There had to be a Power she could use. She had to think of something, anything. As if reading her mind, the Ayah tightened her grasp.

'Don't even think of trying,' she snarled.

Nowhere to run. Nowhere to hide. No chance of summoning up her Powers. Kumari fought to breathe. It felt as if the labyrinth was swallowing her whole. All at once, they were through, the labyrinth opening out into a ledge of rock. From the ledge, rough stone steps wound down to the ground below. In the moonlight, Kumari could make out the shapes of scattered conifers. Further ahead, the trees grew denser. Above the trees, the mountain peak loomed, its bird-like shape distinctive.

Kumari's heart plunged. She was looking at the World Beyond. The ledge on which she now stood marked the border. Take but a few steps beyond it and she was finished.

'Look over there, Kumari,' crowed the Ayah, indicating a tree some five metres away. Tethered to it, a familiar creature.

'Badmash, no!' cried Kumari.

With a gleeful chuckle, the Ayah scrambled down from the ledge and strode across to the tree. Picking Badmash up by his neck, she held him as high as his leash permitted. He let out an agonised squawk.

'Put him down!' yelled Kumari.

The Ayah merely laughed. 'Come and get him, Kumari,' she crooned. 'Or I'll finish him off here and now.'

Once more, Badmash squawked, looking straight into

Kumari's eyes. It was a sound of abject fear, a desperate plea to the person he trusted most. Kumari choked back a cry of anguish. The Ayah was clearly pure evil. Whatever it took, she must not play into her hands. It was obvious the woman wanted the cruel pleasure of making her walk to her death, of watching her face as she took each fatal step. And if she could add to her terror by torturing her beloved pet, then so much the better.

Kumari turned her head away, forcing herself to act indifferent. The Ayah might just spare Badmash if Kumari did not give her the satisfaction of her reaction. With a grunt of disgust, the Ayah let Badmash drop. He did his best to hobble back under the tree. Kumari thought her heart might truly break. He was only a baby after all.

'Of course,' said the Ayah. 'You might prefer to come and get your hands on these.'

She was rooting under a rock, pulling out a bundle of waxed material. With a flourish, she unrolled it, revealing a collection of scrolls. Kumari could see the prominent imperial seal.

'Come on then, Kumari,' said the Ayah. 'Come get the Secrets and your stupid bird.'

Once more she snatched Badmash by the neck, holding both scrolls and bird aloft. Staring at her, Kumari faced an impossible choice. Except that whatever she chose did not matter now. The Ayah would never relinquish the Secrets. If she tried to save Badmash she would surely die, but then she would surely die anyway. The five metres that separated her from him might as well have been five leagues.

She could jump down and know that she had tried to save

her pet, her Papa and her Kingdom. Or she could wait to be pushed into the World Beyond. Behind her, Razzle and his cronies blocked the way. In front of her, death beckoned. And all the while the Ayah stood, laughing at her dilemma. She looked at Badmash, into his frightened eyes.

She could not betray his trust.

CHAPTER 27

'I'm counting, Kumari,' shrieked the Ayah. 'Thirty seconds and he's history.'

Badmash could not even raise a squawk. Instead, his eyes dulled with misery.

At that moment, an image flashed through Kumari's mind. Mamma riding on her lion. Goddesses ruled spirits in all their forms. Use Power No 8 and she could summon a spirit up. Spirits were elemental, after all. Each element had its own spirit: the spirits of Earth, Fire, Air and Water. And Power No 8 gave her command over all the elements.

She had nothing left to lose. Kumari threw her head back.
'OM BANZEN TARE SARVA
SHINDHAM KURU SOHA . . . '

On and on she went, at full volume, no longer caring if anyone heard. Howling, ululating the words, chanting for all she was worth. She could hear the Ayah shrieking at her to stop, but it only fuelled Kumari's fire. Glancing behind her, she saw the Razzle crew held fast by a screaming blast of wind, pinned to the rocks by its force. It was as if she was no longer in her own body, but a part of the chant she hurled to the heavens.

An enormous crack lashed the air like a whip. A low rumble followed it and then a slash of lightning slammed, white hot, into the pinnacle of Eagle Beak Mountain. With eyes still smarting from the brightness of the flash, Kumari could see a shape swooping from the very spot where it had struck.

Enormous wings beat air that fizzed with static. A great neck extended from a feathered body that ran three metres from feet to beak. The beak itself was long, tapering to a point. But it was the colour of this creature that caused Kumari to gasp. Luminous with a divine light, the crane shone like burnished gold. The underside of its throat was a darker shade, the rest of its feathers gilded with a lighter touch. The golden crane from the portrait. A creature of myth. Except that this one seemed all too real, an elemental spirit made flesh.

It soared, encircling them once, twice, three times, then dived, its razor-sharp claws just missing the Ayah's face. As she clutched at her eyes, trying to shield them, the crane sliced through Badmash's restraints. Hooking the vulture tenderly with one foot, it used the other to snatch the Secrets from the shrieking Ayah's grasp. It was all over in seconds and yet it felt as if aeons had passed.

Almost in slow motion, the great bird glided towards Kumari. Still holding Badmash gently, it let out one, haunting cry. That was all the signal Kumari needed. Without even thinking about it she was calling upon Power No 7, the Power to Move Freely Through the Earth, Mountains and Solid Walls.

'OM BEMA TARE SENDARA
LOKA WASHUM KURU SOHA . . . '

She felt it again, that surge of energy. Suddenly, she was riding the crest of a goddess wave, soaring past the thunderstruck Razzle and his henchmen on the rock ledge, powering, astonishingly, through the rock itself. Bursting out the other side of the labyrinth in time to see the crane flying overhead, its claws holding Badmash and the Secrets tight. It inclined its graceful head back towards the labyrinth and Kumari thought she read the glint in its eye.

The labyrinth. Of course. If she could seal the entrance she would trap them all there on the other side. Swing the stone door to and jam it shut. Otherwise, they could simply open it from the far side. But what to use? Frantically, she searched the ground. All the boulders were too big. She could hear shouts from within, the Ayah's shrieks. They were coming after her.

Through the whirl of her thoughts, Kumari felt something grow white hot in her palm. Opening her hand, she saw the shard of stone. It was the perfect size. Her fingers fumbled as she tried to wedge it tight, shaking with fear and haste. Finally she shoved it in between the stone door and the rock surrounding it – hard enough to hold, if only temporarily. Within seconds she could hear dull thuds. They must be trying to break through. Any moment now the shard would work loose. She needed another blast of Power No 8 to seal the deal. Focusing all her energy on the rock face, Kumari called upon the elements once more.

A popping in her ears and then a malevolent cloud rose, black, above the rock wall. Spitting from it, showers of sparks. A low rumble shook the ground. With a satisfying crack, a bolt of lightning struck halfway up the sheer cliff, where another ledge protruded. Like a hot knife through butter, it sliced the ledge cleanly from its anchorage, sending it hurtling down to land in front of the door with a terrifying crash, sealing it like a tomb. Now there was no way out of the labyrinth except to the World Beyond. And only Razzle could survive there.

Shuddering at the noise, Kumari clenched her fist and felt something sharp prick her palm. It was a small fragment of the stone she had used to wedge the labyrinth door. Tucking it into her pocket, Kumari glanced up at the golden crane, the Secrets safe in its grasp. Time for one last blast at her Powers. Might as well go for a hat trick.

She had to get back to the palace as fast as possible and the best way to do that was by using Power No 3, the Power to Run with Incredible Swiftness. Should be a doddle after the other two. One, two, three. *Chant.*

Nothing. Oh no, not now, of all times. The other Powers had worked. She had to get this one right.

'TUTTARE TURE SARVA . . . '

Had she run out of steam?

Take a breath, Kumari. That's it. Now let go. You're trying too hard, darling. Just believe and let it be.

They were exactly the words Mamma would have used. It was almost as if she was whispering in Kumari's ear. *Let go.*

That was the trick. *Let go and believe.*

'ATA SIDDHI SIDDHI KURU SOHA . . . '

She was off and running for her life. Not just her life but Papa's and those of every single person in the Kingdom, feet moving at impossible speed, lungs working fit to burst. Racing over rock-strewn pathways, speeding across terraced paddy fields. All the while the crane kept pace overhead, Badmash letting out the occasional squawk. Now she was passing silent villages, the inhabitants fast asleep, on through the town, dark and still, the palace looming ahead.

As she ran, her lips moved, working in fervent prayer:

'Please, let it not be too late. Please let the shadow still be there.'

There was time, still, to get to the throne room. The moon was at its apex. She had to get there before it slid down through the stars, taking its silver light with it. At this angle, the moonlight hit the window just right, casting its shadow upon the throne-room floor. There was one more segment to be revealed, the last location for the ingredients.

It was as she burst through the palace gates, the guards jumping to startled attention, that a sudden, awful thought brought her to a juddering halt.

She had not collected anything from the cave.

Nothing except a shard of stone. And there was no shard of stone amongst her sketches. But there was no time to worry about it now. Kumari glanced at the sky once more. The moon was definitely lower. She had to get to the throne room before its shadow disappeared, taking with it the final image. The haze was all but gone.

Tonight could be her last chance.

***

226

In the throne room, all was still. Kumari staggered up the steps of the dais. Her legs shook so much she could barely stand. Steadying herself, she stared down. The moonshadow lay before her on the floor. Her eyes searched out the final segment, the others by now obscured. This was it. Her final hope.

At first it seemed nothing more than a series of shapes. Was she already too late? And then the shapes fell into place. At the sight of them, she stumbled.

'No, no!' Kumari moaned.

This was not possible.

She dropped her head into her hands and wept.

So near and yet so far.

All that effort, all the pain.

And still she had failed.

It was there, clear as the stars that shone outside. The outline of a bird's head. Eagle Beak Mountain. Unmistakable. But the mountain was in the World Beyond. She could never have got there alive. And yet the shadow taunted her. It had been she who sealed the labyrinth. Now there was no way anyone could reach the mountain in time.

She could hear voices calling out her name, the throne-room door banging open. She could dimly see Ma and Theo, the Ancient Abbot. Someone must have summoned them. But they all seemed so very far away, like she was under water, unable to reach them. And then a great whirlpool of sorrow sucked her down as she sank to her knees in despair.

CHAPTER 28

'Kumari?'

They were all babbling at her at the same time – Ma, the Abbot. Theo.

'Kumari, are you OK?'

'Thank god you're back. We were so worried!'

'Speak to us, child!'

'Kumari, sweetie, just lift your head.'

'Leave me alone!' she howled. 'Don't touch me.'

She couldn't bear it. To go through all that just to return home empty-handed. She'd tried so hard, kept Mamma's secrets, and all for nothing. Without the final ingredients they could never start the fires. The crane had seemed to hold such promise, but it had disappeared. Kumari let out another sob. It was hopeless.

Another figure pushed through the small group.

'Kumari.'

It was the RHM.

Kumari raised a tear-stained face. 'You're all right!'

'Indeed I am.'

He was smiling. The RHM was smiling.

'And so are you, I see.'

With that, he took her by the hand and helped her to her feet, too stunned now to protest.

'It is Theo here I have to thank,' said the RHM. 'He came to my rescue.'

'I found the entrance to the passage at last,' smiled Theo. 'All I had to do was follow the sound of the RHM yelling.'

And then Ma's arms were about her, pulling her in to the comforting cushion of her chest.

'Kumari, honey, thank god you're safe. The RHM here told us what happened. I can't believe that Razzle guy. Sneaking in past everyone. The nerve of the man, pretending to be some holy type.'

'It's OK,' Kumari whispered. 'He's gone, at least for the moment. I trapped him and the others in the World Beyond. But the ingredients for the fires. I didn't get them all. I'm so sorry. I failed.'

'How do you know you didn't get them all?' asked the RHM.

'There were these images. In Mamma's portrait.'

Too late now for secrets.

'And the shadow on the floor. It led me to places where I found the ingredients.'

'Images? What images? What shadow?' The RHM was staring at Mamma's portrait.

'I don't see no shadow on the floor,' said Ma. 'There ain't nothing but a chink of moonlight.'

They were all looking at her now, the concern visible upon their faces. Kumari could read it, knew just what they were thinking.

'You've been through a lot,' murmured Ma.

They thought she had lost her mind. Again.

'It's only me who can see them,' she mumbled. 'But believe me, they *are* there. Or at least they were.'

She pulled the sketches from her pocket and flapped them in front of their faces.

'See? Now do you believe me?'

'I believe you,' said Theo. 'I'm sure we all do. Let's take a closer look.'

He peered at the sketches in Kumari's hand, the RHM looking over his shoulder.

'How many ingredients do you have, Kumari?' the RHM asked.

'I've got the flowers, the sap. The rest must still be out there. But we're wasting time. Can't you see? We could still go back, find the others.'

'And where are they?'

'In the cave. And out at Eagle Beak Mountain.'

And then she clapped a hand over her mouth.

'The Secrets,' she whispered.

At that moment, a cry rang out.

From behind the throne, the crane emerged. In the light from the butter lamps its feathers shone with that unearthly brilliance that lent it the appearance of burnished gold. Behind it shuffled Badmash, seemingly entranced. The crane raised one long, elegant leg and released the Secrets from its grasp.

As the scrolls unfurled across the throne-room floor, a respectful silence fell.

'Are they all there?' whispered the Abbot.

'As far as I know,' said Kumari. 'Razzle gave them to the Ayah. She'd actually taken them into the World Beyond. It was the crane that got them back.'

'Kumari, the Ayah is dead,' said the RHM.

'No she isn't. She's just kind of chewed up. Mamma's lion, it dropped her off in the World Beyond. She made her way back to New York. That's where she hooked up with Razzle again. They got those people in the cave to help them – Cook, Lopsang and that other man. Cook, she's been putting something in the pepper for Papa's soup. He must not have any more of it.'

'I don't believe it!' said Ma. 'Me and her, we were that close. I told that woman everything. I did her hair, for heaven's sakes.'

The RHM looked at Theo.

'It's my fault,' said Theo heavily. 'I persuaded the RHM here to let Lopsang go. I suspected him as soon as I realised he spoke English and I thought he'd lead us to his masters.'

So that explained Theo's actions that day. Kumari felt the last vestige of suspicion dissipate.

'It was my decision,' said the RHM. 'We were not to know he would move so fast. It's a terrible shame. Lopsang was one of our brightest monks. No wonder they recruited him.'

'He was going to translate the Secrets for them,' said Kumari.

A horrified glance from the Abbot. 'But that is a desecration. None but a person of holy blood should touch the Secrets. And only a person of holy blood can understand them. The Ayah was wasting her time. No mere monk could translate them.'

'Kumari,' said the RHM. 'You must be the one to pick them up.'

Kumari bent and took the scrolls. As she did so, the crane moved closer. The moment they were all safely in her arms, it dipped its head as if in blessing.

'There you go,' said Theo. 'You got the Secrets back. You haven't failed at all, Kumari.'

'But what about the ingredients?' she mumbled.

'Let us worry about those later. At least we have the Secrets.' The Ancient Abbot laid a gentle hand on her arm. 'You have done a great thing, Kumari.'

Kumari gazed into his kindly face. Written upon it was the wisdom of the ages. She trusted the Ancient Abbot more than almost anyone.

'How is my Papa?'

'The same.'

The sooner they got to work on the Secrets the better. She might not have all the ingredients for the fires but maybe the Secrets would reveal another way? Kumari glanced up at the great circular window. In a few hours the dawn would come, taking with it the silver sliver of the waning moon. The haze of Happiness was all but gone. This might be their last chance.

'We're wasting time,' she cried.

'Then let's get to the lab,' said Theo.

All the way back to the monastery, the crane flew escort, its gaze fixed on Kumari. The Abbot himself flung open the doors. This was no time for protocol. The Secrets of the Kingdom must be deciphered and in record time. It was all up to Kumari. As they spread the scrolls across the lab tables, Kumari took a deep breath. Read the Secrets correctly and they might yet succeed. Her Papa would be saved.

OK, think goddess.

Failure was not an option. She stared at the nearest scroll. The words on it swam before her eyes. They looked normal at first. She read on, trying to discern what they had to reveal. It was then she realised they were gibberish. A meaningless collection of words and phrases, cunningly designed to seem profound. But what lay beneath these sentences? How to find the real Secrets?

This was going to be even harder than she had thought.

And all the while the moon was sinking.

CHAPTER 29

Everyone appeared to be holding their breath and still Kumari was staring. She could feel the small group willing her on. But the scrolls did not seem willing to give up the Secrets. None of it made sense. She looked up to see the Abbot's anxious face.

'Take your time, Kumari,' said Theo. 'You have to think laterally. Sometimes we end up looking too hard to see.'

Oh great, now *Theo* was spouting deep stuff. But actually, that made a lot of sense. *Looking too hard to see.* What if you looked a different way? Only a royal was supposed to read these. And only a royal had Powers. Think laterally, Theo had said. What could be more lateral than a goddess take on things? Say a little burst of Power No 2, the Power of Extraordinary Sight. Kumari threw back her head.

'DARA DARA DIRI DIRI . . . '

'What's she doing?' she heard Theo whisper.

'Shhhh!' hissed Ma, and then nothing. She'd managed to blank them out. Concentrating, focusing, taking this higher and higher. *Come on, you can do it.* Chant, chant, chant.

She looked again at the scrolls, this time with the eyes of a goddess. Power No 2, her best so far, but she'd never yet tried to work this intensely. So much detail, so many words, apparently scrambled. *Keep the faith, Kumari. There has to be something to see.*

And there it was, a sentence painted in the space between the others. Then more of them, hundreds of them, covering the other scrolls. It was as if the words hovered off the page, ephemeral, but shimmering with meaning. Hastily, Kumari began to read aloud, afraid they might suddenly disappear. *It's OK*, she told herself. *They're here as long as you need them.* The words seemed to glow a little brighter. An amazing thing, belief.

'*The Secrets of Happiness. The Secrets of Lasting Vigour.*'

On and on Kumari read while the RHM scribbled notes as fast as he could. At last, she came to the final scroll:

'*The Secrets of Eternal Life.*'

Her head was spinning. She had no idea what she was saying. She was in some other place now, calling out the Secrets. As the last word died on her lips, Kumari collapsed to the floor. She was completely spent, her Power used up. From somewhere far away, she heard Ma calling.

'Kumari, come on now, honey. Someone help me here, for

goodness' sake.'

Then they were gently hoisting her on to a chair, bidding her to sit and take some deep breaths. She could feel a small, rough tongue licking her face.

'Badmash!' she muttered. 'Badmash, get off. That's disgusting.'

Lifting her head, she stared into a pair of beady eyes. Badmash was clinging to her chest.

Extricating herself from his anxious claws, Kumari looked at the RHM.

'Did you get it all?'

'Every word.'

'You've done it, Kumari,' smiled Theo.

'So what do they say? Did we get what we need?'

The RHM was consulting his notes.

'Interesting,' he murmured. 'There is nothing here about the holy fires.'

Interesting? Unbelievable. Gut-wrenchingly disappointing. How could the RHM be so calm? Kumari held her head in her hands, feeling the now familiar weight of defeat.

'Nothing?' she stammered.

The Ancient Abbot looked similarly stunned.

'Wait,' said the RHM, flipping through his notes. 'I recall something . . . ah, yes, here it is. A list of eight ingredients for what it calls "Her Majesty's Mixture". It says we must take these and blend them in the cup of double life. All eight must be blessed first. The number can be no coincidence. How many ingredients do we have here?'

Kumari snatched the list from the RHM's hand and read it out loud:

'*Dragon's Blood Sap*
Rock Primula
Saffron Crocus
Mustard Flower
Powdered Ruby
Feather from the Bird of Eternal Youth
Chrysanthemum Stone
One Drop of Royal Blood
All to be blended in the Cup of Double Life until a white plume of smoke arises.'

Kumari looked up from the list.

'B-but these are the images in Mamma's portrait,' she stuttered. 'That must be what it means by "Her Majesty's Mixture". Papa told me Mamma guarded eight secrets. Maybe the gods foresaw the theft of the scrolls after all.'

She glanced at Theo as she said this, remembering his scepticism.

'The three flowers I already gave to Theo, and the sap too. The royal blood, well that's easy, but the others are still out there somewhere.'

She pulled the sketches from her pocket once more and flung them on the table.

A silence reverberated around the room.

'Astonishing,' muttered the RHM.

'It would make sense,' said the Ancient Abbot. 'Who better to look after the Secret of the Holy Fires than the Queen?'

Ordinarily his gentle smile would have warmed Kumari's heart, but today it could not dispel her misery.

'We can't do it,' she said, with flat finality. 'We don't have all the ingredients.'

'OK,' said Theo. 'So we have a problem. But we may also have the solution. Let's lay out the ingredients we've got, then we know what is missing. Once we know what we need to find we can somehow go get them.'

'But we can't,' wailed Kumari. 'We can't get to Eagle Beak Mountain.'

'Let's worry about the *how* later. Right now we need the *what*. What exactly do we have and what exactly are we looking for?' Theo was already moving about the lab, pulling the ingredients from where he had kept them hidden. Carefully, he placed them on the table. They looked so insignificant. One he set aside from the others. It was a flower Kumari did not recognise.

'That one's a dummy I gave to Lopsang,' Theo said in answer to Kumari's enquiring look. 'I was trying to flush him out. I told him it was something really important, possibly even an ingredient of the Holy Fires. I was trying to see how much he knew. He passed it back to me that time he was arrested. I guess he thought it might incriminate him.'

'I see,' said Kumari. That explained an awful lot. Theo flashed her a brief smile then bent his head to study what lay before them.

'OK, we have the sap and these are the flowers – rock primula, saffron crocus, mustard flower. But as for this "Feather from the Bird of Eternal Youth . . ."'

The crane let out a cry. Kumari glanced at it, then looked again. Something stirred in her memory; a story told to her by Mamma long ago: *The Legend of the Golden Crane*.

'Of course!' she exclaimed. 'The crane is the bird of

eternal youth. In the story it lives for over six hundred years. The feather we need is right here.'

They all stared at the crane standing sentry by the door. It bowed its head as if in benediction. Kumari felt a tiny surge of hope. Maybe they could do this after all.

'But powdered ruby? Chrysanthemum stone? And what about this double life cup?' Theo was silent for a moment. Suddenly, his head snapped up. 'I get it!' he shouted. 'Frog. Double life. Amphibian. That's what it means. Amphibians live on land and water so the name translates to "double life".'

'Of course,' murmured the Abbot. 'Frogs have always been considered powerful beings. They represent rebirth, metamorphosis. A most magical totem.'

'And there's a frog cup right over there. The silver one. It was Lopsang's.'

'It was certainly not Lopsang's,' said the RHM. 'It is one of the most precious objects in this laboratory. No doubt it was one of the things he was planning to loot when the Abbot here caught him.'

'Great, so we solved that one,' said Kumari. 'But what about this powdered ruby? There's no ruby here, never mind a chrysanthemum stone. At least I can supply the drop of blood.'

She held up her hand, displaying the deep cut caused by the broken shard back at the labyrinth. The blood had dried to a rusty streak, the skin puckered at its edge.

'How did you get that?' cried Ma. 'Looks nasty to me.'

'From this,' said Kumari, pulling the shard of stone from her pocket. 'It broke off from the piece I used to jam shut the labyrinth. Yet another ingredient we don't have. I wasn't thinking at the time.'

239

'Let me see that,' said Theo, holding it up to the light. 'Well, looks like we've found our ruby. See, how it shines out? It's the softer stuff around it that broke. Kumari, you got the perfect bit.'

Now that she looked at the stone, Kumari could see it the ruby, glistening red against the grey stone in which it nestled. It was beautiful and she hadn't even noticed. So much for her powers of observation.

'That's limestone surrounding it,' said Theo. 'Where did you get this?'

'The hermit's cave.' *The ex-hermit's cave. The one studded with blood-red gemstones.*

'Well, that makes sense. Rubies are often found in limestone caves. There's probably a whole lot more up there.'

And a dead hermit for starters.

'It's a shame for Mr Razzle he never spotted them. Otherwise he could have taken those as well, although he was in something of a hurry.' The RHM permitted himself a wry smile as he touched his bruised forehead.

'The ruby,' said the Ancient Abbot, 'is the symbol of the heart. Of life.'

Kumari felt a surge of excitement. It was like putting together a jigsaw puzzle, the pieces all making a perfect whole. And then she thought again.

'But what about the chrysanthemum stone?'

'Most rare,' said the Abbot. 'I have only ever seen one. It came from a village out near the western border. These stones sit on the bottom of the river there.'

'Of course,' cried Kumari. 'The Village of the

Chrysanthemums! Why didn't I realise? And it's so close to Eagle Beak Mountain!'

Her face lit up, then fell again. 'But it's much too far – we'll never get there in time.'

The crane let out another of its startling cries.

They looked up to see it perched on the windowsill, all but filling its lofty arch. And then it was gone, flying out into the night. On the sill, a single feather. As mementoes went, it was priceless. Then again, without the chrysanthemum stone, the feather was little use. Kumari could have wept. So close and yet so far.

'Hey, why don't we prep these other ingredients anyway,' said Theo, seeing her face. 'Try some more combinations. We have nothing to lose after all. We might just get the reaction we need. Maybe a ninety per cent result. Any scientist would tell you it's worth a go. Experimentation is what it's all about.'

'You must not forget each ingredient has another significance. There is a metaphysical element to this.' The Abbot's voice was gentle but firm. 'You must think beyond mere science.'

'Brother Theo is well qualified,' butted in the RHM. 'And science is, after all, proven.'

'Science cannot solve everything,' retorted the Abbot. 'It has yet to solve the mystery of life for instance.'

'Erm . . . DNA,' Kumari muttered.

The Abbot stared at her askance.

'Actually, the Abbot's right,' Theo countered. 'We might have the code for life but where it comes from is still a mystery.'

'Will you guys quit yakking,' said Ma. 'There's work to be done here. Call it whatever you like, but we got a fire to make. And we ain't got a lot of time.'

As Kumari looked gratefully at Ma, Ma dropped her a slow wink. *Don't you worry*, the wink seemed to say. *This is nothing more than magic. And you and I know what magic takes.*

Magic took belief. It would take a whole lot of magic, though, to relight the fires without the missing ingredient. But what did they have to lose? They might as well try anyway. As Ma began to shred the flowers into the frog cup, Kumari tried to dig the ruby from its surrounding stone with her fingernails.

'Allow me,' said Theo. 'Abbot, a pestle and mortar please.'

A marble bowl was produced and Theo set to with a solid pestle, bashing and mashing the shard of stone, grinding the ruby within to a fine powder.

'Haven't done this since school. Great way to get your angst out. Here, Kumari, you have a go. You look like you need it.'

'Gee, thanks,' she muttered, thumping the pestle thing up and down. Actually, Theo was right. It did help get it all out. Not that getting rid of her angst was going to help the fires any. Suddenly, she threw the pestle down.

'This is all a waste of time!'

They were all looking at her again in that careful way.

'It's a waste of time,' she repeated. 'Without the chrysanthemum stone this is useless.'

'Kumari, where's your belief?'

The Abbot's voice was soft, without a hint of reproach.

Nervously, Kumari rubbed her amulet. *In the heart and in the mind. Believe, Kumari.*

A haunting cry from outside and then the crane was swooping through the window. Its feathers were wet, plastered to its skin. Its legs trembled as it landed, exhausted, from its mercy dash. In its beak was a black stone inlaid with an intricate white pattern. Dropping the stone in Kumari's outstretched palm, the crane bowed its head.

'Look,' breathed Kumari. 'Chrysanthemums. You can see them.'

Sure enough, the white streaks burst out into the shape of the flower.

'A truly magnificent specimen,' said the Abbot. 'The crane must have dived to the bottom of the river to retrieve this.'

'Near where Mamma grew up,' Kumari whispered, almost to herself.

'That's amazing,' said Theo. 'This must have formed millions of years ago.'

'According to legend, it was the daughter of a heavenly empress who planted the stones,' said the Abbot.

At that, the RHM snorted in derision. The Abbot looked at him in astonishment.

'You do not believe me, RHM?'

'I do not believe in legends.'

A silence while the Abbot took this in and then he shook his head sorrowfully. 'After all that I taught you,' he murmured. 'It seems it was not enough.'

Kumari averted her eyes. The tension in the air was palpable. She stared for one last, long moment at the chrysanthemum stone.

'It's so beautiful,' she said. 'It's such a shame to break it up.'

With a sigh of regret, she dropped it in the mortar bowl then lifted her pestle and began to pound. Whatever it took, they had to save Papa and restart the holy fires. Soon now dawn would break. Thud, thud, thud she pounded, bashing out all her hopes and fears. Now and then Theo lent a hand whenever her wrists began to ache.

At last they had a powder fine enough to blend. Carefully, Kumari tipped it into the frog cup.

'How do we know we have enough of each ingredient?' she asked.

'There are no quantities stated here,' said Theo.

'In alchemy, quantity is immaterial,' said the Abbot. 'The very presence of an item is enough.'

'OK, let's make sure we have everything,' said Kumari. 'The three flowers are already in here and so are the two stones. We need to add the feather and the Dragon's Blood sap.'

With great precision, Theo snipped the crane's feather into tiny fragments. They fluttered like golden snowflakes into the frog cup. Then he spooned in the sap, thick and syrupy, spreading in a crimson pool. All they needed now was the final ingredient, a drop of royal blood.

'Has anyone got a knife?' said Kumari.

'I have here a ritual dagger,' said the RHM. He produced a bejewelled stiletto from his robes and pulled it from its scabbard.

'Man, are you crazy?'

Ma's eyes flashed as she shoved her way between Kumari and the RHM.

'There ain't no way she's using that. Child will likely slice her finger off or somethin'. Now you just put that away right this minute.'

Peering over Ma's shoulder, Kumari saw the look on the RHM's face. It was a mixture of annoyance, amazement and something she could not identify.

'Very well,' he said. 'Do you have a better suggestion?'

All of a sudden, the crane leaned over and pecked Kumari's finger. It was swift, painless and clean. A drop of blood rose instantly, welling scarlet from her veins.

'Quick!' said Theo. 'Hold your finger over the cup.'

Despite her shock, Kumari managed to do just that. Badmash was already berating the crane. She could hear his angry squawks as she squeezed her fingertip and watched her blood fall into the cup. Almost at once it disappeared, mingling with the sap.

'Now mix,' urged the Abbot, handing her a spoon.

Round and round she turned it, gently scooping up all the ingredients. All the while, she prayed, *Please, please let it work. No, it will work. I know it will. This will work. It has to.* All the while stirring until the blood-red mixture began to thicken and bind.

'Is it ready yet?' she called out, not missing a beat with her spoon. Twist, twist, turn, turn. *Come on, you have to work.*

'I don't know,' said the Abbot, peering over her shoulder.

'Search me,' said Theo, also taking a peek.

Great, neither the scientist nor the alchemist had the answer. In that case, she would decide. One last big effort. Her amulet rattled against her wrist as she went for it big time, working that spoon, believing with all her might. *You will work, you will work. For Papa, for the Kingdom. Help me, Mamma, I know you're out there. Is this ready? Have I done enough?*

Was it her imagination or was there smoke rising from the frog cup? A tiny wisp, to be sure, but definitely a white spiral. It carried a fragrance she recognised. And what a fragrance it was. The perfume of a thousand roses. Underpinning it, another note, the musk-laden scent of power. A third scent mingling, resonant. The sweet kiss of frangipani.

'It's ready,' cried Kumari.

A tiny spark shot from the mixture. It was popping now and fizzing, a miniature cauldron of fireworks.

But would it save Papa and relight the fires?

There was only one way to find out.

CHAPTER 30

Papa's room looked exactly the same, the curtains drawn, butter lamps burning. Kumari could scarcely believe he was lying as she had left him. So much seemed to have happened. She leaned so her lips almost touched his, feeling the barest whisper of his breath.

'We're going to save you, Papa,' she murmured. 'You need to breathe this in deeply.'

She glanced at the silver cup in Theo's hand, her mind drifting back to the flask. His eyes met hers. He understood. She wanted to be the one to give it to Papa. Without a word, Theo handed her the cup. Kumari gazed at the mixture, then back at her Papa's face. If this did not work, there was no hope. They had run out of options.

'Let me help you,' Ma murmured, tucking her hand under

247

Papa's head. 'Come on, Pops, that's it, honey. Let's prop you up a little bit.'

Hovering by the foot of the bed, the RHM and the Ancient Abbot looked on anxiously. Kumari's eyes met Ma's. *Don't be afraid*, they seemed to say. Fear was the enemy of hope, she knew that. It was what her Mamma had always taught her. And without hope, there was nothing. No future. No kingdom. She would do anything to have her Papa back. Kumari raised the cup to his face so he could inhale its fumes. If this was the correct mixture, these fumes would be a concentrated form of the haze of Happiness.

All at once, Papa let out a sudden sigh. In her fright, Kumari almost dropped the cup. What was he trying to say to her? Was this all a big mistake? She tried to steady her shaking hand, terrified of spilling a precious drop. This potion was all they had. *Please, oh please, let it work.*

Papa took a gulp of air and then another. Kumari saw his chest rise and fall and then a shudder ran through him. The colour was returning to his cheeks, a faint bloom that banished the waxy pallor. His eyelids fluttered but did not open. And then his mouth quirked into a smile.

'It's working, isn't it?' Kumari gasped, looking up for reassurance.

'It seems to be,' said the RHM, tears in his eyes.

'Oh thank the heavens!' cried the Ancient Abbot. 'His holy majesty is restored to us.'

'Well, what do you know,' grinned Theo. 'That stuff did the trick.'

'But why is he not awake? Should I let him breathe some more in?'

'He has already inhaled several lungfuls. That should be more than sufficient.' The RHM was looking at her now with an expression of great gravity. 'Kumari, we need to relight the fires. Any moment now dawn will break.'

Kumari gaped at the RHM. She could not believe what she was hearing. If Papa needed the entire cup that was what he would get. Her Papa meant everything.

'Go.'

The merest whisper, but it was enough.

'Go now.' Her Papa had spoken.

All those weeks of silence, and at last his voice. Kumari let out a whoop of joy then was overcome by a surge of tears. She gulped the sobs back, scared of frightening Papa. He still looked so frail, so delicate.

'Papa? Are you all right? Papa, talk to me.'

'The fires, Kumari. Go.'

He must have heard them. Papa was conscious! Kumari dropped her head on to his chest and wept. She could hear his heart beating beneath his ribs. Strong, rhythmic, soothing. His nightshirt was damp against her cheek, her tears soaking through to his skin. She wanted to stay there for ever, listening to him breathe, feeling his chest rise and fall and rise again.

She felt a cool hand touch her shoulder, did her best to shrug it off.

'Come, Kumari, we must go to the hearth. Your friends will take care of his majesty. Your Papa has been asleep a long time. He needs to come round slowly.'

She looked up into the RHM's face. Behind him, the Abbot, nodding.

Kumari stared at her Papa helplessly. He was hardly back

249

and she had to leave him. The holy hearth was perhaps a hundred metres away, situated in the turret closest to Papa's quarters. And yet the short distance seemed a yawning chasm to cross when it meant tearing herself from his bedside.

'Don't you worry,' said Ma, smoothing her hair. 'We'll take good care of Pops here.'

'Trust us,' said Theo. 'It'll be all right.'

The smile he gave Kumari said everything. It spoke of things that would remain unsaid. It gave her the strength she needed.

'I'll see you soon,' she whispered, kissing Papa's cheek. In answer, he let out another deep sigh. On his breath was a note of pure Happiness. It was all the spur Kumari needed. Happiness was the lifeblood of the Kingdom, as necessary as the air they breathed. It was her sacred duty to relight the fires. Already, the inky sky was giving way to grey.

Soon the blush of dawn would warm the earth, taking with it the last remnants of the haze of Happiness. Kumari could not, would not, let that happen.

'Come on!' she cried. 'Let's light the fires!'

She could only hope they were not too late.

CHAPTER 31

The holy hearth looked grey and sad, its ashes cold within their grate. As Kumari knelt before it, she heard the Abbot murmur something. It sounded like a prayer. With the utmost care she poured the blood-red mixture all over the ashes. Then, taking the firestick the RHM held out, she held it high above the hearth and looked to the heavens.

'Let there be flames!' she cried out.

And then she dropped her firestick.

A fizz, then a sputter. She held her breath. Was that a tiny flame? Oh yessssss. Another flame and another, licking and dancing. As the holy fires burst into life, the tears poured down Kumari's face. Tears might not be a goddess thing, but there were times when she could not help it.

The smoke began to rise, drifting higher and higher, drawn up through the chimney, the dawn winds blowing it towards the town. For a moment, Kumari felt pure relief. She'd done it, *they'd* done it. Together they'd relit the fires of Happiness. Outside, the sun's fingers began to caress the sky. The Kingdom was saved. And so was her Papa.

She heard the sound of running footsteps.

A guardsman, his voice urgent.

'The king is asking for you.'

Her Papa, asking for her? All at once, she was on her feet, racing down the steps and along the passage towards his bedroom door. It stood wide, the guards outside smiling. Inside, Papa was sitting up. At the sight of Kumari, Ma glanced at Theo. Wordlessly, they left the room. Kumari looked at her Papa and beamed. Her world was almost complete.

'Kumari? My child, why are you so out of breath? Has something happened? You must tell me.'

So he had forgotten about the fires. Maybe he thought it was a dream.

'Nothing's happened, Papa,' said Kumari, sitting by his bed. She would tell him everything soon enough. Right now all she wanted to do was hold his hand and gaze upon his face. But still Papa looked thin and weak. She looked round and saw a guardsman hovering.

'When did my Papa last eat?'

'Yesterday evening, your holy highness.'

'And who brought his food to him?'

'The kitchen maid, your holy highness. She brought soup for his holy majesty. Unfortunately, it was not the one the king prefers. I understand Cook did not turn up for work.'

Of course she didn't. She was too busy stealing the treasures of the Kingdom. Not to mention aiding and abetting Kumari's kidnap. Kumari sighed.

'Is anything the matter, Kumari?'

'No, no, Papa. Just a headache.'

'Been studying too hard again?'

Kumari smiled. Papa was teasing her! And if Papa was teasing her it meant he was seriously on the mend. He might look frail, but they could soon do something to fix that.

'I hardly think so,' came a voice from behind. Kumari turned to see the RHM. Behind him the Abbot, Theo and Ma, all of them smiling. The RHM, smiling again? Now this had to mean things were looking good. But if all of them were here, then who was by the holy hearth?

'Who's looking after the fires?' she demanded.

The RHM raised a soothing hand. 'I have left young Asha's father in charge.'

'An excellent man,' said her Papa. 'Although it's time I got back on my feet to tend those fires myself. I have been neglecting my sacred duty.'

Kumari looked at the RHM. Almost imperceptibly, he shook his head.

'Of course, your holy majesty,' he murmured. 'All in good time.'

An unease stirred in Kumari's stomach. *Was* it right to keep this from Papa? He was the king, for goodness' sake. He needed to know what was what. He was also ninety-nine per cent god, practically superhuman. Cook's poison had only attacked the weaker mortal part of him. Now that he was recovering, his Powers would soon be restored. Just look at him sitting up, all alert. He needed to get back on his feet fast. The people needed him. *She* needed him. But she also owed him the truth.

'Kumari, stop looking so worried,' said Papa. 'I've had a slight fever, that's all.'

'Slight fever, phooey. You've been out cold for almost an entire moon.'

Now they all looked positively uneasy. Kumari stuck out her lower lip.

'Well, it's true. I think Papa needs to know now.'

'Needs to know what?'

'The holy fires. They went out.'

A long, long pause. And then the king's face turned purple.

'The fires went out? I must go and see at once.'

He was scrambling out of bed, looking round for his robes.

'Your majesty, your majesty . . . ' pleaded the RHM. 'You must lie down. You have not been well at all.'

'RHM, I will decide if I am well or not. Now get me my robes!'

At this, Kumari flung her arms round him. Papa was back, big time. Her instincts had been right. He had needed one last kick into life.

'Kumari, Kumari,' said her Papa. 'Why the tears, sweetheart?'

'I'm just glad to see you better,' said Kumari.

He'd called her sweetheart. That was nice. If only he would do that more often. Actually, she had a feeling he would. There was something about Papa that was softer. She could see it in his eyes when he looked at her; hear it in the way his voice lowered. The thing that had started in the jacaranda tree had finally fallen into place. Something had shifted between them and it was all to the good. It was something she wanted to hug to herself and yet she could not put a name to it.

It's love, she heard a voice whisper in her ear. Kumari looked round and murmured, 'Mamma?'

'Right, RHM,' Papa was saying. 'I want a full report on what has been going on.'

She so wanted to tell him, but Mamma was calling. *Leave it to the RHM*, she told herself. There will be plenty of time later. Plenty of time. That felt so good. Time to spend with her Papa. She had been robbed of that with her Mamma. The best she could do was speak to her portrait. Quietly, she slipped out of the door and headed for the throne room. It was time for one more chat.

Light-headed, Kumari slumped in front of the empty throne.

'Hey, Mamma,' she murmured. 'We did it. You did it.'

In the pale morning light, the portrait appeared to glow. Picking it up, Kumari moved to the window. She held it as high as she could and stared at the painted background. Nothing. No images. Perhaps a quick rub of her amulet? No, she did not need to do that. The images were definitely gone. And so, she suspected, was the moonshadow.

She knew that as surely as she knew her Powers were hers for the taking. All right, so she only had five. But she was still more than halfway to being a goddess.

'Thank you Mamma,' she whispered. 'Thank you for everything. And now it's your turn. It's time you were properly avenged.'

The Ayah could not survive for ever in the World Beyond. Like everyone else in the Kingdom, she had but a year and a day before she succumbed to the effects of Time. Her comings and goings to New York had already started to eat into it. When her time was up, it would be a slow, horrible death. A fitting sentence for a woman who had destroyed so much that was dear to Kumari, who had nearly taken Papa too, out of hatred and spite. And when she had breathed her last breath, Kumari would be waiting. Waiting to consign her spirit to the outer darkness from which she would never return.

'I'll know when,' said Kumari. 'I'll know because you'll tell me.'

Mamma gazed out from her portrait. Was that a ghost of a smile?

'I love you,' said Kumari. 'Come back and see me soon.'

Her fingers traced Mamma's lips and then she bent and dropped a kiss. Mamma's lips felt warm beneath her own, so warm that Kumari drew back, startled.

'Mamma?'

She reached out and touched. Paint. It was just a portrait, after all.

Weary now, Kumari staggered to her feet, the tears welling in her eyes.

'Goodnight, Mamma,' she called out.

Who cared that it was morning? She was off to sleep at last.

My bedroom

The Second Dark Moon

I can't believe everything that's happened. I mean, in one moon my whole world turned upside down. Now that it's turned right way up again, it's almost like it was all a dream. Except that I know it wasn't. For one thing, Papa came to wish me goodnight tonight. He has never, ever done that before, not even when I was really little. It was always Mamma who told me a bedtime story.

We had a really good talk, all about what's gone on. He told me how proud he was of me. When he said that I nearly cried, because it felt so, so good. I mean, I feel good about everything that's happened and I guess it was me who saved the Kingdom. But it was Papa saying it that made it feel real. I am proud of me, too. When I told Papa about Mamma's portrait and the shadow, he looked like he might cry. I knew I could tell Papa – it's what Mamma would have wanted. We were – we are – a family. We can tell each other anything. That's exactly the words Papa used – 'you can tell me anything, Kumari.' And looking at him I knew I could – all right, maybe not absolutely everything.

But anything about the Kingdom, about getting my Powers and being a goddess – I know the RHM and the

Abbot teach me a lot, but ultimately Papa is the only one who can really understand. He probably won't understand quite like Mamma did – he said that to me as well. And then he took my hand and squeezed it tight and told me he would do his very best.

The wonderful thing is, there are people I can talk to about other stuff. I saw them out the window today – Asha and Tenzin. They were in the courtyard during break, just hanging out together. I know I can count on them to be my friends, especially Asha. She really helped when I needed her most. She's someone I can trust. It feels so good to have friends here now. I've missed Chico and all my friends from the World Beyond so much. But especially Chico. Oh and Charley and Hannah too, they're on my special list. I'm also going to miss Ma and Theo big time when they go, and they have to do that really soon.

With the New Moon, they must leave. I wish they could stay longer. I know that's selfish of me, because they have things to do and people to see – CeeCee, LeeLee; Ms Martin (although he probably calls her Helen). Anyway, even though I know they have to go, I really, really wish they wouldn't. And if they do have to go, which they do, I wish they could come back. But that's not going to happen because Papa won't allow it. Rules are rules, he always says. One moon is all an outsider gets.

You know, much as I love my Kingdom, I wish sometimes there weren't so many rules. But then there are rules everywhere, I guess. It's just some make more sense than others. At least we still have a Kingdom, with a haze of Happiness hanging over it. Now the people are content again and the place is peaceful once more. We have the Secrets back, safely locked away and we now know how to light the holy fires. Almost everything is back the way it should be. Everything except my Mamma.

CHAPTER 32

'You were right about the soup,' said Theo.

'Of course I was,' said Kumari.

They were sitting in the tomato patch again, the three of them, Badmash pecking at the produce. Only this time they were here to pick tomatoes for Ma to take back home. Idly, Kumari scrabbled at the rich, dark earth.

'And you were also right about the pepper,' said Theo. 'But not in the way you think. Whoever dreamed that one up was ingenious. It was all to do with poisonous snails. I rather suspect our monk friend had a hand in it.'

'You mean that guy Lopsang?'

'Correct. I noticed from the beginning that Lopsang was really talented in the lab. And it would take someone with his level of skill to pull this off. He actually managed to separate out the toxins he needed from the hundred or so in snail venom. He put one in the pepper and one in the soup pot. They would only work in combination so the soup would get past any taste test no problem.'

'Eugh!' said Kumari. 'I thought snails only had slime.'

'Gross,' said Ma, pulling a face.

'Not this particular snail. It's a very small one called the cone snail and it's deadly poisonous. Its venom can easily kill. Amazingly, your Papa was merely paralysed. '

'That's because he's only one per cent mortal.'

Theo smiled into Kumari's eyes. 'I have to admit I think you're right.'

A tiny snail. Kumari shuddered. Was that what had happened to Mamma? No, Mamma had died suddenly, with no evidence of poisoning. Someone had got to her another way. Correction, the Ayah had got to her another way. And soon Mamma would have her vengeance.

'But here's the interesting thing,' Theo went on. 'You normally only find the cone snail on coral reefs. Which makes the ecosystem here even more remarkable than I had thought. I've noticed flora and fauna that should by rights be in the tropics or the Mediterranean, not high up in some mountain range. Take these tomatoes, for instance. They shouldn't be doing so well at this altitude. But just look at them, all red and juicy, like they grew under the Italian sun. And that lyrebird feather you keep. Lyrebirds only exist in Australia. What I'd give to study this place some more. '

'I know,' said Kumari sadly. 'I wish you guys could stay longer.'

'We do too, honey,' said Ma. 'I've really grown to like this place.'

'But I thought you hated it,' said Kumari. 'I thought you missed your pizza and TV.'

'I did at first,' said Ma. 'But that soon wore off. Anyways, there was too much going on to notice. You folks sure do have some wild times here.'

'It's not always like that,' said Kumari. 'Usually it's pretty boring. Especially in the evenings. Unless you're a fan of tiddlywinks.'

'Maybe and maybe not. I think it's kind of nice to stare at the moon sometimes instead of at a TV screen. It's real sad we have to go, but I'm taking something special with me.'

'Now Ma,' said Theo. 'You know Kumari's not allowed out.'

'I didn't mean her,' said Ma, cuffing him round the head. 'I meant my memories. Although taking Kumari with us would be just wonderful. But you know what, I wouldn't mind swapping for a month. I could stand to be a rootin' tootin' hoodoo goddess.'

'You can be an honorary goddess any time you like,' said Kumari. 'Trust me, you wouldn't want to be a real one.'

'Yeah, I know. Tough life,' said Ma. 'That big ol' palace. All those servants. Don't know what you're going to do without me.'

'I think I'm a bit old for an Ayah now,' said Kumari. 'And you're too hard an act to follow.'

Ma let out a heartfelt sigh and dropped a kiss on Kumari's head.

'Come on folks, let's get picking,' she said. 'I want to bring some tomatoes back for my girls. You never know, they might just contain a little of that ol' magic that makes you folks look so good.'

'Careful,' said Kumari. 'You're beginning to sound like Simon Razzle.'

'I don't think you're so far from the truth, Ma,' said Theo. 'I can believe youth is in the air here. This whole micro-climate seems to foster it.'

'In that case, you'd better take some of that too,' said Kumari, pretending to catch some air in her hands.

'Kumari!'

They looked up to see the Ancient Abbot waving from the edge of the field.

'Kumari, Ma, Theo, you must all come at once. The king has summoned everyone to the throne room.'

Papa, conducting a throne-room session? He really must be feeling better.

'Isn't it wonderful?' smiled the Abbot. 'His holy majesty feels it has been far too long since he has addressed his people.'

'Come on,' said Kumari, linking arms with Ma and Theo.

'But my tomatoes!' wailed Ma.

Tomatoes would have to wait.

***

Kumari hurried to her room. She had to change into her ceremonial robes. It would be unthinkable to appear before the people in anything less. And this was one very special occasion. For the first time in many moons, Papa was well enough to address his people. She was so looking forward to seeing him back on his throne. It would make the misery of the past few weeks worthwhile.

Badmash clung to her shoulder, letting out the occasional squawk of protest. It always made him feel queasy when she rushed like this. For once, he would just have to put up with it. Kumari rounded a corner and ran slap bang into someone.

'Oof!'

'Ouch!'

'Oh my goodness, I didn't see you there. Are you OK, Asha?'

'I will be when I can breathe. Where are you going in such a hurry? I've been trying to find you for days. I've been worried about you.'

Kumari felt a stab of guilt. 'I'm sorry. Things got really complicated. I'm on my way to my room to get changed. Why don't you come along and I can tell you all about it?'

A few moments later, Asha was sitting on Kumari's bed while Kumari rifled through her wardrobe.

'I don't believe what these people wanted to do to you,' said Asha. 'Especially your Ayah. Why didn't you tell me about her before?'

'I thought I should keep it secret.'

Kumari had given Asha the potted version. The details would wait for later. She felt she owed it to her to be straight. It was no good being friends unless they shared their secrets. They would have all the time in the world to talk when the day was done. Right now, she needed an outfit. Kumari examined her three sets of ceremonial robes. The crimson ones. Perfect. Throwing them on, she twirled for Asha to see.

'Think these will do?'

'*Do?* Those are gorgeous. Just like your room. It's amazing.'

Kumari glanced round the room, trying to see it through Asha's eyes. OK, it was nice but it was just her room. She had stopped noticing it long ago.

'I'm sitting here,' went on Asha, 'and I'm thinking about the time you came to my place. I mean, look at *this* and look at where I live. There's just no competition. I remember you changing into my clothes and then I compare them to those robes. I will never own anything like them.'

'That's right. There *is* no competition,' said Kumari. 'We're friends, and that's it. Yes, we live in different places and wear different clothes. But do you think that makes *us* so very different?'

She looked at Asha and saw something in her eyes that made her heart sink. It was a look Kumari had known all her life. The one that set her apart. Asha was looking at her in awe, as if she was someone very special, very different. She had seen it on the faces of the kids at Rita Moreno in the World Beyond, but, in the end, she had won them over. It was so much harder here, in the place she was born to rule. She could not bear to lose her friend over stuff that was so trivial.

'Feel this,' commanded Kumari, seizing Asha by the hand. 'It's just like yours. Except my nails are dirtier.'

They both looked down and Asha began to giggle. 'What on earth have you been up to?'

Kumari's nails were ringed black with mud.

'Being a grubby goddess,' grinned Kumari.

Tension broken, they smiled at one another.

'You really are a scruff,' said Asha.

'I might be a scruff, but this will have to do. We have to get to the throne room.'

At her bedroom door, Kumari hesitated.

'Friends?'

'You bet.'

'No more secrets?'

'Never.'

A swift hug and they were on their way, charging along the corridors to the throne room.

**

Kumari and Asha squeezed through the throne-room door. In front of them, a sea of people stood shoulder to shoulder. Outside, yet more crowds thronged the walls. The entire town had turned out to catch a glimpse of their king. Kumari could see the RHM standing on the dais behind Papa's shoulder, the Abbot alongside him. Beside Papa, Mamma's empty throne. But Mamma's portrait was no longer propped against it. Instead, it hung on the wall behind. Kumari could not tear her eyes from it.

'Kumari.'

Papa was beckoning her forward, summoning her to his side.

'Go on,' said Asha, giving her a little push.

The people parted like a wave receding. At the foot of the dais stood Ma and Theo, smiling, willing her on. She mounted the steps one by one, conscious of everyone staring. Papa was indicating she sit on Mamma's throne. Kumari shook her head, appalled.

'Papa, I cannot sit there.'

'You can, child. You've earned it. Your Mamma would

want you to sit beside me now and help me carry on her good work.'

Kumari gazed at her Papa. She was not even sure she wanted this. To sit on Mamma's throne felt like an intrusion. But to refuse would upset Papa.

'But Papa,' she said in desperation, 'I have not passed all my Powers. I've barely managed four . . . five . . . I don't know. Anyway, I'm still only a trainee goddess.'

'Kumari does have a point, your holy majesty,' said the RHM. Kumari looked at him gratefully. 'May I suggest she sits on the throne's footstool,' he continued, 'until she has passed all eight tests?'

'An excellent solution,' murmured the Ancient Abbot.

It felt as if the entire throne room was holding its breath, waiting for the king's decision. He looked at Kumari with eyes that were infinitely sad, but also shining with love.

At length, he nodded. 'Very well. The footstool it is, Kumari.'

'Thank you, Papa,' said Kumari, dropping a kiss on his extended hand.

Gently, Papa smoothed the hair from her forehead. 'I am very proud of you, Kumari.'

He'd said it again. And in public. Kumari felt her eyes prickle.

'Now that's settled,' Papa went on, raising his voice, 'it is time to formally thank our guests from the World Beyond. Ma, Theo, I cannot express how grateful we all are for what you have done.'

'Aw, it was nothing, Pops,' said Ma. The king visibly winced.

'It was an honour to help, your majesty,' said Theo.

'*Holy* majesty,' murmured the RHM.

The king waved an impatient hand. 'Majesty, holy majesty, it does not matter. These people do not know the ways of our land. We must allow them some understanding.'

'Of course, your holy majesty,' said the RHM.

His face was a picture. Papa actually telling off the RHM! Kumari smothered a smirk. Out in the audience she could see her class, in the middle of them Tenzin, smiling. As their eyes met, Tenzin dropped her a slow wink. Kumari had to look away fast. Asha and Tenzin – her two best friends. It made her heart feel warm. She had friends here now, as well as Badmash. Ah yes, her naughty pet. She could see him edging towards the ceremonial cakes.

'Badmash,' she hissed. 'Come here at once.'

Inevitably, he ignored her. Selective deafness was a Badmash specialty. Especially when there was food at stake.

'As a mark of our gratitude,' Papa was saying, 'we have some gifts for Ma and Theo.'

At a click of the king's fingers, two bearers appeared, each carrying a small carved chest.

Papa took the first and, rising, handed it to Ma. 'For all you have done for my daughter.'

'Aw shucks,' said Ma. 'It was nothing, Pops. I love that girl as my own.'

'I know you do,' smiled Papa. 'You have shown that in all your actions.'

Even when you stole my pillows, thought Kumari, trying to fight back the lump rising in her throat.

Opening the chest, Ma let out a squeal of delight. Inside lay a magnificent necklace.

'Would you help me with this?' she asked Papa.

'I would be delighted,' he said.

A murmur ran through the assembled throng as the king began to fasten the clasp. His holy majesty, touching a mortal person! It simply was not done. And a stranger at that. Even the king had acknowledged it. Now that he had, the gossip could really begin. Foreigners honoured in the Kingdom!

From her vantage point on the podium, Kumari could see the ripple run round the room. Before the events of this past moon, Papa would never have touched a mortal person. It just proved that progress could be made, that things could be different. Although, knowing Papa, progress would be slow. He was nothing if not a traditionalist. Then again, look at him now, handing Ma a bag.

'Some tomatoes for you,' he said.

'Oh my . . . but how did you know?' said Ma.

'I have ways and means,' smiled Papa.

Behind him, the RHM coughed. It was a discreet signal.

'And now for Theo,' said Papa.

Theo shuffled from foot to foot, his face bright red. Although it went white when he opened his wooden chest.

'I . . . I . . . ' he stuttered, staring at the contents.

'So you can continue your studies,' said the king.

Craning forward, Kumari could see an odd collection of items in the casket. Some roots, a pile of leaves, a few pebbles and a couple of old bones. Hardly exciting and certainly not worthy of Theo's reaction.

'My samples,' Theo was saying as he touched each one lovingly. Ah, now she got it. Papa, allowing these to leave the

Kingdom? Maybe that long sleep had done something to his brain. This new Papa was far more relaxed. She glanced at the RHM. On his face was a look of quiet satisfaction. The RHM was such a fan of science, but he still might object to the solar charger hidden in her room.

Formerly Theo's, it now sat at the back of her wardrobe. Papa might seem more laid back, but she knew this would be a step too far. For now, she would have to charge her iPod in secret. Oh no – *another* secret. She thought she'd dispensed with all of them. It was no fun being a goddess of secrets. It cut you off from your friends. Looking at Ma and Theo's faces now, Kumari thought her heart might burst. Soon now, so very soon, they would be gone. Back to the World Beyond. And, just like Chico and all the others she cared about so much there, she would never see them again.

For a moment, Kumari thought she might start to cry right there on the podium. It took a very big bite into her lower lip to stem the tears. Crying in public was another goddess no no. Sometimes this goddess thing was just too hard. Look at them all, a sea of people. In the middle of them, her new friends. They were allowed to cry, for goodness' sake. But not her, not the girl-goddess. She would always be slightly apart. One of them, and yet not one of them.

Destined to tread another path.

CHAPTER 33

It lay on her pillow, cylindrical, shiny. A small silver orb with three holes pierced in the top. Looped through a hook was a slender chain. The whole thing formed an exquisite pendant. Underneath it she could see a card poking out. Kumari extracted it and began to read:

Dear Kumari,
A special present for you in the hope that you will be able
to use it to come visit us very soon.
With lots of love,
Theo & Ma xxx

Lifting the pendant so that it swung from its chain, Kumari

stared at the white wisp of smoke that floated out. A scent filled the air, the perfume of a thousand roses mixed with something else.

'B-but . . . ' Kumari stuttered.

'Surprise!' yelled Ma and Theo, leaping out from behind the window shutters where they had been hiding.

'Oh my god . . . You scared me!' gasped Kumari.

'Like your present?' smiled Theo.

'I . . . I . . . what is it?' asked Kumari, hardly daring to hope.

'It's a miniature fire of Happiness. I made the pendant from Ma's thermal Yankees mug so it will stay insulated. All you have to do is wear it around your neck and breathe in its fumes. The insulation stops it from feeling hot.'

'No way!'

'Yes, way. I devised it so it will last about a month. After that, you'll have to come back and top it up. But this means you can now visit the World Beyond. This will act like your own personal oxygen tank, Kumari. You can take your own haze of Happiness everywhere you go. It will literally keep you alive.'

'But how?'

Kumari could not tear her eyes from the pendant. Could it, would it, really work? If it did, it meant she was free. She could go see her friends. See Chico. Stay with Ma. Well, in theory, at any rate. If Papa and the others would allow it. And that was about as likely as a pizza joint opening up in the hidden Kingdom. Hope died as fast as it had come.

'It's amazing,' she said sadly. 'But you know I can't use it. Papa will never let me out of the Kingdom again. Not after what happened last time.'

'Aaark!'

A sudden cry from Badmash. Kumari looked up to see someone standing in the doorway.

'Papa!' she exclaimed. Behind him, the RHM and the Ancient Abbot.

'I see you have your present,' said Papa.

'You know about this?' said Kumari, incredulous.

'Theo spoke to me before he gave it to you. Your friend here is very gifted. It almost endears me to science.'

Absolutely unbelievable. Kumari looked from one face to another. They were all smiling, the Ancient Abbot nodding his head.

'You deserve to see your friends, child.'

'Indeed you do,' said Papa. 'The RHM here has persuaded me. It seems you learned a great deal from your sojourn in the World Beyond. I am happy for you to return. Provided that,' and here Papa raised an admonishing finger, 'you are accompanied there and back by Ma and Theo. This will then give us all a chance to keep in touch. We have learned much from your friends.'

'You mean it?' said Kumari. 'You actually mean I can go stay in the World Beyond?'

'For a maximum of one moon each year, Kumari,' said Papa. 'After that you must return home.'

Kumari could only gawp at him.

'But how will Ma and Theo know when to come?'

'We have ways and means,' said the RHM. Kumari's eyes flicked to his. The note she had found on her pillow when Badmash intercepted his carrier pigeon.

'There are of course conditions,' added Papa. 'You must

not bring in anything that might corrupt our Kingdom. This place will remain as it has always done. No more showing off to your classmates, Kumari.'

'Yes, Papa,' she whispered. So the RHM had split on her about the iPod. It was going to be pretty hard to keep it all to herself. Then again, it was worth it. Glancing up, she saw the RHM's face. There was a strange look written across it. One almost of sympathy. Underpinning it, something deeper and more disquieting. It looked suspiciously like envy.

Flinging her arms around Papa, Kumari squeezed him tight.

'Thank you, Papa, thank you so much.'

'It's the least you deserve, my child,' said Papa, patting her gently on the head. Lovely Papa, he did not mean to be distant. It was just the way he had been brought up. That was what Mamma had always said, that Papa needed extra love because of it. Well, Mamma might not be here in the flesh to give that love, but she still made sure they both received it.

Her cheek laid against Papa's chest, Kumari gazed out the window at the hazy skies. From the town came the distant sound of laughter. All at once, she thought she saw something flying through the clouds, a great golden creature. Not a lion, but a bird. A crane, to be exact. Could it possibly have been sent by Mamma? Far stranger things had happened.

She would find out soon enough. In a few days there would be a New Moon. Then Kumari would once more climb the slopes behind the palace and gaze at the Holy Mountain. From its foothills, she would attempt to summon Mamma. Of course there were no guarantees. But her Powers had grown so much this past moon. She had a feeling she might just succeed.

She could feel Papa stroking her hair. Under her ear his chest reverberated as he spoke.

'Your Powers will get stronger and stronger, Kumari. Each one feeds the others.'

Sometimes she could swear he could read her mind. Was that because he was a god-king or her Papa?

'You will make a fine goddess, Kumari.'

'You think so?'

'I know it.'

Kumari snuggled closer to her Papa. For some reason she felt a sudden chill.

KUMARI'S JOURNAL
(TOP SECRET. FOR MY EYES ONLY.
EVERYONE ELSE KEEP OUT!)
THIS MEANS YOU!

My bedroom

Eve of the Second New Moon

In the morning Ma and Theo are leaving, and they're taking some special letters with them. I feel so sad – I'll miss them so much. And Badmash is beyond devastated. He's worried about his honey cakes. I tried to tell him the nice kitchen maid has been promoted to Cook and she'll make sure he still gets them, but he's gone into one of his sulks. I think he's really going to miss Ma. She always made sure he got his ration. I will miss both her and Theo a whole lot, but I also know I'll see them soon. Well, in a few moons at any rate. Papa says I can go for summer break.

I still cannot believe that Theo did that, actually made me a miniature fire pendant. What is even more unbelievable is that Papa actually agreed to let me use it. So much has changed in just one moon. So many things happened that were awful. But out of them came stuff that is really good. It's weird how that happens.

Now I have friends here as well as in the World Beyond. They're different, and yet strangely the same. I mean, we hang out here and we hang out there. It's just we do different things. Maybe Papa is right. It would be awful to spoil the Kingdom. But I think there are some things about the World Beyond that would make this a better place and vice versa. Mental note: Work on Papa!

Wouldn't you know it, for once Ma isn't snoring. I said we had to share as it's her last night here. You know, I think I might even miss her stealing my pillows all the time. Then again, maybe not. Anyway, once she goes I'll have Badmash doing his snorty demon pigs. Really, there is no peace anywhere. You'd think a girl-goddess could get some sleep. Oh no, now he's gone and set Ma off. It's the snorty demon pig chorus. Come to think of it, the real demon didn't sound too much like that. I'm pretty sure that was one in the cave. Right before the RHM grabbed me, that thing behind me was no human. Weirdest of all, it left me in peace. At least demons show some respect.

I wonder if it's peaceful in limbo? Somehow I doubt it. It must be so awful for Mamma to be stuck there. I keep asking for a sign that the Ayah is dead. I'm sure Mamma will show me when that's happened. Funny, I don't feel anything for the Ayah any more. Not hate or anger, just indifference. When I told Papa that he smiled. He said it was a sign of enlightenment. It's one of the Gifts of a Goddess, the Gift of Wisdom. Maybe, just maybe I'm getting there with it. I know I still have a long way to go, but now I really do think one day I can be a full goddess.

In the meantime, I can look forward to the day Mamma is finally avenged. I can also look forward to going back to the World Beyond. It would be wonderful if somehow my friends from both places could meet. I know Charley and Hannah would like Asha. Don't know how Tenzin would get on with Chico, though. That one is way too complicated to think about. I think I will just let it all unfold, the way I've learned to do with my Powers. No more secrets, no more trying so hard. I am what I am and that's good enough for me. An upfront girl-goddess. And proud of it.

THE EIGHT GREAT POWERS OF A GODDESS

1. The Power to be Invincible in Battle with the Sacred Sword

2. The Power of Extraordinary Sight

3. The Power to Run with Incredible Swiftness

4. The Power to Become Invisible

5. The Power of Rejuvenation

6. The Power to Levitate or to Fly Through the Sky

7. The Power to Move Freely Through the Earth, Mountains, and Solid Walls

8. The Power to have Command over the Elements

THE FIVE GREAT
GIFTS OF A GODDESS

1. The Gift of Eternal Life – and the power to grant the same

2. The Gift of Beauty – inner and outer

3. The Gift of Tongues – the ability to speak or understand any language

4. The Gift of Courage – often exhibited *in extremis*

5. The Gift of Wisdom – usually displayed by the more mature goddess

GLOSSARY

The spelling of these words can vary.

Ayah   South Asian word for nanny or nurse-maid.

Badmash   Hinglish (a mixture of Hindi and English) for 'naughty'.

Butter lamp   A metal container in which clarified yak butter or vegetable oil fuels a flame – often found in Himalayan temples.

Hoodoo   African-American folk magic.

Karali   Ancient martial art still practised in some parts of India today.

Kumari   From the Sanskrit, meaning 'princess' or 'maiden'. Although there are living goddesses in Nepal known as Kumaris, there is no connection with our heroine.

Momo	Little dumpling filled with savoury mixture (yum!).
Naan	Round flatbread made of wheat flour.

Find out how it all started!

KUMARI

GODDESS
OF GOTHAM

AMANDA LEES

'*Manhattan Mystery Girl!*' *screamed the newspaper headlines.*

New York is full of thirteen-year-old girls who think they're goddesses. But Kumari is the real deal. And she doesn't have a clue how she got there.

Kumari is a goddess-in-training who lives in a secret valley kingdom. She is destined to stay young forever, unlike people in the World Beyond. But Kumari longs to break out of her claustrophobic life at the Palace, where her only real friend is a baby vulture, and there's nothing to think about – except the mystery of her mother's death.

It's hard to kill a goddess, but someone did. And so Kumari steals away to the Holy Mountain, determined to summon Mamma back from the dead and to find out the truth.

But the next thing Kumari knows, she's in Manhattan. Surrounded by strange buildings and even stranger people, and running for her life . . .

The first book in the Kumari trilogy

'*Powerful and touching*' Glasgow Herald

ISBN 978 1 85340 956 1

Loved this book?
Find out what Kumari does next

KUMARI

GODDESS
OF DESTINY

AMANDA LEES

Kumari has saved the Hidden Kingdom from disaster, and
she's longing to return to the World Beyond. Then an
unexpected invitation arrives, and the girl goddess sets out on
the most important mission of her life.

As her plane touches down in New York, questions fizz
through Kumari's brain. Will her friends still be there for her?
What if Chico's feelings have changed? And is the World
Beyond ready for the secrets she has to share?

But soon Kumari faces an impossible dilemma. With a chance
to fulfil her destiny as a goddess, must she renounce her
friends, her freedom and her happiness forever?

The third book in the Kumari trilogy

'Kumari is a great heroine' WriteAway

ISBN 978 1 85340 992 9
Coming soon to the World Beyond

Find out more about Kumari at:

www.amandalees.com

☆ Read the latest news about future *Kumari* books

☆ Enter competitions with fabulous prizes

☆ Download free *Kumari* wallpaper and banners

☆ Get to know author Amanda Lees

☆ Chat with other *Kumari* fans at the exclusive members' forum